PAUL TEMPLE
AND THE
MADISON MYSTERY

Francis Durbridge

WILLIAMS & WHITING

Titles by Francis Durbridge published by Williams & Whiting

Murder At The Weekend – the rediscovered newspaper serials and short stories

Also published by Williams & Whiting:
Francis Durbridge : The Complete Guide
By Melvyn Barnes

Titles by Francis Durbridge to be published by Williams & Whiting

A Game of Murder
Breakaway – The Family Affair
Breakaway – The Local Affair
Farewell Leicester Square (writing as Lewis Middleton Harvey)
Johnny Washington Esquire
Murder On The Continent (Further re-discovered serials and stories)
One Man To Another – a novel
Operation Diplomat
Paul Temple and the Alex Affair
Paul Temple and the Canterbury Case (film script)
Paul Temple and the Conrad Case
Paul Temple and the Geneva Mystery
Paul Temple and the Jonathan Mystery
Paul Temple and the Lawrence Affair
Paul Temple and the Margo Mystery
Paul Temple and the Vandyke Affair
Paul Temple: Two Plays For Radio Vol 2 (Send For Paul Temple and News of Paul Temple)
The Man From Washington
The Passenger
Tim Frazer and the Salinger Affair
Tim Frazer and the Mellin Forrest Mystery

INTRODUCTION

Those not familiar with the multi-faceted career of Francis Durbridge (1912-98) might welcome a brief résumé. He began in 1933 as a writer of sketches, stories and plays for BBC radio, mostly light entertainments, but a talent for crime fiction became evident in his early radio plays *Murder in the Midlands* (1934) and *Murder in the Embassy* (1937). The *Radio Times* (11 February 1938) mentioned that Durbridge had by then written some one hundred radio pieces, and Charles Hatton commented in *Radio Pictorial* (28 October 1938) that "He is one of the very few people in this country who have succeeded in making a living by writing for the BBC."

Although Durbridge continued to write plays and serials for BBC radio for many years, using his own name and the pseudonyms Frank Cromwell, Nicholas Vane and Lewis Middleton Harvey, his future was assured when he had a particular brainwave. In 1938 he created the dream team of novelist/detective Paul Temple and his wife Steve, with the audience reaction to his radio serial *Send for Paul Temple* leading to sequels over several decades that gained for him an impressive UK and European fanbase. So following *Send for Paul Temple* in 1938, Durbridge responded later the same year with *Paul Temple and the Front Page Men* and continued with many more. From 1939 to 1968 there were another twenty-six Paul Temple cases, of which seven were new productions of earlier broadcasts.

Then in 1952, while continuing to write for radio, Durbridge embarked on a run of BBC television serials that attracted huge viewing figures until 1980. And additionally, from 1973 in the UK and even earlier in Germany, he became known for intriguing stage plays in the style of Frederick Knott's *Dial M for Murder* or Ira Levin's *Deathtrap*.

Paul Temple and the Madison Mystery was first broadcast on the BBC Light Programme in eight thirty-minute episodes from Wednesday 12 October to Wednesday 30 November 1949, and the episodes were repeated on Friday each week. With Temple played by Kim Peacock (1901-66), it was the twelfth outing for Temple and Steve. Although Peacock had a long run in the role, beginning in 1946 with *Paul Temple and the Gregory Affair* and ending in 1953 with the one-hour play *Paul Temple and Steve Again*, he was replaced by Peter Coke (1913-2008) for *Paul Temple and the Gilbert Case* (1954). Coke then made Temple his own in the ten subsequent serials until the concluding *Paul Temple and the Alex Affair* in 1968.

Marjorie Westbury (1905-89), as Steve Temple, partnered both Peacock and Coke in all their appearances, and before Peacock she had already played Steve opposite Barry Morse in *Send for Paul Temple Again* (1945) and Howard Marion-Crawford in *A Case for Paul Temple* (1946). In total she was Steve on twenty-two occasions until the final serial *Paul Temple and the Alex Affair* (1968) – which coincidentally was a new production of her first appearance as Steve in the 1945 *Send for Paul Temple Again*. But mention must also be made of the veteran actor Lester Mudditt, who as Sir Graham Forbes of Scotland Yard appeared on nineteen occasions from the original serial in 1938 until *Paul Temple and the Spencer Affair* (1957-58).

Recordings of many Paul Temple radio serials were released over the years by the BBC on audiocassettes and CDs, but *Paul Temple and the Madison Mystery* remained elusive until 2008 for those who had not heard the original production in 1949 or the new production starring Peter Coke (20 June to 8 August 1955). This was rectified when another new production was broadcast from 16 May to 4 July 2008, one of five Paul Temple serials using re-discovered scripts, produced by Patrick Rayner and starring Crawford Logan as

Temple and Gerda Stevenson as Steve. And this time a set of CDs was released (BBC Audio, 2008), later also included in the CD box set *Paul Temple : The Complete Radio Collection : Paul Temple Returns 2006-2013* (BBC, 2017).

Turning to Temple's popularity on the Continent, the Dutch radio version was broadcast as *Paul Vlaanderen en het Madison mysterie* (14 January to 4 March 1951, eight episodes), translated by J.C. van der Horst and produced by Kommer Kleijn, with Jan van Ees as Vlaanderen and Eva Janssen as Ina; and the German radio version was *Paul Temple und der Fall Madison* (13 January to 2 March 1956, eight episodes), translated by Helmut Schrey and Dagmar Schorr-Nick and produced by Eduard Hermann, with René Deltgen as Temple and Ursula Langrock as Steve.

The Temples also proved to be a hit with cinemagoers - played by Anthony Hulme and Joy Shelton in *Send for Paul Temple* (1946, based on the original 1938 radio serial); John Bentley and Dinah Sheridan in the two films *Calling Paul Temple* (1948, based on the 1945 radio serial *Send for Paul Temple Again*) and *Paul Temple's Triumph* (1950, based on the 1939 radio serial *News of Paul Temple*); and John Bentley and Patricia Dainton in *Paul Temple Returns* (1952, based on the 1942 radio serial *Paul Temple Intervenes*). These movies have fortunately been preserved by Renown Pictures, are shown regularly on Talking Pictures TV, and were collected as the DVD box set *The Paul Temple Collection Limited Edition* (Renown Pictures, 2011).

As with many of Durbridge's radio and television serials, *Paul Temple and the Madison Mystery* was novelised – but not until nearly forty years after the original radio broadcast, and slightly retitled as *Paul Temple and the Madison Case* (Hodder & Stoughton, November 1988). It was published in Germany as *Paul Temple und der Fall Madison*, in the Netherlands as *De zaak Madison*, and in Denmark as *Madison* *mysterie*t. In the UK, *Paul Temple and the Madison C*ase was much later marketed as an audiobook in five audiocassettes and six CDs, read by Michael Tudor Barnes (ISIS Audiobooks, 2001).

Melvyn Barnes
Author of Francis Durbridge: The Complete Guide (Williams & Whiting, 2018)

This book reproduces Francis Durbridge's original script together with the list of characters and actors of the BBC programme on the dates mentioned, but the eventual broadcast might have edited Durbridge's script in respect of scenes, dialogue and character names.

PAUL TEMPLE AND THE MADISON MYSTERY

A Serial in Eight Episodes

By FRANCIS DURBRIDGE

Broadcast on BBC Radio

12th October – 30th November 1949

CAST:

Paul Temple	Kim Peacock
Steve	Marjorie Westbury
Sir Graham Forbes	Lester Mudditt
Sam Portland	MacDonald Parke
Charlie	Desmond Carrington
George Kelly	John McLaren
Stella Portland	Catherine Campbell
Percy	Stanley Groome
Hubert Greene	Ivan Samson
Mark Kendell	Andrew Faulds
A purser	Hugh Manning
Moira Portland	Wendy Gibb
Chris Boyer	Donald Gray
George Denson	Raf de la Torre
Maitland	David Enders
Archie Brooks	John Dodsworth
Eileen	Grizelda Hervey
Sergeant Carver	Ellis Chesney
Inspector James	Alan J Aldridge
Owen Scaley	Malcolm Farquhar
Telephone operator	Gladys Spencer
Dr Elzec	Olaf Olsen
Inspector Vosper	Arthur Ridley
Don Alfaro	Ian Sadler
Harry	Geoffrey Bond

Other parts played by Denis Lehrer, Joan Hart, Frank Coburn
and members of the cast

NEW PRODUCTION
Broadcast on BBC Radio
20th June – 8th August 1955
CAST:

Paul Temple	Peter Coke
Steve	Marjorie Westbury
Charlie	James Beattie
Sir Graham Forbes	Lester Mudditt
Sam Portland	John Gabriel
George Kelly	Stan Thomason
Percy	Brian Haines
Stella Portland	Marjorie Mars
A Purser	Richard Waring
Hubert Greene	Richard Williams
Mark Kendall	Michael Turner
Moira Portland	Peggy Hassard
Chris Boyer	Simon Lack
Archie Brooks	Derek Hart
George Denson	Richard Waring
Inspector James	Manning Wilson
Doctor Elzec	John Carson
Owen Scaley	Hugh David
Eileen	Grizelda Hervey
Sergeant Carver	Geoffrey Matthews
Telephone Operator	Michael Turner
Don Alfaro	Ian Sadler
Harry	Richard Waring
Bennett	Brian Haines
Inspector Vosper	T St John Barry
Sergeant Finley	Geoffrey Matthews
Sergeant Baker	Hugh David

Other parts played by Belle Chrystall, Peter Claughton, Edward Jewesbury, Mairhi Russell and Rolf Lefebvre

NEW PRODUCTION

Broadcast on BBC Radio
16th May – 4th July 2008

CAST:

Paul Temple . . . . Crawford Logan

Steve . . . . .Gerda Stevenson

Charlie . . . . .Greg Powrie

Sir Graham Forbes . . . . Gareth Thomas

Sam Portland . . . . Angus MacInnes

George Kelly . . . . Robin Laing

Barman . . . . .Richard Greenwood

Stella Portland . . . . Emma Currie

Hubert Greene . . . . Richard Greenwood

Telephone Operator . . . . Nick Underwood

Mark Kendall . . . . Nick Underwood

Sergeant . . . . Michael Mackenzie

Cloakroom Girl . . . . .Emma Currie

Maitland . . . . Michael Mackenzie

Moira Portland . . . . .Lucy Paterson

Chris Boyer .Nick Underwood

George Denson . . . . .Robin Laing

Robert . . . . Michael Mackenzie

Inspector James . . . . .Nick Underwood

Dr Elzec . . . . Greg Powrie

Eileen . . . . Eliza Langland

Sergeant Carver . . . . Greg Powrie

Owen Scaley . . . . Gareth Thomas

Archie Brooks . . . . Greg Powrie

Operator . . . . .Lucy Paterson

Inspector Vosper . . . . .Michael Mackenzie

Girl . . . . Lucy Paterson

Man 1 .Richard Greenwood

Stewardess . . . . Emma Currie

Man 2 . . . . .Robin Laing

Young Man . . . . Greg Powrie
Don Alfaro . . . . Jimmy Chisholm
Harry . . . . .Nick Underwood
Waiter . . . . Michael Mackenzie
Bennett . . . . Robin Laing
Sergeant Finley .Greg Powrie
Sergeant Baker . . . . Robin Laing
Constable . . . . .Nick Underwood

EPISODE ONE

A PENNY FOR YOUR THOUGHTS

OPEN TO:

SCENE 1: The TEMPLES' Bedroom in their London Flat.
STEVE is unpacking various suitcases. TEMPLE is making rather a nuisance of himself.

STEVE: Paul, I do wish you'd get out of my way.

TEMPLE: Now don't be irritable, Steve.

STEVE: Darling, we've been away for six weeks and I'm trying to unpack!

TEMPLE: Yes, all right, all right. (*A moment*) Where's that hat – the one I bought in New York?

STEVE: Now what on earth do you want that for?

TEMPLE: I want to try it on.

STEVE: You can't try it on now, not in your pyjamas, you'll look ridiculous. Besides, you've been trying it on ever since you bought it.

TEMPLE: Oh, here it is! (*A moment*) I think it's too big.

STEVE: Of course it's too big. I told you that in the shop.

TEMPLE: It looked all right in New York.

STEVE: Yes, well, we're not in New York. Now Paul, please go into your study and read a book or go to bed or have a bath or something!

TEMPLE: By Timothy, I am popular!

STEVE: You're just getting in the way. Now where did I put that skirt? Oh, here it is …

There is a knock at the door.

TEMPLE: Come in.

The door opens. CHARLIE enters.

TEMPLE: What is it, Charlie?

CHARLIE: Sir Graham Forbes is here, sir. He'd like to have a word with you.

TEMPLE: (*Surprised*) Sir Graham?

CHARLIE: Yes, sir. I put him in the living room, was that okedo – all right, sir?

3

TEMPLE: Yes, that's all right, Charlie.
STEVE: Paul, what does he want – do you know?
TEMPLE: No, darling. Where's my dressing gown?
STEVE: It's on the bed.
TEMPLE: Oh, thanks …
STEVE: Paul, dear.
TEMPLE: (*Turning*) Yes?
STEVE: I shouldn't wear the hat.

SCENE 2: The TEMPLES' Drawing Room.
The door opens, TEMPLE and STEVE enter.
FORBES: Ah, welcome home, Temple! Good to see you again!
TEMPLE: (*Approaching*) Hello, Sir Graham. How are you?
SIR GRAHAM and TEMPLE shake hands.
FORBES: I'm fine. Did you have a nice trip?
TEMPLE: Splendid.
FORBES: Hello, Steve.
STEVE: Hello, Sir Graham.
FORBES: My word, you do look well. Are you glad to be home?
STEVE: Well, I don't know. It all depends what you've got up your sleeve!
FORBES: (*Laughing*) I haven't got anything up my sleeve, so don't you worry, my dear!
TEMPLE: Then what is this, a social call?
FORBES: Not exactly. I want some information.
TEMPLE: What about?
FORBES: Well … when you were on the boat coming back over from America did you meet a man called Portland – Sam Portland?
TEMPLE: Yes, we did.
FORBES: Did you see much of him?

4

TEMPLE: Well – I had a long talk with him. As a matter of fact I was going to phone you about it.

FORBES: Oh? Why?

TEMPLE: Because there's something about Portland you ought to know.

FORBES: What, exactly?

STEVE: Wouldn't it be better if you start the story at the beginning, darling?

FORBES: Yes do, Temple.

TEMPLE: Well, we left America last Thursday or rather early Friday morning. I was feeling rather tired because I'd had a pretty hectic time. It was just after one o'clock when the boat sailed. (*START SLOW FADE*) Steve was on deck staring at the skyscrapers and waving a last farewell to New York …

SCENE 3: The Deck of a large Atlantic liner.
The ship is leaving New York for Southampton. The noises of the Hudson River traffic is heard: tug-boat sirens; the ship's siren, etc. There is a general atmosphere of noise and excitement.

TEMPLE: (*Approaching*) Oh here you are, Steve. I've been looking all over the ship for you!

STEVE: Doesn't New York look wonderful! Oh, Paul, I wish we weren't leaving.

TEMPLE: (*Yawning*) I wish I was in bed! Golly, I'm tired. I can't keep my eyes open.

STEVE: You go to bed, darling. I'll join you later. I'm staying on deck for a little while.

TEMPLE: Yes, all right, but don't catch cold.

STEVE: Oh, what's the number of our cabin?

TEMPLE: 52 – It's on the main deck. Goodnight, darling.

STEVE: Goodnight, Paul.

For a moment or two, we hear the noises from the Hudson River. Then SAM PORTLAND speaks. He is a stout, prosperous, self-made American.

SAM: (*Proudly*) That's the George Washington Bridge over there. Isn't that something?

STEVE: It certainly is! What's that place over on the right?

SAM: Oh, that's Staten Island.

STEVE: Yes, of course. (*Laughing*) I ought to know that by now, but things look different at night.

SAM: How long have you been over here?

STEVE: About four weeks.

SAM: In New York?

STEVE: Most of the time in New York.

SAM: How did you like it?

STEVE: I liked it enormously.

SAM: (*Pleased*) It's some city, isn't it? You know, I've heard a lot of English people say they wouldn't like to live in New York, but I just can't imagine why they say that. It's got everything.

STEVE: That's probably why they wouldn't like to live there.

SAM: Oh? (*He laughs*) That's too subtle for me.

STEVE: Is this your first trip to England?

SAM: (*Nodding*) M'm-m'm, I guess it is. (*Seriously: an afterthought*) At least, I don't think I've been there before.

STEVE: You don't think …? Don't you know?

SAM: (*Hesitating*) No, I don't … (*Pleasantly changing the subject*) Maybe we ought to introduce ourselves. My name is Portland. Sam Portland.

STEVE: I'm Mrs Temple.

SAM: Oh, was that your husband, the tall, tired-looking gentleman?

6

STEVE:	Yes, that was my husband.
SAM:	I've heard quite a lot about your husband, Mrs Temple, but somehow never imagined he looked like that.
STEVE:	At the moment he's suffering from an overdose of American hospitality.
SAM:	(*Laughing*) Oh, so that's it!
STEVE:	He'll look quite different tomorrow.
SAM:	Maybe we'll all look different tomorrow.
STEVE:	Is it going to be rough?
SAM:	(*Amused*) Why, aren't you a good sailor?
STEVE:	Not very.
SAM:	Well, I'll fix it. I'll have a word with the Captain, Don't worry, Mrs Temple, it'll be as smooth as a glass of milk … I hope.

STEVE laughs. A nervous little laugh.
FADE UP music.

FADE DOWN music.
SCENE 4:   The Promenade Deck.
The next day. The ship is now at sea. TEMPLE is in a deckchair. PORTLAND approaches.

SAM:	(*Pleasantly*) Excuse me, sir … Mr Temple?
TEMPLE:	Yes.
SAM:	My name is Portland.
TEMPLE:	(*Friendly*) Oh, good morning, Mr Portland.
SAM:	I had the pleasure of meeting your wife last night, Mr Temple …
TEMPLE:	Yes, so she told me.
SAM:	I was wondering how the little lady was feeling this morning?
TEMPLE:	She's not too good, I'm afraid.
SAM:	On a diet?
TEMPLE:	Strictly on a diet.

SAM: Well, now, that's too bad. If there's anything I can do for Mrs Temple, please let me know.

TEMPLE: That's very kind of you. Won't you sit down?

SAM: Why thank you, sir! (*He lowers himself into a deckchair*) Does my smoking bother you?

TEMPLE: Not at all.

SAM: Would you like a cigar?

TEMPLE: Thank you, not at the moment.

SAM: Mr Temple, I was very thrilled when I saw your name on the passenger list last night.

TEMPLE: Indeed?

SAM: I've been an admirer of yours for some considerable time. As a matter of fact I once wrote you a letter.

TEMPLE: I can't recall ever having received a letter from you, Mr Portland.

SAM: No, you didn't receive it, for the simple reason that I didn't post it. (*A moment*) My wife persuaded me to change my mind.

TEMPLE: I see.

SAM: Mr Temple, forgive me talking shop at this time of the morning but have you heard of a private investigator – a detective – by the name of Madison?

TEMPLE: Madison? No.

SAM: (*Surprised*) I rather imagine he's pretty well known in your country.

TEMPLE: Well, he can't be very well known or I should have heard of him.

SAM: Are you sure you haven't? Madison. M.A.D.I.S.O.N.?

TEMPLE: Quite sure.

SAM: Well now, that's very curious. (*A shrug*) Still, why should I worry if he gets the results.

8

TEMPLE:	Is he working for you?
SAM:	Yes. Actually he's employed by my London representative, a man called Hubert Greene.
TEMPLE:	What exactly is Madison doing?
SAM:	(*Quite simply*) He's trying to find out who I am.
TEMPLE:	Who you are?
SAM:	Yes.
TEMPLE:	But you know who you are. You're Sam Portland.
SAM:	Sure. Sure, I'm Sam Portland. Samuel L. Portland, President of the Portland Yeast Company. New York, Chicago, Detroit, Michigan and all points west. I'm one of the wealthiest men in America, Mr Temple, did you know that?
TEMPLE:	I had a shrewd idea.
SAM:	Right now I could lay my hands on twenty million dollars. It's an awful lot of dough.
TEMPLE:	(*Smiling*) It's an awful lot of dough, Mr Portland.
SAM:	(*Thoughtfully*) Twenty million bucks and I don't know who I am. (*Suddenly*) Mr Temple, would you like to hear my story?
TEMPLE:	Well, as a matter of fact, I did promise my wife …
SAM:	(*Laughing*) You're going to hear it anyway, so you might just as well relax!

TEMPLE laughs.

SAM:	Thirty five years ago, on October 9th 1914 to be precise, a Chicago policeman by the name of Dan Kelly arrested a young man for jay-walking – you know what I mean, trying to beat the traffic. The young fella turned out to be something of a problem. He was suffering from

what the doctors called amnesia, or to put it bluntly, just plain loss of memory.

TEMPLE: (*Interested*) Go on.

SAM: The young man was acquitted and the policeman – Kelly – took him under his wing. Kelly was convinced that sooner or later the young man's memory would return and he'd establish his identity. His memory never did return, Mr Temple, and the young fella never established his true identity.

TEMPLE: Go on, Mr Portland.

A moment.

SAM: I lived with Kelly for the best part of seven years. We got along famously together. I guess he was like a father and the proverbial big brother rolled into one. In 1920 I moved to New York and started the Portland Yeast Company. The rest you can guess. It was just a long, long trail leading to twenty million dollars.

TEMPLE: What made you choose the name Portland?

SAM: Well, I had to call myself something. (*Laughing*) I was on Portland Avenue when Kelly arrested me.

TEMPLE: But couldn't you remember anything?

SAM: Not a thing.

TEMPLE: Hadn't you any marks of identification?

SAM: No. When I was arrested I had three dollars in my pocket, a white handkerchief, a fountain pen and, curiously enough, an English penny.

TEMPLE: An English penny?

PORTLAND reaches for his watch-chain.

SAM: Yes, I've still got it. Look, it's on my watch-chain.

A slight pause.

10

TEMPLE: How does this fellow Madison fit into the picture?

SAM: (*Leaning towards TEMPLE*) I'll tell you. For years now I've been making inquiries in the hope of finding things out about myself. If you were in my shoes wouldn't you want to know who your parents were, where you came from, and why on a certain afternoon in the year 1914 you were suddenly discovered wandering down Portland Avenue in Chicago? Well, two weeks ago Hubert Greene, my London representative, phoned through to New York. He told me that a man called Madison – a well-known private inquiry agent in London – had discovered certain facts concerning my identity. As you can imagine, this sort of thing wasn't exactly new to me so I told Hubert to look into the matter.

TEMPLE: Did he?

SAM: Yes, he did. Three days ago he cabled me. He said he was convinced that Madison was on the level.

TEMPLE: M'm.

SAM: Frankly, I was rather surprised just now when you told me that you'd never heard of Madison.

TEMPLE: Well, I can soon check on him for you. I've got some very good friends at Scotland Yard.

SAM: I hope that won't be necessary, but if it is I'll let you know. (*Suddenly*) Oh, by the way, if you happen to meet Mrs Portland don't mention this Madison story. She doesn't know anything about it.

TEMPLE: No?

SAM: No, you see my wife, she takes the attitude that I should let the past take care of itself. "Why

	should you worry, Sam," she says, "you're sitting pretty anyway."
TEMPLE:	Well, that's certainly a point of view. Is your wife an American, Mr Portland?
SAM:	No, she's English, although she's lived in America for a great many years. As a matter of fact we've only been married for six weeks.
TEMPLE:	(*Faintly surprised*) Oh, well, congratulations!
SAM:	Thanks.
TEMPLE:	Why are you making this trip? For business reasons or simply to meet Madison? Is this a business trip?
SAM:	Well, my wife thinks I'm making it because of Moira. Oh, Moira's my daughter by my first marriage of course. She works in a London office. Actually, however, I must confess I'm coming over simply because of Madison. I'm sold on Madison, Temple. I believe he's found something – Hello, here's George! Now what does he want?

GEORGE KELLY arrives. He is an American of about forty. He has a tough, dry sense of humour.

KELLY:	There's been a call from the New York office. I couldn't find you so I told 'em to ring through this evening. They seemed to be all steamed up about something.
SAM:	Yes, all right, George. How's Mrs Portland?
KELLY:	(*As he leaves*) About the same. She don't look too good. (*He laughs*) I reckon she don't feel too good either.
SAM:	O.K. I'll be right down. (*A pause*) That's George Kelly. When poor old Dan died I promised to find his son a job. He's my secretary. I guess you wouldn't think so though to hear him talk!

12

(*Contemptuously*) He hasn't got the old man's guts, personality or anything else. Still, what can you do? (*Rising from his chair*) Well, I'll go down and see how the old lady's getting on. Nice to have met you, Mr Temple. Let's all have a drink together sometime.

TEMPLE: Yes, let's do that.

SAM: Say we meet in the cocktail bar at seven o'clock? I'll bring Mrs Portland along. How's that?

TEMPLE: Fine.

SAM: And don't forget to bring Mrs Temple.

TEMPLE: (*Laughing*) Well, I will if she can make it.

SAM: She'll make it all right!

SCENE 5: The Cocktail Bar.

We hear the rattle of a cocktail shaker above the background hum of conversation. TEMPLE and STEVE are seated at the bar.

TEMPLE: Are you feeling all right, Steve?

STEVE: Yes, darling. I'm all right now, Paul.

TEMPLE: You certainly look better than you did this morning.

STEVE: I certainly feel better.

BARMAN: What can I get you, madam?

TEMPLE: What would you like, darling? Have a champagne cocktail.

STEVE: Is that a good idea?

TEMPLE: It's a very good idea. Two champagne cocktails.

BARMAN: Yes, sir.

STEVE: I don't see Mr Portland.

TEMPLE: No, he hasn't arrived yet. Oh, here's his secretary …

STEVE: (*Softly*) Who's he with?

TEMPLE: I don't know, unless it's Mrs Portland.

13

STEVE: She's rather young, surely.

GEORGE KELLY and STELLA PORTLAND approach the bar.

KELLY: Excuse me. Have you seen Mr Portland?

TEMPLE: No. We arranged to meet here at seven o'clock but I'm afraid he hasn't shown up yet.

STELLA: I'm beginning to feel very worried, George.

STELLA PORTLAND is a woman of about thirty-eight.

KELLY: There's nothing to worry about. He's probably found a quiet corner somewhere and fallen asleep.

STELLA: (*Impatiently*) That's not like Sam. He doesn't do that sort of thing. (*Turning pleasantly*) Are you Mr Temple?

TEMPLE: Yes.

STELLA: I'm Stella Portland.

TEMPLE: I'm glad to meet you, Mrs Portland. This is my wife.

STELLA: How do you do, Mrs Temple? I hope you're feeling better now. My husband told me that you were not too good this morning.

STEVE: I'm much better, thank you.

STELLA: Seasickness must be really dreadful. I always feel frightfully sorry for anyone who suffers from it. Fortunately, I'm a very good sailor.

KELLY coughs.

STELLA: George, I do wish you'd go and look for Sam. I'm really dreadfully worried.

KELLY: (*Going*) O.K., O.K., Stella.

STELLA: I don't know what's happened to Sam. No one seems to have seen him since lunch time.

STEVE: Have you looked in the gymnasium?

STELLA: My husband's hardly the sort of man to spend an afternoon in the gymnasium.

14

TEMPLE: Well, what would you like to drink, Mrs Portland?

STELLA: May I have a Scotch?

TEMPLE: Yes, of course. What would you like with it?

STEVE: (*Quietly*) Darling, here's the Purser.

The PURSER arrives. He is a man of about forty. His manner is quiet and rather nervous.

PURSER: Excuse me, sir. Mrs Portland?

STELLA: Yes.

PURSER: I'm the Purser. The doctor would like to see you, Mrs Portland.

STELLA: (*Surprised*) To see me?

PURSER: (*Hesitantly*) Yes.

STELLA: But why should – What is it? What's happened?

PURSER: I'm afraid Mr Portland's met with an accident, madam. One of the passengers found him in the swimming pool. The doctor seems to think it was a heart attack.

STELLA: (*A note of desperation in her voice*) Where is he? Where is Sam?

PURSER: Well –

TEMPLE: Is he dead?

PURSER: (*Softly*) Yes, sir.

STELLA: Oh, no! No, no …

STELLA gives a sudden cry and faints, knocking a glass from the bar as she falls.

STEVE: Paul, she's fainted!

FADE up of music.

FADE DOWN.

SCENE 6: The TEMPLES' Drawing Room, as before.

FORBES: Did you speak to the doctor?

15

TEMPLE: Yes. He seemed pretty convinced it was a heart attack. Apparently the old boy had a weak heart, he ought never to have gone into the pool.

FORBES: Did you see Portland?

TEMPLE: Yes.

FORBES: There was no suggestion of foul play?

TEMPLE: So far as I could see, none whatsoever.

FORBES: How did Mrs Portland take it?

TEMPLE: She seemed stunned by the whole business. You just couldn't get any sense out of her,

FORBES: (*Bluntly*) Do you think Portland died from a heart attack, Temple?

TEMPLE: Yes, I do, but what caused the attack I wouldn't like to say. However, I haven't quite finished my story.

FORBES: Go on …

TEMPLE: When we arrived at Southampton Hubert Greene came aboard. Greene, you remember, was Portland's London representative. Well, I asked to see Greene and we met in the main lounge. He was a smart well-dressed man of about fifty. Just the sort of man you'd expect Sam Portland to have in charge of his London office …

CUT TO: The Ship's Main Lounge.

GREENE: Mr Temple?

TEMPLE: Yes.

GREENE: I'm Hubert Greene. I understand you want to see me?

TEMPLE: Yes. Do sit down, Mr Greene.

GREENE sinks into an armchair. He mops his forehead with his handkerchief.

GREENE: This is a most distressing business … I've just been on the phone to Moira …

TEMPLE: Portland's daughter?

GREENE: Yes – by his first marriage of course. The poor girl was heartbroken.

TEMPLE: I rather expected Miss Portland to come on board with you.

GREENE: No, as a matter of fact she couldn't leave town so I – (*He stops: curious*) Do you know Moira?

TEMPLE: No, but her father spoke to me about her. I understand she works for you.

GREENE: Well, she's attached to my office, yes. Whether she does any work or not is open to question. Poor Sam! He thought the world of Moira. (*Suddenly*) How did this business happen? You know it seems perfectly extraordinary to me. Do you think he did have a heart attack, or …

TEMPLE: Or what?

GREENE: Or was it an accident?

TEMPLE: The doctor seems convinced it was a heart attack.

GREENE: (*Suddenly: looking up*) How well did you know Sam?

TEMPLE: Not very well, I'm afraid. We met for the first – and the last time unfortunately – on Friday morning.

GREENE: Sam was a great guy. A real American. That's the only way you can describe him.

TEMPLE: Was he an American?

GREENE: But of course!

TEMPLE: I mean, was he born in America?

GREENE: Why, yes, I've always thought so. I was always under the impression he was born in Chicago.

TEMPLE: (*Slowly: significantly*) I think perhaps I ought to tell you, Greene, before we go any further.

Portland took me into his confidence: he told me why he was coming to England.

GREENE: (*Surprised*) He did?

TEMPLE: Yes.

A moment.

GREENE: Well, I hope you won't say anything about it, Temple. Now that the old boy's dead, I don't see any reason why we should go ahead. After all, it puts rather a different complexion on it. Don't you agree?

TEMPLE: Yes, but if you've no objection, I'd like you to do me a favour.

GREENE: By all means.

TEMPLE: I want you to introduce me to Mr Madison.

GREENE: Mr Madison?

TEMPLE: Yes.

GREENE: Who's Mr Madison?

TEMPLE: (*Surprised*) The private inquiry agent, the man who – (*He stops: quietly*) Are you trying to tell me you've never heard of Madison?

GREENE: Of course I haven't heard of him! Who is he?

TEMPLE: Two weeks ago you telephoned Portland that a private detective called Madison had discovered something about his identity.

GREENE: (*Bewildered*) Whose identity? Portland's?

TEMPLE: Yes.

GREENE: Look here, I don't want to be rude, old boy, but have you been drinking?

A pause.

TEMPLE: (*Watching GREENE*) You've never heard of Madison?

GREENE: I've already told you that I haven't.

TEMPLE: Then why was Sam Portland in such a hurry to get to England?

GREENE: I thought you knew why. You said he told you. (*A moment*) I was having trouble with Moira. I've been having trouble with her for weeks now. Thc girl's a little … well – she gets completely out of hand. I tried to keep it from Sam but in the end it was quite impossible. Three days ago I made up my mind that I wasn't going to stand any more of her damn nonsense. I cabled her father and offered my resignation.

TEMPLE: I see.

GREENE: If you don't believe me, ask George Kelly. He knows about Moira, he knows what's been going on. Now, if you'll excuse me, I've got to see if the car's ready for Mrs Portland.

CUT TO: The TEMPLES' Drawing Room, as before.

FORBES: Did you speak to the secretary, George Kelly?

TEMPLE: Yes, Sir Graham. He confirmed Greene's story. He said he'd actually seen the cable from Hubert Greene offering Portland his resignation.

FORBES: Did you ask him about Madison?

TEMPLE: He'd never heard of him.

FORBES: M'm.

STEVE: (*Curious*) Sir Graham, how does Scotland Yard come into this?

FORBES takes a note out of his pocket.

FORBES: Just over a week ago one of my men – an Inspector James – received this note. Here we are, Steve – read it.

STEVE takes the note.

STEVE: (*Reading*) "An American millionaire called Sam Portland intends to visit England. He must be stopped from doing so – if not a … murder will be committed."

19

TEMPLE: Is there a signature?

STEVE: No, it's typed, no signature.

FORBES: At first we thought it was a hoax, then James decided to take it seriously and contacted New York. They told him that Portland hadn't the slightest intention of coming to England.

TEMPLE: He probably hadn't at that time.

FORBES: We took no further interest in the matter until we heard that Portland was on his way over here and …

TEMPLE: … and had died of a heart attack.

FORBES: Yes.

There is a knock and the door opens.

CHARLIE: Excuse me, sir.

TEMPLE: What is it, Charlie?

CHARLIE: There's a Mr Greene to see you, sir. I didn't say you was in.

TEMPLE: (*Quietly*) That's all right, Charlie. I'll see him.

CHARLIE: (*Leaving*) O.K.

STEVE: What can he want?

TEMPLE: We'll soon see.

A moment, then:

CHARLIE: (*Off*) This way, please, sir.

GREENE is shown in.

TEMPLE: Hello, Greene! Come in. What can I do for you?

GREENE: I'm awfully sorry to disturb you, especially at this time of the night, but … (*He stops*) I beg your pardon, sir, but haven't we met before?

FORBES: My name is Forbes.

TEMPLE: This is Sir Graham Forbes of Scotland Yard.

GREENE: (*Laughing*) Oh, I beg your pardon! I was under the impression that we'd met somewhere. (*Shaking hands*) How do you do, sir?

FORBES: How do you do?

20

TEMPLE: I think you've met my wife.

GREENE: Yes, we met at Southampton. Good evening, Mrs Temple.

STEVE: Good evening.

GREENE: Temple, I've just left Mrs Portland. She's in a pretty bad way I'm afraid, and she seems very upset about – well – what seems to me rather a trivial matter!

FORBES: What is Mrs Portland upset about?

GREENE: Well, it seems that somebody's stolen Mr Portland's watchchain.

FORBES: Stolen his watchchain?

GREENE: Yes.

FORBES: Was it very valuable?

GREENE: (*Faintly exasperated*) From the way Stella's going on about it I should say extremely valuable!

STEVE: She's probably thinking of the sentimental value.

GREENE: I daresay she is, Mrs Temple, yes, but surely at a time like this ... to bother about a watchchain – it seems most odd.

TEMPLE: Have you been in touch with the Shipping Line?

GREENE: Yes, I've even been on to Southampton.

TEMPLE: Well, quite frankly, I don't see what I can do.

GREENE: I was wondering if, by any chance, you remember seeing the chain. If I remember rightly you saw Sam shortly after – after he died.

TEMPLE: The only time I remember seeing it was the morning he introduced himself to me. It was a thin gold chain with an English penny on the end. He kept the penny in his waistcoat pocket.

GREENE: I don't know anything about that. All I know is I wish to goodness we could find the chain!

TEMPLE: Where is Mrs Portland staying?

21

GREENE: She's at The Ritz but there's some talk of her coming down to my place for the weekend.

STEVE: Is she alone?

GREENE: No, George Kelly's with her and Moira's moving in tomorrow morning.

FORBES: Who's Moira?

GREENE: It's her stepdaughter.

TEMPLE: Have they met before, by the way?

GREENE: Yes, they met about six months ago in New York.

FORBES: Mr Greene, I understand from what Temple tells me, that you're in charge of the Portland Corporation in this country.

GREENE: Yes.

FORBES: When did you last see Portland?

GREENE: About four years ago.

FORBES: Was Portland over here?

GREENE: No. I was in America. So far as I know this was Sam's first trip to Europe. Well, I'm sorry to have bothered you, Temple. I thought perhaps you might be able to throw some light on the missing watchchain.

TEMPLE: If I were you I should get in touch with the Purser.

GREENE: Yes, I'll do that.

FORBES: Can I give you a lift? I was just about to make a move.

GREENE: Well, actually I'm on my way to Park Lane. If you could drop me I'd be very grateful.

FORBES: Yes, certainly.

TEMPLE: I'll see you to the door.

TEMPLE leads FORBES and GREENE into the hall.

GREENE: Goodnight, Mrs Temple.

STEVE: Goodnight.

FORBES:	Goodnight, Steve.
STEVE:	Goodnight, Sir Graham.
CHARLIE:	Is there anything you'd like, Mrs Temple, before I pop off to bed?
STEVE:	No, that's all right, Charlie.
CHARLIE:	O.K. Goodnight.
STEVE:	Goodnight.

TEMPLE comes back into the room.

CHARLIE:	I'm off to bed, Mr T. Goodnight.
TEMPLE:	Goodnight, Charlie.
STEVE:	Paul, do you think the doctor was mistaken about Portland? Do you think we've all been mistaken and – he was murdered?
TEMPLE:	No, I don't. But there's one thing I'm rather curious about, Steve.
STEVE:	What's that – the watchchain?
TEMPLE:	Yes …

A moment, then TEMPLE lifts the telephone receiver and starts to dial.

TEMPLE:	I'm going to have a word with Mrs Portland.
STEVE:	Oh, darling, not at this time of night.
TEMPLE:	I've got a hunch it's important.

We hear the ringing tone and then the telephone receiver being lifted at the other end of the line.

OPERATOR:	Good evening. Ritz Hotel …
TEMPLE:	Could I speak to Mrs Portland please?
OPERATOR:	Who is it calling?
TEMPLE:	My name is Temple.
OPERATOR:	One moment, please.

A moment.

A clicking noise can be heard and then a receiver is lifted.

STELLA:	(*Quietly*) Hello?
TEMPLE:	Mrs Portland? This is Paul Temple here.
STELLA:	Oh, good evening, Mr Temple!

TEMPLE: Forgive me ringing at this time of the night, Mrs Portland, but I've just been having a chat with Mr Greene. He tells me that you've lost your husband's watchchain?

STELLA: Is Hubert with you at the moment?

TEMPLE: No, he's just this second left.

STELLA: (*Hesitatingly*) I've got the chain, Mr Temple, there's no need to worry about it.

TEMPLE: (*Surprised*) You mean you've found it?

STELLA: No, I mean it was never lost. I – I had it all the time.

TEMPLE: (*Puzzled*) Oh. Oh, I see.

STELLA: (*A faint smile*) I doubt very much whether you do see, Mr Temple. Are you likely to be passing my hotel tomorrow?

TEMPLE: Yes, I might be. Probably in the morning.

STELLA: I'd like you to drop in for a few minutes.

TEMPLE: Yes, all right. Shall we say eleven o'clock?

STELLA: That will do nicely. Goodnight, Mr Temple.

TEMPLE: (*Deep in thought*) Goodnight, Mrs Portland.

TEMPLE replaces the receiver.

STEVE: What's happened?

TEMPLE: She's got the watchchain. Apparently it was never lost.

STEVE: Then Greene was lying?

TEMPLE: No, I don't think he was lying, darling. He really did think it was lost.

STEVE: Paul, there's something very odd about this business. Very odd.

TEMPLE: You're telling me. (*He yawns*) Let's go to bed, darling.

SCENE 7:   The TEMPLES' Bedroom.

TEMPLE and STEVE are in bed. TEMPLE is breathing very heavily, almost snoring.

Somewhere in the background, a clock chimes the hour. It is three o'clock.

There is a pause.

STEVE: (*Softly*) Paul, are you asleep?

TEMPLE: (*Quietly*) M'm?

STEVE: I said: are you asleep, darling?

TEMPLE: No. Is anything the matter?

STEVE: I thought I heard something.

TEMPLE: What?

STEVE: I don't know. It sounded as if there was someone on the balcony.

TEMPLE: Nonsense. Get to sleep, Steve.

STEVE: Darling, I'm sure I heard something.

TEMPLE: Of course you didn't.

There is a slight noise from the balcony, as if someone is removing a small pane of glass from a leaded window.

STEVE: Well, did you hear that?

TEMPLE: Sh!

There's another slight noise.

STEVE: What is it?

TEMPLE: You were right, there is someone on the balcony
            …

STEVE: Paul, who is it?

TEMPLE: I don't know.

STEVE: Is it a man?

TEMPLE: Yes?

STEVE: Can you see him?

TEMPLE: (*Very softly*) Yes …

STEVE: What are you going to do?

The man on the balcony slowly opens the window and enters the room.

TEMPLE:	He's coming into the room. Now don't move, Steve …
STEVE:	Paul, I don't like this …

TEMPLE is slowly climbing out of bed.

TEMPLE:	There's no need to be frightened. Keep quiet.
STEVE:	Paul, what are you going to do?
TEMPLE:	Sh.

A pause.

TEMPLE:	(*In his normal voice*) Are you looking for anything in particular, my friend – or is this just a social call?

The intruder is MARK KENDELL. He is a very well-built man of about forty.

KENDELL:	Why, what the …!
TEMPLE:	Put the light on, Steve!

STEVE clicks the light on.

STEVE:	Look out, he's got a gun!
TEMPLE:	(*Jumping at MARK*) No, you don't, my friend!
KENDELL:	(*Struggling*) My wrist! Leave go of my wrist! Leave go!
TEMPLE:	Drop it! Drop the gun!
KENDELL:	You're twisting my wrist!
TEMPLE:	Drop it!

The revolver fires.

TEMPLE:	Now drop it!

MARK drops the revolver to the floor.

KENDELL:	Please leave go!
TEMPLE:	Who are you? What are you doing here?
KENDELL:	(*Gasping for breath*) If you'll just wait a minute, I'll tell you. Please leave go of my wrist … Thank you … I came here because I wanted to …

MARK suddenly throws himself at TEMPLE.

STEVE: Look out!

TEMPLE and MARK are struggling. A table is over-turned, a vase crashes to the floor.

Then the sound of a smashing blow and TEMPLE gives a cry and collapses. He continues to groan throughout the following dialogue.

STEVE: Paul! Paul, darling!

KENDELL: Stay where you are! Do you hear me – stay where you are!

STEVE: If you come near me I'll scream. I'll scream! I warn you … (*She starts to scream*) Help! Charlie! Help!

KENDELL: Shut up!

STEVE: Charlie!

KENDELL: Do you hear me, shut up!

STEVE: Charlie!

KENDELL: (*In a panic*) Oh, my God, I've got to get out of here!

KENDELL rushes out through the window.

TEMPLE is still groaning: he is slowly coming to his senses.

STEVE: Paul, are you all right?

TEMPLE: What happened? Where is he? Steve, where is he?

STEVE: He's gone.

TEMPLE: What did he hit me with, a sledge-hammer?

STEVE: (*Faintly amused*) No, he just hit you.

TEMPLE: Just hit me! … What are you laughing about?

STEVE: I was just thinking – if this was in a novel – you'd be out on the balcony blazing away with a revolver!

TEMPLE: (*Annoyed with himself*) Yes, well, this isn't in a novel and I'm blazing away in here! Oh, my head … Steve, for heaven's sake stop giggling and go and get some ice …

27

SCENE 8:   The TEMPLES' Dining Room.

Breakfast time the following day. STEVE is at the table, drinking coffee. Then the door opens and TEMPLE enters.

STEVE: I thought you were never coming, Paul. I've poured your coffee out.

TEMPLE shuts the door and sits at the table.

TEMPLE: Oh, thanks, dear.

STEVE: I've told Charlie to make you an omelette. Is that all right?

TEMPLE: Yes, that's fine.

STEVE: How does your head feel this morning?

TEMPLE: It's not too bad. I could kick myself for letting that fellow get away.

STEVE: (*Laughing*) Oh you know, Paul, last night I was worried but I couldn't help laughing – nerves, I suppose.

TEMPLE: I don't know why the devil you didn't hit him with something! I'm afraid you didn't come up to scratch, darling.

STEVE: You didn't exactly come up to scratch yourself.

TEMPLE: (*Clearing his throat*) Er –

STEVE: Have you been in touch with the Yard?

TEMPLE: Yes, I spoke to Vosper. He's calling round after breakfast.

STEVE: Paul, do you think you'd recognise that man again?

TEMPLE: Yes, I think so. Wouldn't you?

STEVE: He was a dark … a very big man … about six foot two, I should imagine. I think he had a moustache.

TEMPLE: Yes, he had. I'd recognise the swine all right.

A slight pause.

STEVE: Paul, I've been thinking …

TEMPLE: Yes, I've been thinking too, dear …

28

STEVE: Paul, do you think he had anything to do with this Portland affair?

TEMPLE: (*Thoughtfully*) I don't know.

There's a knock and then the door opens.

CHARLIE: I beg your pardon, ma'am …

STEVE: Yes, what is it, Charlie?

CHARLIE: A Mrs Portland has called – she wants to see Mr Temple.

TEMPLE: Yes, all right. Ask her in.

CHARLIE: In here, sir?

TEMPLE: Yes.

CHARLIE: (*Leaving*) O.K.

STEVE: I thought you'd arranged to see Mrs Portland at her hotel?

TEMPLE: I did. I said I'd drop in about eleven.

A moment.

CHARLIE: (*At the door*) Mrs Portland.

STEVE: (*Rising: pleasantly*) Good morning, Mrs Portland. We're just having some coffee, won't you join us?

STELLA: (*Tired and emotional*) That's very sweet of you, Mrs Temple. A cup of coffee certainly would be very welcome.

STEVE: Won't you sit down. You look tired.

STELLA: Yes, I'm afraid I didn't sleep very well last night. (*Suddenly, an attempt to pull herself together*) I've just been for a walk in St James's Park. It's a lovely park, isn't it? You know, there's no place quite like London is there? I don't know why, but I always think the trees look so different. (*A sigh*) Sam would have loved it over here … It's an awful pity that … (*A moment*) Poor Sam.

STEVE passes STELLA a cup.

STEVE: Here's your coffee, Mrs Portland.

STELLA: Thank you.

TEMPLE: (*Pleasantly*) I think we had an appointment at eleven o'clock?

STELLA: Yes, we did, Mr Temple, I'm awfully sorry dropping in on you like this.

TEMPLE: That's all right. We're delighted to see you.

STELLA: I thought we might be able to talk better here than at my hotel, you see … (*Almost a note of desperation in her voice*) Mr Temple, did Sam talk to you about his watchchain? Did he show it to you?

TEMPLE: Yes, he did. Mrs Portland, what is this all about? Hubert Greene came here last night, he told me that you'd lost the chain and yet when I telephoned you at your hotel you –

STELLA: (*Quickly*) No. No, I haven't lost it. It's here –

STELLA removes the watchchain from her handbag and passes it to TEMPLE.

STELLA: I want you to have a look at it, Mr Temple. Please …

A pause.

TEMPLE: Well?

STELLA: Is that the chain that my husband showed you?

TEMPLE: Yes.

STELLA: Are you sure?

TEMPLE: (*Slowly*) Yes, I'm pretty sure. It's got the penny on the end and it looks exactly the same. Yes, this is it all right.

STELLA: Did my husband tell you about the penny?

TEMPLE: He said it was in his pocket when a policeman called Dan Kelly arrested him for jay-walking. That was in Chicago in 1914.

STELLA: Yes.

TEMPLE:	Your husband told me rather a remarkable story, Mrs Portland. He said that, from the moment he was arrested his memory was a complete blank, and he simply couldn't recall … (*He stops dead*)
STELLA:	What is it?
STEVE:	Paul, what's the matter?
STELLA:	What's the matter, Mr Temple?
TEMPLE:	Steve, look at the date on this penny!
STEVE:	(*Amazed*) 1919!

END OF EPISODE ONE

EPISODE TWO

THE MANILLA

ANNOUNCER: On their way home to England, after a visit to the United States, Paul Temple and Steve meet a Mr and Mrs Sam Portland. Portland is an American millionaire and he tells Temple that he is coming to England in order to consult a private investigator called Madison. Portland dies however before the boat reaches Southampton. The morning after their arrival, Temple and Steve are visited by Stella Portland. Mrs Portland shows Temple a watchchain which belonged to her husband …

SCENE 1: THE TEMPLES' Dining Room, as at the end of Episode 1.

STELLA: Is that the chain that my husband showed you?

TEMPLE: Yes.

STELLA: Are you sure?

TEMPLE: (*Slowly*) Yes, I'm pretty sure. It's got the penny on the end and it looks exactly the same. Yes, this is it all right.

STELLA: Did my husband tell you about the penny?

TEMPLE: He said it was in his pocket when a policeman called Dan Kelly arrested him for jay-walking. That was in Chicago in 1914.

STELLA: Yes.

TEMPLE: Your husband told me rather a remarkable story, Mrs Portland. He said that, from the moment he was arrested his memory was a complete blank, and he simply couldn't recall … (*He stops dead*)

STELLA: What is it?

STEVE: Paul, what's the matter?

STELLA: What's the matter, Mr Temple?

TEMPLE: Steve, look at the date on this penny!

STEVE: (*Amazed*) 1919!

STELLA: Why, that's impossible! If the penny wasn't made until 1919, Sam couldn't have had it in his pocket when he was arrested …

STELLA's voice dies away: she is confused and bewildered.

TEMPLE: Mrs Portland, when I met your husband, the first morning we left New York, he told me a very unusual story. He said that although he was known as Sam Portland, Portland was not in fact his real name. He told me that he didn't know his name, didn't even know his true identity.

STELLA: That's perfectly true. Thirty-five years ago a policeman called Dan Kelly found Sam wandering aimlessly down Portland Avenue in Chicago. He was suffering from amnesia: he just couldn't remember a single thing. He couldn't remember who he was or where he'd come from. (*Quietly*) Is that the story my husband told you?

TEMPLE: It's part of it, yes – but your husband also told me that Hubert Greene, his London representative, had cabled him about a private detective called Madison.

STELLA: (*Puzzled*) Madison?

TEMPLE: Yes. He was supposed to have discovered certain facts about your husband's past. But when I spoke to Greene about this he said he'd never heard of Madison.

STELLA: I've never heard of him either! All this is news to me!

TEMPLE: Your husband was pretty interested in Madison – he even went so far as to say that Madison was his sole reason for coming over here.

STELLA: (*A note of indignation in her voice*) That's ridiculous. We all know why Sam wanted to come to England. Moira, his daughter, works over here and the silly girl's been making a fool of herself. She's got herself engaged to a sleek young man called Chris Boyer, and I know for a fact that Sam was very worried about it.

STEVE: Chris Boyer? The name's familiar.

STELLA: He's a professional dancer. He works – if one can call it work – at the Manilla Club.

TEMPLE: Mrs Portland, you still haven't told us about the watchchain.

STELLA: Oh, yes! Yes, I was forgetting. Just before we left New York Sam said a rather peculiar thing. Actually, I thought he was joking.

TEMPLE: Oh? What did he say?

STELLA: He said: If anything should happen to me, Stella, please take great care of my watchchain. You'll probably find it's the most valuable thing I possess.

TEMPLE: Is that all he said?

STELLA: Yes.

TEMPLE: He didn't mention the penny at all.

STELLA: No.

STEVE: Mrs Portland, why did you tell Hubert Greene that the chain was missing?

STELLA: Because he was so curious about it. All the way down from Southampton he kept on asking me about the chain, throwing out veiled hints that he'd like to see it. (*The note of indignation returning*) I made up my mind that I wasn't going to let him see it.

TEMPLE: (*Slowly: examining the watchchain*) Well, it looks a perfectly ordinary watchchain. The only curious point is the date on the penny.

STELLA: Yes, that rather worries me. It almost makes me feel that Sam's story about himself was a fabrication.

TEMPLE: Well, that's one explanation of course, but there is another one.

STELLA: (*Curious*) What?

TEMPLE: (*Quietly*) Somebody's changed the penny.

SCENE 2: The TEMPLE's Study / The Hall / The Drawing Room.

Paul is busy typing. After a little while the front door buzzer goes. TEMPLE is a little irritated at being interrupted.

He stops typing, gets up, walks through to the hall and opens the front door.

TEMPLE: Hello, Sir Graham! I didn't expect you until four o'clock.

FORBES: I've been lunching with some friends in Berkeley Square. They started to talk a lot of high-falutin' nonsense about crime so I walked out on them. Why the devil don't people realise I'm just a flat-footed copper!

TEMPLE: (*Laughing, as he closes the door*) Because you don't look like a flat-footed copper! What you need is a whisky and soda.

FORBES: I couldn't agree with you more.

TEMPLE and SIR GRAHAM move into the drawing room, SIR GRAHAM to a chair, TEMPLE to the drinks table to pour two whiskies.

FORBES: Where's Steve?

TEMPLE: She's been down at Bramley all the week. She's due back on the 3.15.

FORBES: I expect you've got the boy down there?

TEMPLE: Yes, but – would you like soda with this or water?

FORBES: Water, please.

TEMPLE siphons in some soda, then hands the glass to FORBES.

TEMPLE: Here we are.

FORBES: Thank you.

TEMPLE: I'm seriously thinking of selling Bramley Lodge. It's very inconvenient always trotting down to Evesham. I've got my eye on a place outside Dorking.

FORBES: It's certainly a very nice part of the world.

TEMPLE: Yes, it is. (*He raises his glass*) Skoal!

FORBES: Skoal!

They drink.

TEMPLE: Well, did you go to the inquest?

FORBES: No, I was too busy. I sent Vosper.

TEMPLE: What happened?

FORBES: For your information Mr Samuel L. Portland died from natural causes. The coroner was quite convinced there was no suspicion of foul play.

TEMPLE: M'm.

FORBES: Don't you agree?

TEMPLE: Yes, and yet … There's something behind this Portland business. I don't know what it is, but I'm quite sure.

FORBES: I don't know. We mustn't make a mountain out of a molehill. Let's take the facts, Temple. Either Portland told you the truth about himself and about Hubert Greene getting in touch with him – in which case Greene lied to you when you saw

39

	him at Southampton – or Portland didn't tell you the truth, in which case …
TEMPLE:	In which case his story was a complete hoax.
FORBES:	Yes.
TEMPLE:	M'm.
FORBES:	You think Greene was lying and he did contact Portland about this mysterious Mr Madison?
TEMPLE:	Yes, on the other hand I'm not so sure that Greene wasn't telling the truth about Mrs Portland.
FORBES:	What do you mean?
TEMPLE:	I'm not so sure that Greene is interested in the watchchain. I've got a hunch that the chain was lost for a short time and Mrs Portland kicked up a devil of a fuss about it.
FORBES:	In other words she suspected Greene without, in your opinion, any real justification?
TEMPLE:	Yes.
FORBES:	Well, so far as we're concerned, Temple, there just isn't a case. I'm putting the whole thing right out of my mind.
TEMPLE:	Well I'm not. There's too many coincidences for my liking. First of all, you receive an anonymous letter stating that if Portland comes over here a murder will be committed, and then –
FORBES:	But a murder hasn't been committed!
TEMPLE:	One was very nearly committed, Sir Graham.
FORBES:	When?
TEMPLE:	Five nights ago, here, in this very flat.
FORBES:	(*Not convinced*) Oh, but, now look, that's a coincidence if you like! Just because a man breaks into your flat it doesn't mean to say –
TEMPLE:	You don't think it had anything to do with this business?

40

FORBES: I'm sure it hadn't!

TEMPLE: I don't know. Would you like another drink, Sir Graham?

FORBES: No thanks, I suppose I'd better be getting back to the Yard. Heaven only knows there's enough to do!

TEMPLE: What are you on at the moment?

FORBES: We're awfully worried about this counterfeit business. I expect you've read about it?

TEMPLE: No, I can't say I have.

FORBES: It's serious, Temple. For several months now the Continent has been flooded with counterfeit notes – chiefly dollars, of course. About a week ago the French people stated that in their opinion the gang were not actually working from the Continent but from England.

TEMPLE: You mean the French authorities think that the gang have their headquarters here – in this country?

FORBES: Yes.

TEMPLE: Do you think that?

FORBES: Two months ago I should have said no. Now, I'm not so sure.

TEMPLE: Who are the people behind this – have you any idea?

FORBES: I wouldn't say this to anyone else, Temple, but frankly, at the moment we just haven't a clue.

TEMPLE: Well, there must be somebody behind it. Somebody with a first-class brain if you ask me. Organisations don't run themselves, Sir Graham.

FORBES: (*Rising*) No. Well, now you know why I'm not particularly interested in the late Mr Portland, to say nothing of his watchchain.

The telephone rings.

TEMPLE: Excuse me.

TEMPLE lifts the receiver.

TEMPLE: Hello?

We hear STEVE pressing Button B on the other end.

STEVE: (*On the other end of the line*) Is that you, Paul?

TEMPLE: Hello, Steve. Where are you?

STEVE: Paul, listen! I'm in Harridges. I want you to come here straight away. It's urgent, darling.

TEMPLE: What's happened?

STEVE: I came back from Bramley on the 11.40. When I got to Paddington I was just getting into a taxi to come straight back to the flat when I saw a man cross over to the taxi rank. At first I couldn't place him although I knew jolly well I'd seen him somewhere before. Then suddenly I realised who it was. Darling, it was that man!

TEMPLE: Which man?

STEVE: The man who broke into the flat, the man who knocked you out!

TEMPLE: Are you sure?

STEVE: Absolutely sure!

TEMPLE: Go on, Steve.

STEVE: I didn't know what to do. I waited a bit and then when I saw he was taking a taxi I decided to follow him. Anyway, to cut a long story short, he's here, at Harridges.

TEMPLE: Where are you actually speaking from?

STEVE: I'm in a callbox on the ground floor, you know, darling, next to the flower stall.

TEMPLE: Where's the man?

STEVE: He's in the snack bar. It's all right, he can't come out without my seeing him, in any case he's only just given his order.

TEMPLE: Has he seen you?

STEVE:	No, I don't think so.
TEMPLE:	Steve, are you sure it's the same man?
STEVE:	Absolutely sure.
TEMPLE:	O.K. darling. I'll be there in ten minutes!

TEMPLE bangs down the receiver.

FORBES:	What's happened?
TEMPLE:	Get your hat, Sir Graham! I'll explain in the car.

SCENE 3:	The Ground Floor of Harridges, a smart department store.

We hear the chatter of shoppers passing to and fro. In the background are the sounds of the snack bar.
TEMPLE arrives, a little out of breath.

TEMPLE:	Hello, Steve … Is he still here?
STEVE:	Darling, you've been quick! (*Surprised*) Hello, Sir Graham!
TEMPLE:	Steve, is he still here?
STEVE:	Yes, he's in the snack bar. He hasn't come out yet.
TEMPLE:	Are you sure it's the same man, darling?
STEVE:	Yes, I've told you, I'm quite sure. In any case, if you walk down the corridor over there you can see him through the glass door. He's sitting at the counter.
TEMPLE:	Come along, Sir Graham! Come along, sergeant!
SERGEANT:	Sir.

They move down the corridor.

FORBES:	Well?
TEMPLE:	(*Quietly*) Yes, that's him all right.
SERGEANT:	The chap in the grey suit with the attaché case.

TEMPLE:	Yes, that's him, sergeant, there's no doubt about it.
STEVE:	Well, I'm glad to hear it!
FORBES:	Nice work, Steve!
TEMPLE:	Yes, you did very well, darling.
SERGEANT:	(*Watching*) He's paying his bill, sir.
STEVE:	What are you going to do?
FORBES:	We'll pick him up as soon as he comes out.
TEMPLE:	He's a pretty tough customer, Sir Graham. It's a hundred to one he'll make a dash for it.
FORBES:	Is there another entrance near here?
STEVE:	Yes, just over on the right. It leads into Knightsbridge.
FORBES:	You'd better watch it, Temple.
TEMPLE:	He's probably armed, Sir Graham. I think the three of us ought to tackle this character.
FORBES:	No, you watch the door, Temple. Otherwise if he gets away from us we'll probably lose him.
STEVE:	I think he's right, Paul.
TEMPLE:	Yes, all right. You'd better come with me, Steve.
SCENE 4:	Another Part of the Ground Floor of Harridges, by the Knightsbridge Entrance.
STEVE:	He's rather a long time coming out of the snack-bar.
TEMPLE:	I hope there isn't another entrance to that place.
STEVE:	No, I'm sure there isn't … (*Suddenly*) There he is! He's just come out!
A pause.	
TEMPLE:	The sergeant's talking to him …

There is another pause, then in the background we hear MARK KENDELL struggling, shouting, and trying to free himself.

KENDELL: (*Off*) Take – your – hands – off – me!

There is more struggling, then KENDELL breaks free from the SERGEANT and runs towards TEMPLE and STEVE.

TEMPLE: Look out, Steve, he's coming this way!

SERGEANT: (*Off*) Stop him, sir! Stop him!

TEMPLE makes a grab at KENDELL.

TEMPLE: Oh, no you don't, my friend!

KENDELL: What the devil do you think you're doing! Leave me alone! (*Struggling wildly*) Take your hands off me! Do you hear what I say, take your hands off me!

STEVE: Look out, Paul! Mind the case! Mind the – !

MARK swings the case against TEMPLE and with a cry of pain and annoyance TEMPLE falls to one side. The case drops to the ground.

TEMPLE: (*Breathless*) Blast!

STEVE: Paul, are you all right?

TEMPLE: (*Getting up*) Yes, I'm only winded!

FORBES rushes up.

FORBES: Where is he? Temple, where is he?

TEMPLE: (*On the move*) This way! Come on, Sir Graham!

SCENE 5:   The Busy Street Outside Harridges.

We hear the sounds of traffic and pedestrians.

FORBES: (*Breathless*) He's given us the slip, Temple!

TEMPLE: It looks very much like it!

FORBES: Confound it, if only we'd held on to the fellow you could have –

STEVE: Paul, there he is!

TEMPLE: Where?

SERGEANT:	She's right, sir!
FORBES:	He's just crossing the road, Temple!
TEMPLE:	He's making for the Underground. Come on, Sir Graham! Come on, sergeant! We'll head him off!
STEVE:	Paul, be careful!
FORBES:	He's spotted us, Temple!
STEVE:	Paul, that taxi … He's not looking where he's going, he's running straight into – Oh!

As STEVE speaks there is a tremendous screeching of brakes and several cries of alarm from pedestrians. MARK has been knocked down by a taxi and the screeching of brakes is followed by the voices of an excited crowd and the noises of congested traffic.

FORBES:	He ran head-long into it!
STEVE:	How dreadful!
FORBES:	Go back to Harridges, Steve, there's no need for you to get mixed up in this. We'll meet you there in a few minutes.
TEMPLE:	Yes, go on, darling. We'll see you in the snack bar.
FORBES:	Come along, Temple!

FADE UP of street noises and excited voices.
FADE SCENE completely.

SCENE 6:   Harridges' Snack Bar
There is a background of polite conversation and the muted clink of teacups, etc.
TEMPLE and FORBES approach STEVE.

TEMPLE:	Sorry we've been so long.
STEVE:	What happened?
FORBES:	He was killed, Steve.
STEVE:	Oh dear.
TEMPLE:	It must have been instantaneous.

STEVE: Darling, I feel awful.

FORBES: Now Steve, listen, there's no point in reproaching yourself about this. If he hadn't resisted arrest this would never have happened.

STEVE: Who was he, do you know?

FORBES: According to this diary we found on him, his name's Mark Kendell. (*Reading*) "Address, 78A Nelson Towers, Chelsea." I'll get Vosper to check that.

TEMPLE: Is there anything else in it of interest?

A moment, as FORBES flicks the diary pages.

FORBES: … No, there doesn't seem to be … Just a minute! Apparently our friend had a date this evening!

TEMPLE: (*Leaning over*) Where does it say that?

FORBES: Look – … 8.45. The Manilla. Appointment with C.B."

TEMPLE: The Manilla? That's familiar … Where have I heard that name before?

STEVE: Yes, don't you remember, darling? Mrs Portland mentioned it. She said that her step-daughter was engaged – (*She stops*) That's funny.

TEMPLE: What is it, Steve?

STEVE: She said that her step-daughter was engaged to a man called Chris Boyer – CB – he's a professional dancer at the Manilla Club …

TEMPLE: (*Significantly*) I wonder if that's another coincidence, Sir Graham?

FORBES: By George, this business is beginning to tie-up, Temple! It's beginning to look as if Kendell really was mixed up in the Portland affair.

STEVE: Then why did he break into our flat?

TEMPLE:	It's pretty obvious why he broke into the flat, darling – he was looking for something.
FORBES:	That watchchain?
TEMPLE:	(*Slowly*) It might have been the watchchain, Sir Graham.
STEVE:	Paul …
TEMPLE:	Yes, darling?
STEVE:	I was just thinking. Wouldn't it be quite an idea if we went along to the Manilla Club tonight and simply asked Boyer if he had an appointment with this man Mark Kendell?
TEMPLE:	Quite an idea, but unfortunately neither of us happen to be members of the Manilla.
FORBES:	We can easily get over that, Temple.
STEVE:	Don't say you're a member, Sir Graham!
FORBES:	No, but Archie Brooks is. He'll fix you up all right.
TEMPLE:	Who's Archie Brooks?
FORBES:	One of our bright boys. We keep him on tap for occasions like this. I'll tell him to meet you both at the Manilla at ten o'clock. Is that all right?
TEMPLE:	Fine.
FORBES:	Well, I'll get back to the Yard.
STEVE:	Don't forget the attaché case, Sir Graham. I picked it up when I came back into the store.
FORBES:	Oh yes. (*He picks the case up*) I say, it's pretty heavy, isn't it?
TEMPLE:	You'd think so if you'd been biffed in the tummy with it!
FORBES:	Have you looked inside, Steve?
STEVE:	No. Of course not.

Under the next few words, FORBES clicks open the case's two catches.

48

FORBES: What the devil was the fellow carrying about with him? (*Opening the lid*) Temple, look …

STEVE: What is it? Why – why the case is full of notes!

TEMPLE: By Timothy!

FORBES: They're dollar bills!

SCENE 7:   The Main Hall of the Manilla Club.

At the cloakroom. There is a slight background of people chatting. In the distant background a dance orchestra can be heard playing.

GIRL: Can I take your hat and coat, sir?

TEMPLE: Oh, thank you.

STEVE: (*Off*) I'll be with you in a moment, darling.

TEMPLE: Yes, all right, Steve.

GIRL: Here's your ticket, sir.

TEMPLE: Thank you.

MAITLAND is a man of about fifty with a slightly officious manner.

MAITLAND: Excuse me, sir, but are you a member?

TEMPLE: No, I'm looking for a Mr Brooks.

MAITLAND: (*Much pleasanter*) Oh, are you Mr Temple, sir?

TEMPLE: Yes.

MAITLAND: He's expecting you, sir. He's in the cocktail bar.

TEMPLE: Thank you.

HUBERT GREENE arrives. He is in rather a bad mood.

GREENE: My hat and coat, please.

GIRL: Have you got the ticket, sir?

GREENE feels in his pocket.

GREENE: I've got the confounded thing somewhere. It was No. 74 … Oh, here we are!

TEMPLE: Hello, Greene! I didn't expect to see you at the Manilla.

49

GREENE: (*Surprised*) Oh, hello, Temple! What are you doing here?

TEMPLE: Strange though it may seem, I frequent this type of establishment.

GREENE: You're welcome. It's not my idea of fun and games.

TEMPLE: What is your idea of fun and games?

GREENE: Do you play chess?

TEMPLE: Indifferently, I'm afraid.

GREENE: (*Blandly*) Well, that's my idea of fun and games.

GIRL: Your hat and coat, sir.

GREENE: Oh, thank you.

TEMPLE and GREENE stroll away from the cloakroom.

TEMPLE: Are you a member here?

GREENE: No, but Moira Portland is. I dropped in to have a word with her.

TEMPLE: Is Miss Portland here tonight?

GREENE: Yes, she's with her fiancé Chris Boyer. The silly girl's here every night. I wish to goodness someone would talk to her, Temple!

TEMPLE: Oh – what about?

GREENE: She doesn't seem to realise how serious the situation is. Now that the old man's dead I'm afraid a great deal of responsibility's going to fall on Moira. There's going to be a lot of work to do during the next three or four months. This is no time for gallivanting about. I'm afraid this chap Boyer is a very bad influence on her.

TEMPLE: Is that what you've been telling her?

GREENE: No, I've been trying to persuade her to come down to my place for the weekend. I've got Mrs Portland staying with me and the old

	boy's secretary, George Kelly. There's a great deal to discuss, Temple.
TEMPLE:	Yes, I can well imagine it.
GREENE:	Moira refuses to come unless I invite this fellow Boyer. Why the devil should I invite Boyer? Quite apart from the fact that I can't abide the fellow, he's not a member of the family, and he's got nothing whatever to do with the business.
TEMPLE:	(*Smiling*) Well, it looks as if he's going to be a member of the family, doesn't it?
GREENE:	I wouldn't be too sure about that. This isn't the first boy friend Moira's lost her head over … (*Quietly*) Hello, here she is!
TEMPLE:	Is that Boyer?
GREENE:	Yes.
TEMPLE:	He's very good looking.
GREENE:	(*With sarcasm*) And he dances like a dream – in case you're interested.

MOIRA PORTLAND arrives with CHRIS BOYER. MOIRA is a rather headstrong girl of about twenty-six. BOYER is a sleek gigolo.

MOIRA:	Hello, Hubert! I thought you'd gone!
GREENE:	I'm just leaving, Moira. Oh Moira, this is Mr Temple.
MOIRA:	(*Vaguely*) How d'you do.
TEMPLE:	(*Watching MOIRA*) How d'you do.
MOIRA:	We're just going into the bar, Hubert. Won't you join us?
GREENE:	No, thank you.
MOIRA:	(*Pulling his leg*) You can have an orangeade, darling.
GREENE:	(*Quietly*) I don't like orangeade.
MOIRA:	Oh, I forgot! It's ginger ale, isn't it?

51

BOYER laughs.

MOIRA: Goodbye, Mr … (*She stops: seriously*) Did you say your name was Temple?

TEMPLE: (*Still watching MOIRA*) Mr Greene said so – yes.

MOIRA: (*Rather uncertain of herself*) I've heard Stella talk about you. You know who I mean, don't you? Stella Portland. (*A touch of sarcasm*) My stepmother.

TEMPLE: Yes, we met on the boat coming over from America.

MOIRA: That must have been cosy. Oh, this is my fiancé – Chris Boyer.

BOYER: How do you do, Mr Temple?

TEMPLE: How do you do?

BOYER: This is quite an honour. I've heard a great deal about you, sir.

TEMPLE: From Mrs Portland?

BOYER: No, no! I mean from the newspapers. They say you're the most famous private detective in England.

TEMPLE: That's very nice of them. I wonder if Mr Madison shares that opinion.

BOYER: (*Puzzled*) Mr … Madison?

TEMPLE: He's another private detective – at least, so I'm told. Ah, here's my wife! (*Moving off*) Will you excuse me?

MOIRA: Well, goodbye, Hubert!

GREENE: Goodbye, Moira. (*Swallowing his pride*) I hope I shall see you at the weekend – both of you.

BOYER: Why, that's charming of you! We shall be delighted. Shan't we, Moira?

MOIRA: Of course. Delighted. Goodbye Hubert …

AS MOIRA and BOYER leave, TEMPLE returns with STEVE.

GREENE: Ah, Temple – (*Quietly*) – now you see what I'm up against. (*Pleasantly*) Hello, Mrs Temple, how are you?

STEVE: Hello, Mr Greene. I thought I recognised you!

TEMPLE: Are you ready, Steve? Our friend's apparently in the cocktail bar.

STEVE: Yes, I'm ready.

GREENE: Goodbye, Temple. Goodbye, Mrs Temple – nice to have seen you again.

STEVE: Goodbye.

TEMPLE and STEVE start to walk towards the busy cocktail bar.

STEVE: Is he a member here?

TEMPLE: No, he only dropped in to have a word with Miss Portland.

STEVE: Yes, that's the girl I saw you talking to?

TEMPLE: Yes. The rather sleek young man was her fiancé.

STEVE: What, Boyer? Did you ask him about Kendell?

TEMPLE and STEVE have reached the doorway to the bar. TEMPLE looks round the crowded room.

TEMPLE: No, I didn't want to say anything in front of Greene. Let's go in.

TEMPLE and STEVE move into the bar.

TEMPLE: Now I wonder which one of these bright young things happens to be Archie Brooks?

STEVE: I'll bet a fiver that's him.

TEMPLE: Where?

STEVE: Over there – propping up the bar.

ARCHIE: Well, you'll lose your fiver! I'm much better looking than that! Mrs Temple?

STEVE: (*Taken aback*) Yes?

ARCHIE: I'm Archie Brooks. How are you? Temple?

TEMPLE:	Yes.
ARCHIE:	Glad to meet you. Heard an awful lot about you from Sir Graham. Deuced odd we haven't met before.
TEMPLE:	(*Laughing*) Yes, it is! I hope this date hasn't inconvenienced you?
ARCHIE:	Not in the slightest. I'm usually in some pub or other at this time of night. By the way, shall we go straight to our table? This place is a bit like a bear-garden.
STEVE:	Yes, I think it's a very good idea.
ARCHIE:	Can you push your way through the bods, Mrs Temple, or shall I shout fire?
STEVE:	(*Laughing*) I think I can manage.

As they push through the crowd, they pass GEORGE, a hearty R.A.F. type.

GEORGE:	(*Very surprised*) Hello, Chunky! How are you?
ARCHIE:	Hello, George! How's things?
GEORGE:	Ghastly!
ARCHIE:	Where's Edith?
GEORGE:	She's in Tenby, old boy. Been there for six months.
ARCHIE:	Tenby?
GEORGE:	Yes.
ARCHIE:	How very odd.
GEORGE:	It's all very difficult, Chunky. Tell you next time we meet.
ARCHIE:	Yes, all right, George! Cheers!
GEORGE:	(*Passing on*) Cheers, old boy!

SCENE 8: The Main Hallway of the Manilla Club.
TEMPLE, STEVE and ARCHIE BROOKS are strolling towards the dining room. Through the following few lines, FADE UP the buzz of Dining Room conversation.

ARCHIE: That was George Denson. We were at school together.
TEMPLE: (*Laughing*) I rather gathered that.
STEVE: Why did he call you Chunky?
ARCHIE: Everybody calls me Chunky, Mrs Temple. Do you remember those beautiful pineapple chunks we used to get?
STEVE: Yes.
ARCHIE: Well, I used to eat thousands of 'em when I was at school. Simply couldn't stop. Tin after tin. By Golly, I've eaten some pineapple chunks in my time! (*He laughs pleasantly*)

They've now arrived at the dining room.

ARCHIE: Good evening, Robert.
ROBERT: Good evening, Mr Brooks.
ARCHIE: Have you got my table?
ROBERT: Yes, sir.
ARCHIE: Everything's got to be just right tonight, Robert. Just right. I've got some very distinguished guests.
ROBERT: Yes, sir.
ARCHIE: And don't you dare give me that table near the ventilator. You know, Mrs Temple, I had dinner here last Friday (*START FADE*) and on Saturday morning my shoulder was so jolly stiff I couldn't hold a bally squash racket …

SCENE 9:   The Manilla Club Dining Room

There is a background of after-dinner conversation and a dance orchestra. This is a small combination orchestra playing soft, sweet music.

ARCHIE, STEVE and TEMPLE are at a table.

ARCHIE: Are you sure you won't have a liqueur, Mrs Temple?

STEVE:	Quite sure.
ARCHIE:	What about you, Temple?
TEMPLE:	No, thanks.
ARCHIE:	Well, we'll have a cigar anyway! (*Over his shoulder*) Robert, fetch us a decent cigar, will you?
ROBERT:	Certainly, sir.
TEMPLE:	Did Sir Graham tell you why we wanted to come here tonight?
ARCHIE:	He said you wanted to see Chris Boyer. I can't imagine why.
STEVE:	Do you know him?
ARCHIE:	Vaguely. I know everyone vaguely, Mrs Temple, that's my job.
TEMPLE:	(*Curious*) What exactly is your job?
ARCHIE:	Didn't Sir Graham tell you?
TEMPLE:	No.
ARCHIE:	(*Pleasantly*) Then I should ask him. That's Chris Boyer over there. Shall I invite him over for a drink?
TEMPLE:	No, that might look obvious. Tell him Steve's been admiring his dancing and she'd like to have a dance with him.
ARCHIE:	He'll fall for that all right. He thinks he's Casanova.
STEVE:	(*Quietly*) He's heading this way …
TEMPLE:	He walks exactly like a gigolo.
BOYER:	(*Pleasantly*) Hello, Chunky, how are you?
ARCHIE:	I'd like you to meet some friends of mine – Mr and Mrs Temple. Chris Boyer.
BOYER:	Mr Temple and I have already met. But this is an unexpected pleasure, Mrs Temple.

56

ARCHIE: Now, now, Chris, don't start switching on the charm. Mrs Temple's been admiring your dancing.

BOYER: That's very nice of you, Mrs Temple.

ARCHIE: To me, you're just a rogue elephant with lumbago! (*He laughs*) But what's my opinion against so many?

BOYER: You've taken the words right out of my mouth. Would you care to dance, Mrs Temple?

STEVE: I should love to.

BOYER: (*To TEMPLE*) Do you mind, sir?

TEMPLE: No, of course not.

STEVE leaves the table and commences to dance with CHRIS BOYER.

ARCHIE: (*Quietly*) He's a conceited devil, isn't he?

TEMPLE: (*Watching STEVE and BOYER*) Yes, but he knows how to dance.

Cross to STEVE and BOYER dancing.

BOYER: Is Mr Greene a friend of your husband's, Mrs Temple?

STEVE: We met at Southampton. He came down to meet Mr Portland.

BOYER: Yes, of course. It was very sad about Mr Portland. I was so much looking forward to meeting him.

STEVE: Yes, he seemed to be a very nice man.

STEVE and BOYER dance for a moment.

BOYER: I don't remember seeing you here before, Mrs Temple. Is your husband a member?

STEVE: No, neither of us are members. I suppose we shouldn't be here really, it was entirely Mr Brooks's idea.

BOYER: And a very nice idea if I may say so.

STEVE: Thank you.

STEVE and BOYER continue dancing. BOYER starts to hum the tune – occasionally saying the words of the lyrics to himself.

BOYER: It's not crowded tonight. Usually, at this time, it's impossible to get a table.

STEVE: Is your fiancée a good dancer, Mr Boyer?

BOYER: (*Reluctantly*) Yes – she's about average, I suppose.

A moment.

STEVE: I was awfully sorry to read about that friend of yours.

BOYER: Which one?

STEVE: The one you had the appointment with.

BOYER: Who do you mean?

STEVE: Haven't you read about it? He was knocked down by a taxi outside Harridges.

BOYER: Who are you talking about? I have no appointment this evening – except with my fiancée.

The dance orchestra stops. There is polite applause.

STEVE: There must be some mistake. I thought this man was a friend of yours. His name was Mark Kendell.

BOYER: I've never heard of him. What gave you the impression he was a friend of mine?

STEVE: (*Vaguely*) Something my husband said. I must have misunderstood him.

BOYER: (*Coldly*) I'm afraid you must have done, Mrs Temple. Shall we go back to the table?

STEVE and BOYER return to the table.

STEVE: Mr Boyer's furious with me, darling. He's a heavenly dancer and I've simply trodden all over his feet!

ARCHIE: Good.

BOYER: You've done nothing of the sort. You're a very
            good dancer, Mrs Temple.
ARCHIE: I'll bet you tell that to all the girls!
BOYER: Now if you'll excuse me … Goodbye, sir.
TEMPLE: Goodbye.
BOYER: Goodnight, Mrs Temple.
STEVE: Goodnight!

A pause.

TEMPLE: Well? Did you ask him about Kendell?
STEVE: Yes. He said that he hadn't an appointment:
            that he'd never even heard of him.
TEMPLE: Do you think he was telling the truth, Steve?
STEVE: (*Thoughtfully*) Yes, I do.
ARCHIE: You bet she does! Old Chris is an
            accomplished liar! He lies even better than he
            dances. Oh, by the way, Sir Graham told me to
            give you a message. You know those notes, the
            ones in the attaché case?
TEMPLE: Yes?
ARCHIE: They were counterfeit. Damn good counterfeit
            too. Personally, I couldn't tell the difference.
STEVE: Did Sir Graham tell you about Kendell – about
            what happened?
ARCHIE: Yes. I knew the fellow. He used to be an artist
            with one of the big advertising agencies.
            Temperamental sort of cove from what I
            remember.
TEMPLE: How well did you know him?
ARCHIE: Oh, vaguely, very vaguely. (*Suddenly*) I say,
            look here, Temple – it's a quarter to twelve,
            would you mind terribly if we broke the party
            up?
TEMPLE: No of course not. I was going to suggest that
            we made a move.

STEVE: (*Amused*) Have you got a date, Mr Brooks?

ARCHIE: Good Lord, no! Only I promised to pop in and see my sister. She's got a flat just round the corner.

STEVE: Your sister?

ARCHIE: Yes. (*A little laugh*) She's been my sister for years.

ROBERT: Excuse me, sir.

ARCHIE: Yes, what is it, Robert?

ROBERT: There's a telephone call for Mrs Temple, sir.

STEVE: For me?

ROBERT: Yes, madam.

TEMPLE: Are you sure it isn't for Mr Temple?

ROBERT: Quite sure, sir. The gentleman particularly asked for Mrs Temple. He refused to give his name, sir.

STEVE: (*Rising*) Yes, all right, I'll take it.

ROBERT: There's a box in the hall, madam.

TEMPLE: (*Also rising*) I'll come with you, darling. Goodbye, Brooks. Thank you for the dinner.

ARCHIE: Delighted, old boy! Goodbye, Mrs Temple. See you again sometime.

STEVE: I hope so. Thanks for a lovely evening. (*To TEMPLE, as she moves away*) Who do you think it is on the phone, darling?

TEMPLE: (*Thoughtfully*) I should imagine it's Charlie.

SCENE 10:   The Interior of a Telephone Box in the Manilla Club Hall.

STEVE opens the folding doors and she and TEMPLE squeeze into the box.

STEVE: (*Hesitating*) Shall I take it?

TEMPLE: Yes, of course.

TEMPLE shuts the door. STEVE lifts the receiver.

STEVE: Hello?

KELLY: (*On the other end of the line*) Hello, is that Mrs Temple?

STEVE: Yes.

KELLY: This is George Kelly here. Do you remember me? We met on the boat coming over from the States.

STEVE: Yes, of course, I remember you. You're Mr Portland's secretary.

KELLY: I <u>was</u> his secretary. Yeah, you've got the right guy all right. Mrs Temple, listen. There's something I want to say to you.

STEVE: Well, I'm listening, Mr Kelly.

KELLY: Now don't take this wrong. This isn't a melodramatic warning, it's just a nice piece of friendly advice. I took a liking to that husband of yours, Mrs Temple. He looks a pretty regular fella.

STEVE: Well, I think so. Of course, I may be prejudiced.

KELLY: Regular fellas like that should be taken care of, you know. They shouldn't be allowed to go around pushing their noses into affairs which don't concern them.

STEVE: What do you mean?

KELLY: (*Pleasantly*) Tell your husband to keep out of this Madison case. If he doesn't, he's going to get mixed up with a bunch of very unpleasant customers. (*With a laugh*) I know. I happen to be one of them.

STEVE: (*Sweetly*) I don't think you're unpleasant, Mr Kelly. A little stupid perhaps, but not unpleasant.

KELLY: (*Amused*) You don't know me, baby. Let's
            hope you don't get to know me. Remember
            what I've told you. You have a word with that
            husband of yours. If he's smart, he'll catch on.

STEVE: Mr Kelly, just supposing your wife told –

KELLY: I haven't got a wife, honey!

STEVE: (*Forcefully*) Well, supposing you had a wife
            and supposing you were mixed up in the
            Madison case and supposing she told you to
            keep your nose out of it! What would you do,
            Mr Kelly?

KELLY: (*Seriously*) I'd take a slow boat to China.

*KELLY rings off. STEVE replaces the receiver. TEMPLE and
STEVE are stood together in the telephone box. They speak
quietly, confidentially to each other.*

STEVE: Did you hear that?

TEMPLE: Yes.

STEVE: What did you make of it?

TEMPLE: It sounded to me as if he'd been told to contact
            you. Did you notice, Steve, he said "Tell your
            husband to keep out of this Madison case." Not
            Portland, but Madison. Yet when I spoke to
            Kelly on the boat he said he'd never even heard
            of Madison.

STEVE: Yes, but who is Madison? If Portland was
            telling the truth and Madison's a private
            detective he shouldn't be difficult to find.

TEMPLE: Well, the Yard can't find him. I've had Sir
            Graham on his track for almost a week now.

In the distance the dance band resumes playing.

STEVE: There's another thing, Paul. How did Kelly
            know that we were here – at the Manilla?

TEMPLE: He might have seen us come in – unless of
            course …

62

STEVE: … Someone tipped him off?

TEMPLE: Yes. (*Suddenly*) Come on, Steve!

TEMPLE opens the door of the telephone box and he and STEVE re-enter the hall. The dance orchestra plays in the background.

SCENE 11:   The Street Outside the Manilla Club.

There is distant noise of the main thoroughfare.

STEVE: Where did you put the car?

TEMPLE: It's round the corner in a side street.

A moment.

TEMPLE and STEVE stroll along the pavement.

STEVE: Paul, I've been thinking about Hubert Greene. Do you think he's simply invented that story about Madison in order to get Portland over here?

TEMPLE: According to Greene he'd plenty of excuses for getting Portland over here.

STEVE: His daughter for instance?

TEMPLE: Yes.

STEVE: What did you think of Moira Portland?

TEMPLE: I don't know what to think of her. She's either what Hubert Greene says she is, the spoilt daughter of a millionaire or …

STEVE: Or what?

TEMPLE: Or she's putting on a very good act.

STEVE: Well, I can't say I like her fiancé – although he danced like an angel. Is this the car?

TEMPLE: Yes.

STEVE: You didn't leave your lights on.

TEMPLE: That's funny, I could have sworn –

TEMPLE stops – he's heard something.

STEVE: What is it?

TEMPLE: Steve, listen!

From the car, the low moan of a person in pain.

STEVE: Paul, what is it?

TEMPLE: There's someone in the car – in the back seat!
            Look!

*TEMPLE rushes forward to the car and opens the door. As he
does so the body of ARCHIE BROOKS falls out of the car. He
is obviously in very great pain.*

STEVE: Paul ... Paul, it's Archie.

TEMPLE: Don't touch him!

STEVE: Paul, there's a knife ... It's covered in blood ...

TEMPLE: Steve, listen! Run back to the Club and phone
            for an ambulance, then find out if there's a
            doctor ...

ARCHIE: (*Speaking with great difficulty*) Temple, don't
            ... it's too late ... I ... I ...

TEMPLE: Do as I say, Steve!

ARCHIE: No ... No, wait! Listen, there's something I
            want to tell you ... You know that man, the one
            that was killed – Mark Kendell?

TEMPLE: Yes.

ARCHIE: You ... You thought he had an appointment
            with Chris Boyer, didn't ... you?

TEMPLE: Yes, we did. It was in his diary. "Appointment
            with C.B."

ARCHIE: I'm – I'm the man he had the appointment
            with, Temple. I'm ... C.B.

STEVE: (*Softly: amazed*) You are?

ARCHIE: Chunky ... Brooks ... Everybody calls me ...
            Chunky ...

STEVE: Paul ... what's happened?

A moment.

TEMPLE: (*Quietly*) He's dead.

END OF EPISODE TWO

EPISODE THREE

EILEEN

SCENE 1: A London Side Street, as in the final scene of Episode 2.

TEMPLE: Steve, listen! Run back to the Club and phone for an ambulance, then find out if there's a doctor ...

ARCHIE: (*Speaking with great difficulty*) Temple, don't ... it's too late ... I ... I ...

TEMPLE: Do as I say, Steve!

ARCHIE: No ... No, wait! Listen, there's something I want to tell you ... You know that man, the one that was killed – Mark Kendell?

TEMPLE: Yes.

ARCHIE: You ... You thought he had an appointment with Chris Boyer, didn't ... you?

TEMPLE: Yes, we did. It was in his diary. "Appointment with C.B."

ARCHIE: I'm – I'm the man he had the appointment with, Temple. I'm ... C.B.

STEVE: (*Softly: amazed*) You are?

ARCHIE: Chunky ... Brooks ... Everybody calls me ... Chunky ...

STEVE: Paul ... what's happened?

A moment.

TEMPLE: (*Quietly*) He's dead.

STEVE: Oh no.

TEMPLE: Steve, listen. You know Sir Graham's number. Go back to the Manilla and phone him. Tell him exactly what's happened. If you can't get Sir Graham get through to the Yard.

STEVE: Yes, all right, Paul.

TEMPLE: There's no need for you to come back here, Steve. When you've phoned Sir Graham pick up a taxi and go back to the flat.

STEVE: No, I'll come back, darling. Don't worry, I'll be all right.

TEMPLE: Now do as I tell you, Steve! I'll see you later …

SCENE 2: The TEMPLES' Drawing Room.

We hear the sound of a soda siphon as TEMPLE makes drinks.

TEMPLE: Is that enough soda, Sir Graham?

FORBES: Yes, that's fine.

TEMPLE: Here you are.

TEMPLE hands FORBES his drink.

FORBES: Thank you. (*He drinks*) I'm terribly worried about Brooks, Temple. I'd always looked upon him as being completely trustworthy. Admittedly he was an extravagant sort of person, even inclined to overstep the mark as far as expenses were concerned, but we never doubted his integrity.

TEMPLE: Well, I can only tell you what he said, Sir Graham.

FORBES: (*Slowly, puzzled*) He said that he had an appointment with Mark Kendell, that he was the C.B. referred to in the diary?

TEMPLE: Yes.

FORBES: There's no doubt in your mind that's what he did say?

TEMPLE: No.

STEVE: There's no doubt, Sir Graham. I heard it as well as Paul.

TEMPLE: What exactly did Brooks do? Was he attached to your department?

FORBES: Yes. He had rather a curious position, Temple. He started with us about seven or eight years

68

ago. He had quite an unimportant job to start with and then one day Superintendent Henson asked him to investigate the activities of a certain night club. We'd been having trouble with this particular club and we wanted a detailed report of what was going on behind the scenes. Brooks got it for us – in fact, he made a howling success of the assignment. And since then we've used him almost continually as a contact, a sort of …

TEMPLE: Man about town?

FORBES: Exactly. I was very fond of Brooks, Temple. I'm terribly sorry this happened.

TEMPLE: I can understand that, but it does rather look as if he was mixed up in this affair, doesn't it?

FORBES: Yes, it does. You know, though, I may be dense but I don't quite see how all these pieces fit together. Take Kendell for instance. Kendell was quite obviously mixed up in the counterfeit racket and yet it was Kendell who broke into your flat. Now why on earth should he do that? Was he looking for something? If he was, then it must have been the watchchain.

We hear the sound of the front door buzzer.

STEVE: (*Rising*) I'll go.

Under the next couple of lines STEVE opens the door and goes out into the hall.

TEMPLE: That's precisely what I said this afternoon, Sir Graham. Shall I tell you what I think? I think this Portland affair, the murder of Archie Brooks, and this business about the watchchain are part and parcel of the same case.

FORBES: You think it all ties up with the counterfeit racket?

TEMPLE:	I do, and I'm convinced that we'll never smash that racket until we've solved the mystery of the penny and revealed the identity of Madison – Who is it, darling?
STEVE:	Paul, it's Inspector James.
TEMPLE:	(*Rising*) Oh, hello, Inspector. Come in!
JAMES:	Thank you. (*To SIR GRAHAM*) Good evening, sir. I don't think we've met before, Mr Temple.

INSPECTOR JAMES is a well-spoken man of about fifty.

TEMPLE:	No, I don't think we have. Can I get you a drink, Inspector?
JAMES:	No, thank you, sir.
FORBES:	Well, have you finished?
JAMES:	We've finished with the car, sir. It's been photographed from more angles than Greta Garbo.
FORBES:	Did you find anything?
JAMES:	It rather looks to me as if he was attacked in the mews, sir, and then crawled to the car on his hands and knees. His clothes were in a pretty bad condition.
TEMPLE:	Do you think he knew that it was my car?
JAMES:	I very much doubt it, sir.
FORBES:	How far is the mews from where the car was parked?
JAMES:	About thirty yards. It's a cul-de-sac. I can't imagine what Chunky was doing down there.
TEMPLE:	Was Brooks a friend of yours, Inspector?
JAMES:	I don't think I'd exactly call him a friend, sir. I knew him a little better than most people at the Yard because we once did a double act together at a police concert.
FORBES:	What did you do, James – a song and dance?

JAMES:	No, sir. I did impersonations. Brooks was the song and dance man. And very good he was too. It's a shame about Brooks, sir.
FORBES:	Yes.
TEMPLE:	Have you any idea what time he left the Manilla?
JAMES:	He must have left while you and Mrs Temple were in the phone box, sir. The commissionaire said he saw you leave about four or five minutes after Brooks.
TEMPLE:	He told us he intended to drop in and see his sister; whether he was pulling our leg or not I don't know.
JAMES:	Brooks hadn't got a sister, sir. He was an only child. He'd plenty of lady friends though – that's probably what he meant.
FORBES:	Where did he live, James?
JAMES:	He had a flat at Whitedown Gardens, that's just off the Cromwell Road. As a matter of fact, I'm on my way there now.
FORBES:	Well take a good look at the place. Go over it with a tooth-comb if necessary.
JAMES:	Yes, sir.
TEMPLE:	Would you mind if I went along with you, Inspector?
JAMES:	(*Hesitating*) Well …
FORBES:	No, that's all right, Temple.
JAMES:	I'd be very pleased to have you, sir.
TEMPLE:	Fine (*On the move*) I'll get my things. Oh, you've got a car, I take it?
JAMES:	Yes, sir.
TEMPLE:	(*To STEVE*) Steve, I'll get Charlie to pick my car up first thing tomorrow morning.
STEVE:	All right, darling.

71

JAMES: We've taken it to the garage, sir – the one opposite the Manilla.

TEMPLE: Oh, good. I'll see you at the lift, Inspector.

JAMES: Can we drop you, Sir Graham?

FORBES: No, I've got my car.

SCENE 3:   A Corridor.

By the lift outside the TEMPLES' front door a lift is heard arriving.

TEMPLE: Here it is …

The lift stops and the gates are opened.

TEMPLE: After you.

JAMES: Thank you.

TEMPLE and the INSPECTOR enter the lift: the gates are closed.

JAMES: Which button do I press?

TEMPLE: The last but one. The bottom one's for the basement.

JAMES: Oh, yes, I –

The lift suddenly starts to ascend.

JAMES: What's happened?

TEMPLE: (*Laughing*) We're going up. It must be someone on the floor above!

The lift ascends and then stops at the floor above. The lift gates are opened and ELZEC steps in.

ELZEC: Oh, I beg your pardon! I thought the lift was empty.

ELZEC is a pleasant young Dane of about thirty.

TEMPLE: (*Smiling*) That's all right. You just caught us in time.

ELZEC: (*Puzzled*) Yes?

TEMPLE: We were just going down.

ELZEC: Oh.

TEMPLE: Do you want the ground floor?

72

ELZEC: If you please.

The lift gates are closed. The lift starts to descend.

TEMPLE: My name is Temple. Have you taken Major Hartley's flat?

ELZEC: Yes, I moved in a few days ago. The day you came back from America, Mr Temple.

TEMPLE: Oh.

ELZEC: My name is Dr Elzec.

TEMPLE: We've got the flat underneath yours, doctor. Drop in for a drink one evening.

ELZEC: Thank you.

TEMPLE: We shall be delighted to see you.

ELZEC: That's very kind of you.

JAMES: (*Slowly*) Did you say Dr Elzec, sir?

ELZEC: Yes.

JAMES: Haven't we met before somewhere?

ELZEC: (*Slowly*) No, I don't think so.

JAMES: Oh. Sorry, I thought we had.

The lift stops. TEMPLE opens the gates.

TEMPLE: After you, doctor.

ELZEC: Oh, thank you. (*Hurrying away*) Goodbye.

JAMES: It's all right, sir. I'll close the gates.

The INSPECTOR closes the gates.

TEMPLE: Do you know that fellow?

JAMES: I've seen him somewhere before, but I'm dashed if I can place him.

TEMPLE: Was the name familiar?

JAMES: No, that's the extraordinary part about it. I don't think his name's Elzec at all, in fact I'm sure it isn't.

TEMPLE: Then what is it?

JAMES: I don't know. (*Suddenly*) So he just moved in here?

TEMPLE: Yes, he's taken a furnished flat. It belongs to a
            Major Hartley. Hartley's with the Foreign
            Office, he's been transferred to Washington.
JAMES: M'm. I wish I could remember where I've seen
            the fellow. Elzec ... I'm sure that's not the
            name.

SCENE 4:   On the steps outside the main door of
            BROOKS' flat off the Cromwell Road.
Traffic noises are in the background.
TEMPLE beats on the door with the knocker – rather
energetically.
TEMPLE: I think there's someone coming.
JAMES: Not before time.
After a moment the door is unbolted and the chain removed.
TEMPLE: Who lives here, do you know?
JAMES: A chap called Scaley owns the place. Brooks
            has the top floor.
The door opens.
JAMES: Good evening. My name is –
The INSPECTOR is interrupted by OWEN SCALEY, a volatile
little Welshman.
SCALEY: What the devil do you think you're doing man,
            knocking on the door like that? Why for
            goodness sake don't you use the bell?
TEMPLE: Where is the bell?
SCALEY: It's right under your nose, man! It's staring you
            in the face!
SCALEY presses the bell: it rings out in the house.
SCALEY: There, you see! It's quite unnecessary to be
            making all that noise.
JAMES: Are you Mr Scaley?
SCALEY: I am.
JAMES: Well, I'm a friend of Mr Brooks.

SCALEY:	Then I wish to goodness you'd have a word with your friend. Would you mind telling the gentleman to stop his fancy ladies from ringing up? There hasn't been a moment's peace in this house. His phone's been ringing since seven o'clock this evening.
JAMES:	Yes, well don't worry, Mr Scaley – from now on that's a thing of the past.
SCALEY:	What do you mean?
JAMES:	I'm afraid Mr Brooks has met with an accident.
SCALEY:	Accident? What sort of an accident?

A moment.

JAMES:	He's dead.
SCALEY:	Why man, I don't believe it! You're pulling my leg now! It's a joke, isn't it?
JAMES:	No, it's not a joke, Mr Scaley. I'm Chief-Inspector James of Scotland Yard. This is Mr Temple. May we come inside?
SCALEY:	(*Stunned*) Yes. Yes, of course. Archie Brooks … dead? Why man, I can't believe it. I just can't believe it.

SCENE 5:	The Sitting room of BROOKS' Comfortable Flat.

TEMPLE is searching through some papers. After a moment or two the door opens and INSPECTOR JAMES enters.

JAMES:	How are things going, sir?
TEMPLE:	I've nearly finished. Was there anything in the bedroom?
JAMES:	Nothing of importance.
TEMPLE:	There are quite a lot of papers here, Inspector, and two snapshot albums. I think you ought to go through them.
JAMES:	Yes, I'll take them back with me.

TEMPLE: What time did Brooks go out, do you know?

JAMES: Well, according to our Welsh friend downstairs he went out shortly after ten this morning – or rather yesterday morning.

TEMPLE: Yes, but he must have come back to have changed into a dinner jacket.

JAMES: Yes.

TEMPLE: Is this the first time you've been here, Inspector?

JAMES: Yes, it is. (*Looking about him*) It's a very nice flat, isn't it? You know I reckon Brooks must have had a private income, he couldn't keep a place like this going without one –

The INSPECTOR is interrupted by the telephone ringing.

TEMPLE: Don't touch it, let it ring!

A moment.

JAMES: It's rather late for a call, isn't it? It's nearly two o'clock.

The telephone continues to ring.

TEMPLE: (*Suddenly*) James, you said you could do impersonations. Do you think you could impersonate Brooks?

JAMES: Chunky? (*Hesitatingly*) Yes. Yes, I think I could.

TEMPLE: All right, have a shot at it!

JAMES: You mean – you want me to answer the telephone?

TEMPLE: Yes. Yes, go on. (*Leaving*) I'll listen in the bedroom on the extension.

TEMPLE shuts the door behind him. The telephone continues to ring. A moment, then JAMES lifts the receiver. A woman's voice is heard on the other end of the line.

EILEEN speaks softly, as if frightened of being overheard. It is a pleasant voice: the voice of a woman in the forties.

EILEEN: Hello. Is that you, Chunky?

Throughout the telephone conversation JAMES gives a somewhat nervous impersonation of ARCHIE BROOKS. The part is doubled by the actor who played the part of BROOKS in Episode 2.

JAMES: Yes – this is Chunky. Who is that?

EILEEN: Why, this is Eileen – who did you think it was?

JAMES: I'm sorry. I didn't recognise your voice.

EILEEN: (*Suspiciously*) You sound different – is anything the matter?

JAMES: No. I was asleep, that's all. Where are you? Where are you speaking from?

EILEEN: I'm at home … It's all right – he can't hear. He's in bed, asleep … Chunky, listen … I found out what you wanted.

JAMES: Did you?

EILEEN: (*A tense whisper*) It's tomorrow night.

JAMES: Tomorrow night?

EILEEN: Yes. Eleven o'clock.

JAMES: What?

EILEEN: (*Still whispering*) I said: eleven o'clock …

JAMES: Oh.

A moment.

EILEEN: Well, aren't you going to ask me where?

JAMES: (*A nervous intake of breath*) Where, Eileen?

EILEEN: Do you know Eppingdale?

JAMES: Eppingdale? Yes, I know it. It's a village about twelve miles from Tenterden.

EILEEN: That's right. Well, there's a farm called Foxdale Farm, it's in the meadow about a mile and a half from the village.

JAMES: (*Unintelligently*) Oh.

EILEEN: (*A shade impatient*) Did you hear what I said?

JAMES: No, I'm afraid … I … didn't …

EILEEN: (*Worried: almost frightened*) Oh, Chunky, darling – do try and listen. There's a farm called Foxdale Farm, it's in a meadow about a mile and a half from Eppingdale. Have you got that?

JAMES: Yes.

EILEEN: Be there tomorrow night, Chunky. Eleven o'clock.

JAMES: I'll be there. (*Hesitating*) Shall I … see … you … Eileen?

EILEEN: Me?

JAMES: Er – yes.

EILEEN: No! No, of course you won't! (*Puzzled*) Darling, what do you mean – shall you see me?

JAMES: (*Trying to cover his mistake*) I meant … some other time … perhaps …?

EILEEN: (*Nervously*) I don't know. I've got to be careful. I've got to be very careful, Chunky.

JAMES: Yes I know.

EILEEN: Take care tomorrow, darling. (*Slowly*) You never know what might happen …

EILEEN replaces her receiver. JAMES replaces his receiver and gives a huge sigh of relief. A moment and then the door opens and TEMPLE returns.

TEMPLE: Well done, Inspector!

JAMES: Did you hear?

TEMPLE: Every word.

JAMES: Phew, I feel like a piece of chewed string. I wondered what the devil she was going to say next. Do you think I got away with it?

TEMPLE: Yes, you got away with it all right!

JAMES: I was dying to ask her who she was! Eileen …? Eileen who, Temple?

TEMPLE: Yes. I wonder if Scaley knows her?

JAMES: There's just a chance that he might. Come along, Temple. Let's go down and ask him …

SCENE 6:   A Room in Scaley's Flat.

SCALEY has fallen asleep in an armchair. He is snoring slightly. JAMES shakes him.

JAMES: Wake up, Scaley. Wake up!

SCALEY: Oh … Oh … Oh it's you! … I was fast asleep. Have you finished upstairs?

JAMES: Yes, we've finished. We're just leaving.

TEMPLE: Mr Scaley, was Archie Brooks friendly with a lady called Eileen?

SCALEY: Eileen? I can't recall an Eileen. That's a new one on me. Are you sure you've got the name right?

JAMES: Quite sure.

SCALEY: (*Thoughtfully*) There was a Betty, a Judy, a Phyllis, a Dora, there was a Pat, there … No. No, I can't recall an Eileen. Eileen what? What's the other name?

TEMPLE: Yes, that's the point, Mr Scaley. What's the other name?

SCENE 7:   The TEMPLES' Dining Room.

TEMPLE and STEVE are having breakfast.

STEVE: Pass the toast, darling.

TEMPLE: M'm?

STEVE: I said, pass the toast.

TEMPLE: Oh.

STEVE: You're very quiet.

TEMPLE: What do you mean, quiet? What do you expect me to be like at half-past eight in the morning?

STEVE: What's the matter? Have you got out of bed on the wrong side or something?

TEMPLE: I'm just annoyed, Steve.

STEVE: What are you annoyed about?

TEMPLE: I jumped to conclusions. The wrong conclusions.

STEVE: About Archie Brooks?

79

TEMPLE: M'm.

STEVE: (*Smiling*) Yes, I thought you had.

TEMPLE: (*Looking up*) Why – what did you think?

STEVE: I thought Brooks was mixed up in this business but I felt sure he was on the right side.

TEMPLE: What made you so sure?

STEVE: Oh, just intuition.

TEMPLE: Oh, by Timothy, don't tell me that good old intuition's on the warpath again.

STEVE: Well, the way things are at the moment you can certainly do with it.

TEMPLE: Yes. How right you are.

STEVE: Who was that on the phone a few minutes ago?

TEMPLE: The Inspector. He'd just been talking to Sir Graham about last night.

STEVE: Is Sir Graham going down to Eppingdale?

TEMPLE: We're all going. I told Sir Graham we'd dine with him and then run down in the car.

STEVE: Does that include me?

TEMPLE: Is there the slightest chance of my being able to go without you?

STEVE: Not the slightest.

TEMPLE: Then it includes you. By the way, Steve, have you seen the young fellow who's taken the flat above?

STEVE: Yes, I caught a glimpse of him yesterday morning. They say he's taken it on a six months' lease: supposed to be paying thirty guineas a week.

TEMPLE: Thirty a week! Phew. Dr Elzec must have a pretty flourishing practice.

STEVE: Is he a doctor?

TEMPLE: Well, he said he was. I met him in the lift when I went down with Inspector James. James thought he recognised him.

STEVE: He looks a pleasant sort of person, but he certainly doesn't look like a doctor.

TEMPLE: He'll probably turn out to be an osteopath or a chiropodist. I've asked him to drop in for a drink one evening. (*Yawns*) Golly, I'm still tired.

The front door buzzer sounds.

STEVE: Darling, you answer that – I can't be seen like this.

TEMPLE: You certainly can't.

STEVE: (*Rising*) Give me a second and I'll slip into the bedroom.

STEVE quickly leaves the room. TEMPLE crosses into the hall and opens the door.

TEMPLE: (*Surprised*) Why, hello, Greene.

GREENE: Hello, Temple! Sorry if I've interrupted your breakfast.

TEMPLE: No, we've just finished. Come in.

GREENE enters the flat. TEMPLE closes the front door.

They move into the drawing room.

GREENE: It's a bit of an impertinence dropping in like this, but I did rather want to see you, and since I was passing the door I thought I might as well.

TEMPLE: It's not an impertinence at all. Delighted to see you. Would you like some coffee?

GREENE: No. No, thank you.

TEMPLE: Are you sure?

GREENE: Quite sure.

TEMPLE: Well, let me take your things.

GREENE: No, I won't keep you a minute, Temple. (*Pleasantly*) I only dropped in because – well – I'd like you and Mrs Temple to come to my place for the weekend. Mrs Portland, Moira and George Kelly are coming down. We'd like you to join us, Temple.

TEMPLE: Well, I don't know. This weekend happens to be rather awkward. You see, we – er – we did think of … (*He hesitates*)

GREENE: (*Politely*) It's awfully difficult to think of excuses, isn't it? Especially on the spur of the moment.

TEMPLE: It's not that, but – Look, Greene, why are you inviting my wife and I for the weekend? Let's face it, we're not exactly friends are we – barely acquaintances?

GREENE: Shall I be frank, Temple?

TEMPLE: I would prefer it.

GREENE: The first time I saw you, at Southampton, I said to myself, now there's a man I would like to get to know. An intellectual but at the same time a man of action. It's a combination I've always admired.

TEMPLE: I thought we were going to be frank with each other.

GREENE: What do you mean?

TEMPLE: The first time you met me you thought I was a confounded nuisance. So far as you were concerned I was an unmitigated bore pushing my nose into an affair which didn't concern me.

GREENE: (*Politely*) Was that the impression I gave you?

TEMPLE: I'm afraid it was.

GREENE gives a little laugh.

GREENE: Well, if you must know, I particularly want Moira Portland to come down to my house this weekend. We've quite a lot of family business to discuss and without Moira the whole thing would be quite pointless.

TEMPLE: (*Puzzled*) Yes, you told me that last night. You said she wouldn't accept your invitation unless you included the boyfriend.

GREENE: Moira telephoned me this morning. She said we could expect her on one condition.

TEMPLE: What was that?

GREENE: That you and Mrs Temple were invited.

TEMPLE: But why on earth should Moira Portland insist that my wife and I spend the weekend with you? We barely know the girl. Actually, my wife doesn't know her, she didn't even meet her last night at the Manilla.

GREENE: Moira is a strange girl. A very determined one too. If you don't accept the invitation I doubt very much whether we shall see her.

TEMPLE: I'm sorry, Greene, both my wife and I have other plans.

GREENE: (*Sighs*) Well – thought I'd give it a try.

TEMPLE: Why does Miss Portland want us anyway?

GREENE: I asked her that. She said that if you came down for the weekend she'd feel quite sure that nothing unfortunate would happen.

TEMPLE: Nothing unfortunate?

GREENE: Oh, didn't I tell you? She's under the impression that her life's in danger. Apparently she's been under that impression for weeks now. It's almost a joke at the office.

TEMPLE: Do you think her life's in danger?

GREENE: Of course not! Why should it be?

TEMPLE: (*Suddenly: a complete change: quite friendly*) Where is your place, Greene?

GREENE: It's just outside Leatherhead. Quite a nice little place. I've got about a hundred acres.

TEMPLE: It does sound a nice little place.

GREENE laughs.

GREENE: Temple, I'm so sorry to have issued this invitation in such an unorthodox manner, but the fact is I am in rather a hole. I've got to please Mrs Portland and at the same time keep on friendly terms with Moira. It's not easy.

TEMPLE: I'm quite sure it isn't. And how does George Kelly fit into the picture?

GREENE: Well, as you know, Kelly was Portland's secretary. He now appears to have taken on the job of financial advisor to Mrs Portland. In short, he's making a damn nuisance of himself.

TEMPLE: It does sound a jolly little house-party!

GREENE: (*Laughing*) It certainly could do with an uplift, if that's what you mean.

TEMPLE: What do they call your place?

GREENE: It's called Brown Acres. It's just off the main road, about two miles this side of Leatherhead … Why?

TEMPLE: You can expect us on Saturday. We'll be there in time for lunch.

GREENE: Well, that's jolly sporting of you, Temple. I appreciate it. What made you change your mind?

TEMPLE: Well, the first time I saw you at Southampton, Mr Greene, I said to myself – now there's a man I would really like to get to know …

A moment, then GREENE laughs, but he is not quite sure whether it is funny or not. TEMPLE laughs with him.

SCENE 8: TEMPLE's Car.
TEMPLE is driving very fast.

FORBES: Take it steady, Temple.

TEMPLE: Are you nervous?

FORBES: Well, we're not in a desperate hurry, it's only just gone nine.

A moment.

STEVE: Where are we meeting Inspector James?

FORBES: I said we'd pick him up at the crossroads near Tenterden, it's about ten miles this side of Eppingdale.

TEMPLE: When did he go down there?

FORBES: I sent him down this morning.

TEMPLE: Was that a good idea?

FORBES: I think so. James is a good man, Temple. He's discreet.

TEMPLE: Is he alone?

FORBES: No, he took a Sergeant Carver down with him. Carver's a tough bird, there's nothing he likes more than a spot of action.

TEMPLE: I remember Carver. He was with us on the Gregory Affair.

FORBES: Yes, that's right.

STEVE: Have you heard from the Inspector?

FORBES: He phoned through to the Yard about half past three this afternoon but unfortunately I was out. He didn't leave a message. I say, it's looking rather stormy, isn't it?

TEMPLE: It doesn't look too good.

The car slows down.

STEVE: What's this place called?

FORBES: I think this is Biddenden.

TEMPLE: Yes.

STEVE: Ooh – did you see that?

TEMPLE: What?

FORBES: It was lightning, wasn't it, Steve?

STEVE: Yes, I think it was.

There's a close roll of thunder.

STEVE: Ooh!

The rain starts: it increases very quickly and develops into a downpour.

STEVE: You'd better put the window up, Sir Graham.

SIR GRAHAM winds his window up.

TEMPLE: By Timothy, it's certainly coming down!

STEVE: Ooh … Did you see that, darling? Again!

TEMPLE: Yes.

FORBES: Don't you like lightning, Steve?

STEVE: (*Nervous*) I'm crazy about it!

They laugh.

FADE OUT.

SCENE 9:   TEMPLE's Car.

The car is now travelling more slowly along a wet country road. It is raining very heavily but the thunder is now in the distance.

FORBES: We ought to be somewhere near the crossroads.

TEMPLE: I'm not so sure we're on the right road.

STEVE: Slow down, darling. There's a signpost.

The car slows down and comes to a standstill.

FORBES: Can you see, Steve?

STEVE: It says something about Tenterden, but I can't see what –

STEVE gives a gasp of surprise.

FORBES: What is it?

TEMPLE: Steve, what is it?

STEVE: There's someone in that hedge, Paul … Look, just past the signpost.

TEMPLE: Where?

A moment.

FORBES: (*Peering*) I don't see anyone …

TEMPLE: (*Suddenly*) She's right, Sir Graham! Look!

FORBES: Yes. Is it Inspector James?

TEMPLE: I shouldn't think so.

STEVE: It's probably a tramp sheltering from the rain.

FORBES: Put your window down, Steve.

STEVE winds down the window. TEMPLE switches off the car engine.

TEMPLE: (*Calling*) Hello, there! Hello, there!

FORBES: (*Calling*) Is that you, James?

A pause.

FORBES: (*Quietly*) Let's have a look, Temple.

FORBES and TEMPLE open their doors and get out of the car.

TEMPLE: The fellow's asleep by the look of things.

FORBES and TEMPLE cross the road to the hedgerow, and with some difficulty get close to what they quickly realise is a dead body.

FORBES: Temple …

TEMPLE: Yes … Let's turn him over.

They do so.

FORBES: … He's been stabbed. Look.

TEMPLE: Yes.

FORBES: That's exactly what happened to Chunky Brooks, Temple.

TEMPLE: Exactly. It's even the same sort of knife.

STEVE: (*Calling: approaching from the car*) Paul, what is it? Darling, what's the matter?

FORBES: Don't let Steve see him. Quickly, Temple.

TEMPLE moves to STEVE.

TEMPLE: Go back to the car, Steve.

STEVE: What's happened?

TEMPLE: It's Inspector James. He's been murdered.

SCENE 10: Further down the road.

There's wind in the trees: the rain has stopped.

TEMPLE: (*Softly*) Good evening, Sergeant.

CARVER: (*A sudden start of surprise*) Ah! Oh, you gave
           me quite a turn, Mr Temple! I wondered who the
           devil it was. Good evening, sir.

TEMPLE: You know my wife, Sergeant Carver.

CARVER: Good evening, ma'am.

STEVE: Good evening, Sergeant.

TEMPLE: Is that Foxdale Farm?

CARVER: Yes, that's it, sir, at the bottom of the meadow.

TEMPLE: You've picked a pretty good observation point.

CARVER: Yes, I had a good scout round. You can see
           pretty well everything from here, sir. Did you
           pick the Inspector up, sir?

TEMPLE: Yes, we – picked him up. He's with Sir Graham.

CARVER: How did you get down here?

TEMPLE: I parked my car at the top of the lane. As a
           matter of fact we've had a job finding you;
           we've been strolling around for the past half-
           hour.

CARVER: But I told the Inspector I'd be here, sir. Isn't he
           with you?

TEMPLE: Er, no. What time did he leave you, Carver?

CARVER: About a quarter to eight.

TEMPLE: Have you been here all day?

CARVER: Off and on. We got here about half past ten this
           morning. I suppose the Inspector told you the
           farm's deserted.

STEVE: How do you mean deserted? Doesn't anyone live
           there?

CARVER: No, ma'am. A doodle-bug hit it during the war
           and it's been derelict ever since. The land's

farmed by a man called Fenby, he lives the other side of Tenterden.

TEMPLE: Oh. Have you seen anyone?

CARVER: Not a soul.

TEMPLE: Anything suspicious?

CARVER: Nothing, sir. Are you sure this isn't a wild goose chase, sir?

TEMPLE: I don't think so, Carver. (*A moment*) James was murdered. We found his body in a ditch the other side of Tenterden.

CARVER: What! Good Lord, no sir! You're joking!

TEMPLE: I'm not joking, Carver. He was stabbed ...

CARVER: But it seems incredible, sir. He was here at seven o'clock. We were together ... we sat over there on that bank and smoked a cigarette.

TEMPLE: Carver, listen. Did anyone see you this morning? Did you stop in the village on the way down here?

CARVER: Yes, we stopped at a café in the High Street and had a cup of coffee.

TEMPLE: What time would that be?

CARVER: About ten o'clock. Of course the Inspector made a trip into Eppingdale this afternoon. I believe he made a phone call.

TEMPLE: Yes, I heard about ... (*He is listening*) ... that phone call ... unfortunately ... he ... What's that?

In the distance the sound of an approaching light aeroplane, flying low, is heard.

STEVE: It's a plane ...

A moment.

CARVER: There he is! Look! He's flying pretty low, isn't he?

The plane gets nearer.

TEMPLE: Keep down, Sergeant!

CARVER: What the devil's he trying to do?

TEMPLE: What time is it?

STEVE: I make it just gone eleven.

CARVER: Yes, it's just about five minutes past … Good Lord, do you think this is it, sir? Do you think this is what we've been waiting for?

TEMPLE: I don't know.

The aeroplane is now circling, gradually flying lower and lower.

STEVE: It looks to me as if he's trying to come down …

CARVER: Yes.

TEMPLE: I've got a hunch he's looking for something.

CARVER: Yes, it looks like it.

STEVE: He's probably expecting a light.

TEMPLE: Yes. (*A moment*) I don't see one.

The plane is now coming in to land.

STEVE: He's coming down, Paul!

CARVER: She's right, sir! He's going to land in the meadow!

TEMPLE: By Timothy – that won't be easy!

The plane roars by immediately overhead.

STEVE: He's nearly down …

CARVER: Yes, he's made it all right!

TEMPLE: By Timothy this fellow knows his stuff! That's about the best …

Suddenly TEMPLE, STEVE and CARVER give a quick and spontaneous gasp of surprise.

STEVE: (*Horrified*) Paul!

TEMPLE: He's going to hit the bank!

There is a tremendous crash followed by an immediate explosion as the plane disintegrates.

TEMPLE: Come along, Sergeant!

SCENE 11: By the plane in a field.

The plane is burning fiercely.

CARVER: It's hopeless, sir! We'll never get near it!

TEMPLE: I'm afraid so. The heat's terrible.

CARVER: The whole thing must have just disintegrated.

STEVE arrives.

STEVE: (*Breathless*) Oh, Paul …

TEMPLE: Don't get too near, Steve.

STEVE: Paul, can't we do something? We can't just stand here and watch …

TEMPLE: It's too late, Steve. There's nothing we can do. You stay here, Sergeant. I'll drive back into Eppingdale and see Sir Graham.

CARVER: Yes, all right, sir.

TEMPLE: We should be back in about half an hour.

CARVER: Very good, sir.

TEMPLE: Come along, Steve.

The sound of the burning plane lessens as TEMPLE and STEVE move away.

TEMPLE: What's that you've got?

STEVE: I've just picked it up. It must have been thrown from the plane.

TEMPLE: What is it?

STEVE: It's a key-ring. The keys are buckled but … (*Surprised*) There's a penny on the ring, darling.

TEMPLE: A penny?

STEVE: Yes. It's rather bent.

TEMPLE: Let me have a look at it.

STEVE passes it over.

STEVE: Well?

TEMPLE: It's the same as the one that Sam Portland had.

STEVE: What do you mean?

TEMPLE: (*Thoughtfully*) It's the same date, Steve … 1919 …

91

FADE IN music.

FADE DOWN.
SCENE 12: The Forecourt at Brown Acres.
*TEMPLE's car approaches and pulls up. The engine is
switched off. Car doors open and shut as TEMPLE and
STEVE get out.*
GREENE: (*Pleasantly*) Hello, Temple! Welcome to Brown
           Acres.
TEMPLE: I'm afraid we're a little on the late side, Greene.
           We didn't leave town till just after eleven.
GREENE: Nonsense! You're in perfect time! Delighted to
           see you, Mrs Temple. Leave your things in the
           car, Temple, my man will take care of them.
TEMPLE: Oh, thank you. My word, it's quite a place
           you've got here.
GREENE: I think you'll like it.
TEMPLE: Have all your guests arrived?
GREENE: Yes, they're all here, including Moira. I'm glad
           to say she's behaving herself for a change.
STEVE: What a lovely terrace!
GREENE: Do you like it?
STEVE: It looks heavenly!
GREENE: I'm quite proud of Brown Acres, Mrs Temple.
           Be a pleasure to show you around. Would you
           like to go to your rooms straight away, or would
           you like a drink? Come along, let's join the
           others on the terrace! I'm sure you're both dying
           for a drink!

SCENE 13: The Terrace.
*There is a background of animated conversation. STELLA
PORTLAND, GEORGE KELLY and MRS GREENE are
having a friendly argument.*

92

KELLY:	(*Laughing*) Why you're crazy, Stella! How can you say Americans haven't got a sense of humour! Would you say Thurber hadn't got a sense of humour? George Kaufman? Now you take the Marx Brothers …
STELLA:	No, darling, you take the Marx Brothers!

They all laugh. The laughter dies down as TEMPLE and STEVE arrive with HUBERT GREENE.

GREENE:	Are you still lecturing, George?
KELLY:	Stella's just been telling us that … (*Pleasantly*) Why hello, Mrs Temple! How are you?
STEVE:	Good morning, Mr Kelly.
KELLY:	Hello, there!
TEMPLE:	(*Quietly: watching KELLY*) Good morning, Kelly. How are you?
KELLY:	I'm fine. I think you know Mrs Portland.
TEMPLE:	Yes, of course. How are you, Mrs Portland?
STELLA:	I'm quite well, thank you.
KELLY:	And Mrs Greene.
TEMPLE:	I don't believe …
GREENE:	No, I don't think you've met my wife, have you, Temple? Darling, this is Mr and Mrs Temple.
MRS GREENE:	Hello, Mrs Temple, delighted to meet you. It's awfully nice of you both to join us for the weekend.
STEVE:	It's awfully nice of you to ask us.
TEMPLE:	We've been looking forward to it.
GREENE:	Do sit down.
MRS GREENE:	What would you like to drink?
STEVE:	May I have a gin and French?
MRS GREENE:	Yes, of course. Mr Temple?
TEMPLE:	A … Scotch?

KELLY: A man after my own heart.

STEVE: Isn't it a heavenly view, darling?

MRS GREENE: Do you like it?

STEVE: Oh, I think it's wonderful, Mrs Greene.

MRS GREENE: Oh, please – not Mrs Greene!

GREENE: (*With just a very slight touch of sarcasm*) For some obscure reason my wife dislikes being called Mrs Greene. I've never discovered why.

MRS GREENE: (*Laughing at GREENE*) Darling, don't be silly!

GREENE: But it's true, my dear!

MRS GREENE: Nonsense! None of my friends call me Mrs Greene, you know that! It's always Eileen.

END OF EPISODE THREE

EPISODE FOUR

HUBERT GREENE
ENTERTAINS

SCENE 1:	The Terrace at Brown Acres, as at the end of Episode 3.
GREENE:	I don't think you've met my wife, have you, Temple? Darling, this is Mr and Mrs Temple.
MRS GREENE:	Hello, Mrs Temple, delighted to meet you. It's awfully nice of you both to join us for the weekend.
STEVE:	It's awfully nice of you to ask us.
TEMPLE:	We've been looking forward to it.
GREENE:	Do sit down.
MRS GREENE:	What would you like to drink?
STEVE:	May I have a gin and French?
MRS GREENE:	Yes, of course. Mr Temple?
TEMPLE:	A … Scotch?
KELLY:	A man after my own heart.
STEVE:	Isn't it a heavenly view, darling?
MRS GREENE:	Do you like it?
STEVE:	Oh, I think it's wonderful, Mrs Greene.
MRS GREENE:	Oh, please – not Mrs Greene!
GREENE:	(*With just a very slight touch of sarcasm*) For some obscure reason my wife dislikes being called Mrs Greene. I've never discovered why.
MRS GREENE:	(*Laughing at GREENE*) Darling, don't be silly!
GREENE:	But it's true, my dear!
MRS GREENE:	Nonsense! None of my friends call me Mrs Greene, you know that! It's always Eileen.
GREENE:	Well, would you mind mixing the drinks, Eileen. I'm sure our guests are thirsty.

MRS GREENE moves to a nearby table and makes the drinks.

STELLA:	Did you have a pleasant journey, Mrs Temple?
STEVE:	(*Hesitating*) Well –
TEMPLE:	If you overlook the fact we had a puncture outside Kingston, we had a very pleasant journey.

They all laugh.

MRS GREENE:	Did you say Scotch, Mr Temple?
KELLY:	He did and so did I, Mrs – er – Eileen.
STELLA:	(*Pleasantly*) George, I think you've had quite enough for one morning.
KELLY:	Well, it's a point of view, Stella. (*Laughing*) O.K.
GREENE:	(*Handing STEVE her drink*) Here we are, Mrs Temple.
STEVE:	Thank you.
GREENE:	(*Handing TEMPLE his drink*) Temple.
TEMPLE:	Oh, thank you.
STEVE:	I suppose all this is quite new to you, Mr Kelly.
KELLY:	What do you mean – the Scotch?
STEVE:	(*Laughing*) No, I mean the countryside.
KELLY:	Yeah, kind of takes a bit of getting used to. I like it though. I like all this green stuff.

They laugh.

TEMPLE:	Is this the first time you've been over here?
KELLY:	Yeah. I nearly came over with the Cody Boys in '36 but I changed my mind at the last moment. Wish I hadn't now, it might have been fun.
GREENE:	The Cody Boys?
MRS GREENE:	Who are the Cody Boys?
KELLY:	It was a circus outfit. And boy did we travel. We toured every state in the Union.

GREENE: (*With a touch of sarcasm*) What were you doing with a circus outfit?

MRS GREENE: Don't tell me you were the bare-backed rider, Mr Kelly.

KELLY: Well, I wasn't the bearded lady!

They all laugh.

GREENE: What did you do?

KELLY: Oh, I was a sort of general factotum, handyman. I started the outfit with a knife throwing act – and boy was it corny!

MRS GREENE: A knife throwing act!

STEVE: You mean you used to throw knives?

KELLY: (*Laughing*) That's right! You know the sort of thing, a gal stands up against a door and some phoney looking character throws a lot of knives at her. If it's a good act the knives just miss, if it's a bad act – well – you're pretty soon out of business.

STEVE: What happened to your act, Mr Kelly?

KELLY: We folded. I was no good. I couldn't get near the gal – I was too darned scared. One night I missed the gal, the door and every darn thing! I just wasn't cut out for show business.

GREENE: (*Pleasantly, but with just a touch of malice*) What were you cut out for, George?

KELLY: (*Surprised: pulling GREENE's leg*) Why, didn't you know? I'm a financial wizard!

MRS GREENE: (*Suddenly*) Here's Miss Portland and her fiancé!

MOIRA PORTLAND and CHRIS BOYER arrive.

GREENE: Hello, Moira! Where have you two been?

MOIRA: We've been for a walk. Any objections, Hubert?

99

GREENE: Of course not, but I wanted you to meet Mr
              and Mrs Temple.
MOIRA: We've met. We met at the Manilla.
TEMPLE: I don't think you've met my wife, Miss
              Portland.
MOIRA: (*Casually*) Hello, there. Oh no. How d'you
              do.
STEVE: (*Equally casual: almost mimicking MOIRA*)
              Hello, there. How d'you do.
MRS GREENE: Mrs Temple, this is Chris Boyer.
BOYER: Oh, we're old friends, aren't we, Mrs
              Temple?
STEVE: Well, it's nice of you to say so. After the
              way I danced the other night I'm surprised
              we're even on speaking terms.
MOIRA: Oh, Chris is used to that sort of thing. I'm
              the world's worst dancer, aren't I, sweetie?
BOYER: Positively the world's worst!
MOIRA: Why, you beast, Chris!
STELLA and GEORGE KELLY laugh.
MRS GREENE: (*Rising*) Come along, Mrs Temple. Let me
              show you to your room.
STEVE: Thank you.
GREENE: Would you like a drink, Moira?
MOIRA: Yes, I should like a gin and Dubonnet.
GREENE: What about you, Boyer?
BOYER: Have you a Cinzano?
GREENE: (*Irritated*) Not out here, but I can get it for
              you.
BOYER: No, it's all right. I'll have a gin and French.
GREENE: George?
KELLY: Have I your permission to have another
              Scotch, Stella?
STELLA: (*Pleasantly*) No.

GREENE: Oh, go on, let the poor fellow have a drink. It won't do him any harm. You won't start throwing knives at us, will you, George?

KELLY: (*A gag: pretending to be a little hurt*) Not if you're nice to me I won't.

They all laugh.

SCENE 2:   The TEMPLES' Bedroom.

MRS GREENE: I think you'll be comfortable, Mrs Temple. I'm sure you shall. If there's anything you'd like just let me know.

STEVE: Thank you. It's a lovely room, isn't it, darling?

TEMPLE: Delightful. I was just admiring the view. You seem to be able to see for miles.

MRS GREENE: Yes. When I was a little girl we used to climb on to the roof and stay there for hours on end. We had picnics up there in the summer. On a clear day you could see right across country.

STEVE: How long have you been here, Mrs Greene?

MRS GREENE: Well, off and on, I suppose I've been here all my life. You see, the house belonged to my father – Lord Dalesdon. He died in 1945. After my father died I shut the house up for a short time and went abroad. I was in Naples when I met Hubert.

TEMPLE: When was that?

MRS GREENE: That was just over two years ago.

TEMPLE: Was this house always called Brown Acres?

MRS GREENE: No, good gracious, oh no! It's really Dalesdon Hall. It's been Dalesdon Hall for generations. (*Remembering HUBERT's words about her name*) But for some

101

	obscure reason my husband suddenly took it into his head to change the name to Brown Acres. (*A little wistfully*) I've never discovered why.
TEMPLE:	Mrs Greene – (*He stops: smiles*) Oh, I'm sorry! I forgot, you don't like to be called that.
MRS GREENE:	What were you going to say?
TEMPLE:	I was going to ask you a question – rather a personal one I'm afraid.
MRS GREENE:	That's all right, Mr Temple. Please go on.
TEMPLE:	Was Archie Brooks a friend of yours?
MRS GREENE:	(*Slightly taken aback*) Archie Brooks?
TEMPLE:	Yes.
MRS GREENE:	(*Hesitantly*) I'm afraid I've never heard of anyone called Archie Brooks.
STEVE:	His friends called him Chunky. He had a flat in Whitedown Gardens.
MRS GREENE:	(*Puzzled*) What do you mean, he had a flat in Whitedown Gardens?
TEMPLE:	Brooks is dead. He was murdered.
MRS GREENE:	(*Aghast*) No … no … I don't believe it. You're not serious … You're lying because you want to find out …
TEMPLE:	(*Forcefully: facing MRS GREENE*) I'm telling you the truth, Mrs Greene, because I want to find out how well you knew Archie Brooks.

A pause.

MRS GREENE:	(*Softly; tensely*) When was he murdered?
TEMPLE:	(*Quietly: watching MRS GREENE*) Tuesday night. About two hours before you telephoned.

MRS GREENE: But I spoke to him! I told him … (*A sudden realisation*) That wasn't Chunky! That wasn't Chunky on the phone! I suspected it! I thought there was something different, I … (*Desperately, taking hold of TEMPLE*) Who was it? Who impersonated him?

TEMPLE: An Inspector James.

MRS GREENE: (*Very worried*) I told him about Foxdale Farm, didn't I? I told him that … How did you know that I was a friend of Chunky's – were you at the flat when I telephoned?

TEMPLE: Yes. I heard the whole conversation. I suggested the impersonation.

MRS GREENE: You might have spared me that! You might have had the decency to … Who murdered Chunky?

TEMPLE: The same person that murdered Inspector James.

MRS GREENE: (*Astonished*) Was James murdered?

TEMPLE: Yes.

MRS GREENE: When?

TEMPLE: The night we went down to Eppingdale.

MRS GREENE: (*Hesitantly*) How was … he … murdered?

TEMPLE: They were both stabbed.

MRS GREENE: (*Deeply distressed*) Oh! This is terrible. It's even worse than I thought!

MRS GREENE covers her face with her hands and starts to sob.

TEMPLE: (*Quietly: but persuasively*) Eileen, listen. Who was the pilot – the man that landed at Foxdale Farm?

MRS GREENE: I don't know.

TEMPLE: Then why did you tell Brooks to go down there?

103

MRS GREENE: I had to tell him because – (*She stops*)

TEMPLE: Because what?

MRS GREENE: (*Intensely frightened*) I'm not going to say any more! Please don't ask me!

TEMPLE: Now listen! How was Brooks mixed up in this business? Why did you tell him to go down to Eppingdale?

MRS GREENE: I don't know. Really, I don't know. Now please leave me alone. Don't ask me any more questions.

TEMPLE: Don't you see, I've got to ask you these questions. I've got to know what's behind all this. Now tell me the truth: why did you tell Chunky Brooks about Eppingdale?

MRS GREENE: I had to tell him. I made a promise that once I knew when … when … oh, please leave me alone, Mr Temple! I can't talk now, I'm too upset. I was awfully fond of Chunky, he …

MRS GREENE continues to cry.

STEVE: (*Softly*) Paul, don't go on with this …

TEMPLE: (*Quietly*) Was Brooks a close friend?

MRS GREENE: Yes. We'd – known – each – other ever since we were children. He was always very kind to me.

A moment.

TEMPLE: Eileen, I want you to have a look at this.

MRS GREENE: What is it?

TEMPLE: It's a penny. My wife found it down at Eppingdale. It's attached to a keyring. Have you ever seen anything like this before?

MRS GREENE: What do you mean?

TEMPLE:	Have you ever seen a penny like this on a keyring or a watchchain, or perhaps even on a bracelet?
MRS GREENE:	(*Puzzled*) No. No, I don't think so.
TEMPLE:	Are you sure?
MRS GREENE:	Yes, I'm quite sure.

A moment.

STEVE:	Are you feeling better now?
MRS GREENE:	Yes.
TEMPLE:	(*Sympathetically*) Don't you realise that I'm only trying to help you? Sooner or later, whether you like it or not, you're going to tell me all you know about this business. Why don't you tell me now?

A moment.

MRS GREENE:	Mr Temple, listen! I'll tell you what I'll do. I'll come to your room tonight – late tonight when the others are in bed.
STEVE:	But won't your husband miss you?
MRS GREENE:	No. I have my own room. My room's just along the corridor. I'll come tonight, Mr Temple.
TEMPLE:	Can I depend on that?
MRS GREENE:	Yes, I promise. Honestly …
TEMPLE:	All right.
STEVE:	(*Quickly*) I think there's someone coming, Paul!
MRS GREENE:	Oh dear, I look dreadful!

There is a knock and the door opens.

MRS GREENE:	(*Forced brightness*) What is it, Hubert?

HUBERT GREENE pauses for a moment as he takes in the scene.

GREENE:	(*Quite pleasantly*) Lunch is ready, my dear.

FADE IN music.

FADE DOWN.

SCENE 3: The TEMPLES' Bedroom.

TEMPLE: Did you pack that white handkerchief, darling – the silk one?

STEVE: Yes, here it is.

TEMPLE: Thanks. I enjoyed that walk through the woods this afternoon.

STEVE: Yes, so did I. (*Looking in the mirror*) Does this dress look all right?

TEMPLE: Yes, of course, it looks all right. It ought to look all right, considering what you paid for it.

STEVE: Now don't start on that! Zip the back for me.

TEMPLE: (*Zipping the dress*) What did Boyer have to say? You seemed to be putting your heads together rather a lot.

STEVE: Oh, nothing. He told me he thought I'd make a very good dancer.

TEMPLE: By Timothy, the old technique! I wouldn't trust that tailor's dummy as far as I could throw him.

STEVE: Did you notice Moira Portland this morning when he said she was the world's worst dancer? She looked furious.

TEMPLE: Moira Portland's always looking furious. I'm inclined to agree with Greene about that young woman.

STEVE: Pass me that hairbrush, darling.

TEMPLE: Oh – here.

A moment: STEVE brushes her hair.

STEVE: Paul, I don't know whether you've realised it or not, but George Kelly's avoiding us. He didn't even have tea with us this afternoon.

TEMPLE: He's probably frightened that one of us might mention that telephone call.

STEVE: Yes. (*Curious*) Why do you think he made it, darling? He must have known that sooner or later we'd ask him about it.

TEMPLE: He obviously made it because …

TEMPLE is interrupted by a knock on the door.

STEVE: Come in!

The door opens.

GREENE: Excuse me …

TEMPLE: (*Pleasantly*) Oh, come in, Greene!

GREENE: There's a telephone call for you, Temple.

TEMPLE: For me?

GREENE: Yes, it's a personal call from London.

TEMPLE: Oh. Who is it, do you know?

GREENE: (*With a laugh*) I'm afraid I didn't ask.

TEMPLE: Oh.

GREENE: You can take it in my room if you like.

TEMPLE: Oh, thanks. I shan't be a moment, darling.

SCENE 4: HUBERT GREENE's Bedroom.

The door opens and GREENE and TEMPLE enter.

GREENE: Here we are. The phone's by the bed.

TEMPLE: Oh, thanks.

GREENE: Can you find your way back all right?

TEMPLE: Yes, rather.

GREENE: When you and your wife are ready we're having cocktails in the library.

TEMPLE: (*Nodding*) Fine.

GREENE exits, closing the door.

TEMPLE picks up the receiver.

TEMPLE: (*On the phone*) Hello?

OPERATOR: (*On the other end of the line*) Is that Paul Temple?

TEMPLE: Yes.

OPERATOR: Speaking personally?

TEMPLE: Yes.

OPERATOR: Hold the line, please. You're through!

FORBES: (*On the other end of the line*) Hello? Hello?

OPERATOR: Mr Temple's on the line now. Go ahead, please.

FORBES: Hello, is that you, Temple?

TEMPLE: Oh, hello, Sir Graham!

FORBES: How are you?

TEMPLE: I'm fine.

FORBES: Sorry if I've interrupted your dinner.

TEMPLE: You haven't, we were just going down.

FORBES: You did say to give you a ring, remember?

TEMPLE: Yes, of course.

FORBES: (*Quietly, but with enthusiasm*) I think we're making headway, Temple – at last!

TEMPLE: Oh, good. I thought you sounded optimistic.

FORBES: Well, I don't want to be too optimistic, of course.

There is a click on the line as if someone has lifted an extension receiver and is listening to the conversation. It makes no difference whatsoever to TEMPLE and FORBES: they give no indication that they have noticed it.

TEMPLE: What's happened?

FORBES: Are you alone?

TEMPLE: Yes.

FORBES: Is it all right – to talk, I mean?

TEMPLE: (*Slowly*) Yes, I think so.

FORBES: (*Confidentially*) Well, Temple, listen, We've discovered the identity of the pilot, we know why he came here and we know who was supposed to have met him at Eppingdale.

TEMPLE: Go on …

FORBES: We also know the name – the real name of Dr Elzec.

TEMPLE: How did you discover that?

FORBES: We came across his photograph in a snapshot album; the one you found at Archie Brooks's.

TEMPLE: Oh. Oh, I see.

FORBES: His real name is Weiner. He was mixed up in the Basle counterfeit racket in 1937.

TEMPLE: Are you sure of that?

FORBES: Yes, I'm quite sure.

TEMPLE: What are you going to do about it?

FORBES: There's no point in picking him up. In any case we've nothing on him at the moment. You can't arrest a man for paying thirty guineas a week for a furnished flat.

TEMPLE: Are you watching him?

FORBES: Yes, there's a man on the block night and day. You'll probably spot him when you get back on Monday morning.

TEMPLE: You seem to have been pretty busy since I left town, Sir Graham.

FORBES: Yes. Get in touch with me as soon as you get back.

TEMPLE: Yes, I'll do that.

FORBES: How are things at your end?

TEMPLE: Well, so far, we're having a very quiet weekend.

FORBES: Good. I hope it stays that way. Probably see you on Monday.

TEMPLE: Yes, all right, Sir Graham. Goodbye.

FORBES: Goodbye.

SIR GRAHAM replaces his receiver.

A moment: we hear a click as the extension receiver is replaced, then TEMPLE replaces his receiver.

SCENE 5:   The TEMPLES' Bedroom.

The door opens and TEMPLE enters.

STEVE: Oh, I was just going to go down, darling. Are
           you ready?

TEMPLE: (*Thoughtfully*) Yes, I'm ready.

STEVE: Who was that on the phone?

TEMPLE: Sir Graham.

STEVE: (*Faintly surprised*) Oh. Did he want anything
           special?

TEMPLE: No, he – (*With a little laugh*) – just wanted a
           chat.

STEVE: (*Puzzled*) What's the joke?

TEMPLE: I've got a hunch we shall find somebody rather
           on edge this evening, Steve. It'll be interesting
           to see who it is.

STEVE: Why do you say that?

TEMPLE: Before I left Town I made arrangements for Sir
           Graham to phone and pretend that the Yard had
           discovered the identity of the pilot – the man
           that crashed at Eppingdale. I also told him to
           tell me that they'd discovered who the contact
           was.

STEVE: But what was the point of that? Why should he
           say those things if they weren't true?

TEMPLE: I was pretty certain that any telephone
           conversation I had would be listened to and I
           wanted the eavesdropper to believe that the
           Yard had discovered the pilot's identity.

STEVE: Do you think someone did listen to your
           conversation?

TEMPLE: Yes, I'm sure of it. I heard a receiver being
           lifted.

STEVE: Was it Greene?

TEMPLE: It – it might have been Greene.

STEVE: Paul, you looked puzzled just now. Did Sir Graham say anything else?

TEMPLE: Yes, he did. He said that they'd found out about Dr Elzec.

STEVE: You mean the man who has the flat above ours?

TEMPLE: Yes. Apparently his name's Weiner.

STEVE: Did Sir Graham tell you that on the phone?

TEMPLE: Yes, and that's what I don't understand. He knew as well as I did that the conversation was being listened to.

STEVE: He probably wants to use Elzec or Weiner or whatever his name is as a bait. If the people behind this affair think that Elzec's been found out they'll probably try to get rid of him.

TEMPLE: (*Thoughtfully*) Yes.

STEVE: And that's when Sir Graham'll step in.

TEMPLE: There might be something in that, Steve. I shouldn't be surprised. (*Suddenly*) Come along, darling, let's go down.

STEVE: Paul, who do you think is behind all this? Hubert Greene? Stella Portland? George Kelly?

TEMPLE: You've forgotten your boyfriend – Chris Boyer.

STEVE: Oh, he's just a gigolo, darling. He couldn't have anything to do with this.

TEMPLE: I'm not so sure.

STEVE: Why do you say that?

TEMPLE: He dances far too well for my liking.

SCENE 6: The Library.

There is a background of general chatter.
A door opens and TEMPLE and STEVE enter the library.

111

MRS GREENE: (*Pleasantly*) Ah, so here you are, Mrs Temple!

STEVE: Oh, dear, are we the last?

MRS GREENE: No. Miss Portland isn't down yet.

BOYER: I don't know what's keeping Moira, she was ready ages ago.

GREENE: What would you like, Mrs Temple?

STEVE: May I have a gin and French?

GREENE: Certainly. Temple?

KELLY: He'd like a Scotch.

TEMPLE: (*Laughing*) No, I'd like a glass of sherry.

GREENE: (*Pleasantly*) Would you like a dry sherry?

TEMPLE: Yes please.

GREENE fixes the drinks.

STELLA: What a lovely dress, Mrs Temple!

MRS GREENE: How funny you should say that! I was just admiring it!

STELLA: Did you get it in New York? It's really charming.

STEVE: No, as a matter of fact I bought it in London only –

The door opens and STEVE stops speaking.

There is a significant pause.

GREENE: (*Pleasantly*) Come in, Moira – we've been waiting for you.

BOYER: (*Faintly irritated*) Where on earth have you been, Moira? You were ready ages ago.

MOIRA: (*Nervy and strangely on edge*) I've been for a walk. Is there any particular reason why I shouldn't go for a walk before dinner?

BOYER: No, I suppose not.

KELLY: Say, you look all steamed up about something! You need a drink.

MOIRA:	Excellent advice, Mr Kelly – if a slight understatement. I need several drinks.
GREENE:	(*Quietly: watching MOIRA*) What would you like?
MOIRA:	It's all right, I'll mix it.
GREENE:	(*Firmly*) I'm mixing the drinks, Moira – what would you like?
MOIRA:	I'll have a gin and French.
BOYER:	(*Staring at MOIRA*) Have you been drinking already?
MOIRA:	What do you mean – already? I've had three very small pink gins, if that's what you mean!
STELLA:	(*Laughing at MOIRA*) Where on earth did you have those?
MOIRA:	I drove down into the village.
GREENE:	I thought you said you'd been for a walk?
MOIRA:	I drove down into the village. I got out of my car and I walked – on my own two legs – into a very large pub and ordered three very small pink gins. Is there anything else you'd like to know?
TEMPLE:	(*Quietly*) Yes there is …
MOIRA:	(*Facing TEMPLE: defiantly*) What?
TEMPLE:	(*Smiling*) Where's my sherry?
GREENE:	Oh, I'm sorry, Temple! Here we are …

TEMPLE takes his drink.

TEMPLE:	Thank you.
GREENE:	Mrs Temple … Oh, you asked for a gin and French, didn't you? I'm so sorry.
STEVE:	It's all right, I'll have a sherry.
GREENE:	No, no certainly not! I'll mix you another.
MOIRA:	(*Taking the glass*) Then we won't waste the sherry, Hubert!

MOIRA drinks the glass of sherry in one go, finishing with a final gasp for breath.

KELLY: Boy, that's drinking.

BOYER: Moira, don't be stupid. That's not the way to drink sherry.

MOIRA: It's the way I drink it. Now where's my gin and French, Hubert?

BOYER: Look here, Moira, I think you've had far too much already –

MOIRA: Darling, I'm not interested in what you think. In fact, sweetie, I'm not at all sure that you can think! You're a tall, upright, well – creased slice of sartorial perfection, but when it comes to brains …

MRS GREENE: (*Embarrassed*) Miss Portland, please.

GREENE: Moira, now just pull yourself together!

BOYER: No. No, please. I'm finding this very interesting. This is a new side to my fiancée. It seems to me that I ought to get acquainted with it.

MOIRA: Careful, Chris. Careful! Those are mighty big words!

MOIRA giggles, then turns towards HUBERT.

MOIRA: Where's my drink?

HUBERT: Here.

MRS GREENE: Miss Portland, you really oughtn't to have another drink before dinner.

MOIRA: Do you agree, Mr Temple – do you think I oughtn't to have another drink?

TEMPLE: You're over twenty-one, Miss Portland – you know what you're doing.

KELLY: You'll finish up with a duodenal, baby – that's what you'll finish up with.

114

MOIRA:	Why, Mr Kelly! I didn't know you cared! Don't look so worried, Eileen, I can take it!

MOIRA empties the glass in almost one drink, as before. She gives a final gasp.

KELLY:	(*Almost to himself*) Boy, you certainly can take it!
MOIRA:	A duoden ... a duoden ... What did you say I'd finish up with, Mr Kelly?
KELLY:	A duodenal.
MOIRA:	(*Giggling*) A gigolo and a duodenal! What a horrible thought!
MRS GREENE:	Hubert, I think we'd better go in to dinner.
GREENE:	Yes.
BOYER:	(*Quietly, but intensely angry*) Just a moment. Moira, don't you think you owe me an apology?
MOIRA:	An apology? What for?
BOYER:	You know perfectly well what for.
MOIRA:	Because I called you a gigolo? But you are a gigolo! And if you must know, darling, not a very nice gigolo. (*Suddenly: vehemently*) You're a stinking rotten little gigolo!
GREENE:	Moira, please!
STELLA:	I think you'd better go to your room, Moira.
MOIRA:	I'll do nothing of the sort. Why should I go to my room? I'm not a schoolgirl. I'm not going to anybody's room, I'm going to have another drink. Another little drink.

MOIRA picks up a decanter.

GREENE:	You're going to have nothing of the sort!
MOIRA:	Leave go of my arm!

GREENE:	Moira, now don't be silly, put that decanter down!
MOIRA:	You heard what I said – let go – of – my – arm …
GREENE:	(*Gently; almost in confidence*) Moira, please, now don't make an exhibition of yourself – put the decanter down, dear.
MOIRA:	(*Near to tears now*) Don't you 'dear' me. You're no friend of mine.

MOIRA drops the decanter.

MOIRA:	Never have been. Haven't got any friends. Haven't got a friend in the world.
KELLY:	(*Softly*) Boy, is she high!
BOYER:	(*Gently*) Come along. I'll take you up to your room.
MOIRA:	Don't touch me! Don't put your hands on me. Do you hear what I say, leave me alone! Leave me alone, Chris!
MRS GREENE:	Moira, please!
BOYER:	Moira, what is it?
STELLA:	Whatever's the matter with the girl?
MOIRA:	You know what's the matter! You know what's the matter with me all right! One of you murdered Chunky! I only found that out tonight! (*The tears are flowing now*) He was the only friend I had. He understood me. There was no nonsense with Chunky. He was a real friend.
MRS GREENE:	Come along, Moira. Let me take you to your room.

MRS GREENE and MOIRA depart. The door closes.

STELLA:	Well! You said she was a temperamental young woman but I certainly never thought she was that bad!

GREENE:	Oh, that's nothing. Sometimes she gets completely out of hand. I wonder what the devil we're going to do with the girl.
KELLY:	Who's this guy Chunky she was on about?
TEMPLE:	Chunky was a man called Archie Brooks. He was attached to Scotland Yard.
KELLY:	Was he murdered – or was she just making that up?
TEMPLE:	(*Quite simply*) He was murdered.
KELLY:	When?
TEMPLE:	Three or four nights ago. Outside the Manilla – the night you telephoned my wife.
KELLY:	The night I telephoned your wife?
TEMPLE:	Yes.
KELLY:	You mean – Mrs Temple?
TEMPLE:	Well, I've only got one wife, Mr Kelly.
KELLY:	(*With a puzzled little laugh*) But why should I phone Mrs Temple?
TEMPLE:	I don't know why, but you did.
KELLY:	Well, I'm sorry to disillusion you but I certainly didn't telephone your wife that night, or any other night if it comes to that.
BOYER:	What the blazes does it matter whether he phoned your wife or not? Didn't you hear what Moira said? She said that someone in this room – one of us – murdered Archie Brooks. Now who was she getting at?
KELLY:	Don't look at me, brother! I'd never even heard of Brooks until that crazy dame of yours mentioned him.
STELLA:	(*Significantly*) Did you know Archie Brooks, Mr Boyer?

BOYER: (*Facing STELLA: bluntly*) Yes, I did. I knew him, liked him, and I didn't murder him.

STELLA: Well, that seems conclusive enough. What about you, Hubert?

GREENE: I'd never heard of the fellow until Moira mentioned him.

The door opens and MRS GREENE returns.

STEVE: How's Miss Portland?

MRS GREENE: She's all right now. I've given her three aspirins and she's lying down. Shall we go into dinner, Hubert?

GREENE: I think it might be a very good idea, Eileen.

BOYER: (*Relenting*) I think perhaps I'll just slip upstairs and have a word with Moira.

MRS GREENE: No, I should leave her, Mr Boyer. She'll probably be down after dinner full of apologies.

KELLY: I wouldn't depend on that!

GREENE: Me neither.

SCENE 7:   The Terrace.

BOYER can be heard playing the piano in the room beyond.
GREENE emerges onto the terrace.

GREENE: So here you are, George. I've been out looking for you. Don't you find it cold out here on the terrace?

KELLY: It's not too cold for me.

GREENE: Well, we want a fourth for bridge. How about it, old man?

KELLY: Not for me, sir. I'm tired. It won't be long before I'm hitting the hay.

GREENE: You're as bad as the Temples!

KELLY: Have they gone to bed?

GREENE: They went a quarter of an hour ago.

KELLY: Well, why don't you ask Boyer?

GREENE: I doubt he knows one card from another.

KELLY: Don't kid yourself! I'll bet that boy's a wizard. He can certainly play the piano anyway.

GREENE: Sure you won't change your mind?

KELLY: Quite sure.

GREENE: Well, I suppose there's nothing for it – I'll have to ask Boyer.

KELLY: (*Laughing*) Don't blame me if he skins you alive!

STEVE: (*Quietly*) Excuse me.

KELLY: (*Turning, very surprised*) Oh, I'm sorry, Mrs Temple.

STEVE: I'm looking for my handbag. I think I left it out here when we were having coffee.

KELLY: Oh –

KELLY looks around, then sees and picks up STEVE's bag.

KELLY: Is this it?

STEVE: Oh, yes, that's it.

STEVE takes it.

STEVE: Thank you.

The piano stops.

KELLY: I thought you'd gone to bed?

STEVE: I came down for my bag.

KELLY: Oh. (*Smiling*) Well, there it is.

STEVE: Mr Kelly?

KELLY: Yes.

STEVE: Why did you tell my husband that you didn't speak to me on the telephone?

KELLY: Because I don't remember speaking to you.

STEVE: You don't?

KELLY: No.

STEVE: You must have a very short memory.

KELLY: Maybe.

STEVE: Don't you remember what you said to me that night?

KELLY: Well, if I don't remember speaking to you I'm hardly likely to recall what I said.

STEVE: You told me to tell my husband to keep out of the Madison case.

KELLY: (*Quite simply*) What's the Madison case?

STEVE: Sam Portland had an appointment to see a private detective called Madison. Unfortunately Portland died of heart failure and was unable to keep the appointment. I'm fairly sure that if he had kept it he would have discovered that Madison was no more a private detective than you are. If you want my frank opinion –

KELLY: Sure, let's have your frank opinion, Mrs Temple.

STEVE: I think Madison's a blackmailer and the leader of a racket for distributing counterfeit dollars.

KELLY: (*Still smiling: pulling STEVE's leg*) You do?

STEVE: Yes, I do.

KELLY: You know, you've got some queer notions inside that head of yours! You're quite a gal!

STEVE: I'm glad you think so.

KELLY: I do think so. I do indeed. What else am I supposed to have told you over the telephone?

STEVE: You said: tell your husband to keep out of the Madison case. If he doesn't he's going to get mixed up with a bunch of very unpleasant customers.

KELLY: (*Pretending to be shocked: still pulling STEVE's leg*) Did I say that?

STEVE: You did, Mr Kelly. You also said that you were one of the unpleasant customers.

KELLY: No!

STEVE: Yes!

KELLY: Why that's a dreadful thing to say to anybody,
            it's almost a threat! You don't really think I'm
            an unpleasant customer, do you, Mrs Temple?

STEVE: (*Slowly: watching KELLY*) I think you're a
            very slippery one, Mr Kelly. Goodnight.

GEORGE KELLY chuckles.

SCENE 8:   The TEMPLES' Bedroom.

The door opens and STEVE enters.

TEMPLE: Did you find your bag?

STEVE: Yes, it was on the terrace.

TEMPLE: You've been rather a long time, Steve.

STEVE: I've been talking to Kelly.

TEMPLE: Oh, what did he have to say?

STEVE: I mentioned that telephone call. He still claims
            that he never made it.

TEMPLE: He made it all right. But why did he make it,
            that's the point. Is Eileen downstairs?

STEVE: Yes, she's playing bridge. Do you think she'll
            come tonight, Paul?

TEMPLE: I don't know. What's that good old intuition of
            yours feel about it?

STEVE: Well, she promised to come, didn't she? I hope
            she does because I've got a feeling that Mrs
            Greene knows quite a lot about this affair.

TEMPLE: Yes … you know, Steve, there's one rather
            interesting point about all this. I don't know
            whether you've spotted it or not.

STEVE: Yes, I've spotted it, I think. So far we haven't
            heard from Mr Madison.

TEMPLE: So far.

FADE UP music.

FADE DOWN.

SCENE 9:   The TEMPLES' Bedroom.

A clock is ticking: the ticking continues for a little while and then the clock chimes the hour. It is three o'clock.

STEVE: (*Whisper*) Paul, are you awake?

TEMPLE: Yes.

STEVE: It's three o'clock.

TEMPLE: Yes, I know.

STEVE: It doesn't look as if she's coming, does it?

TEMPLE: No.

STEVE: Did you hear them come up to bed?

TEMPLE gets out of bed and puts on his dressing gown under the following:

TEMPLE: I heard Greene. I don't know whether Eileen was with him or not.

STEVE: What time was that?

TEMPLE: Oh – it must have been about half past twelve … Where's my lighter?

STEVE: It's on the dressing table.

TEMPLE crosses to the dressing table.

TEMPLE: Like a cigarette, darling?

STEVE: No thanks.

TEMPLE: (*Flicking the lighter*) I'm going to give her another half an hour. If she's not here by half-past three, I'm – (*He stops*)

STEVE: What is it?

TEMPLE: I thought I heard something.

A pause.

STEVE: I can't hear anything.

TEMPLE: No … No, I must have been mistaken.

Another pause.

STEVE: Wait a minute!

TEMPLE: What is it, Steve?

STEVE: Sh! Listen!

There is a soft tap on the door of the room.

STEVE: It'll be Eileen!

TEMPLE: Yes.

STEVE gets out of bed and puts on her dressing gown.

STEVE: Good, I thought she'd come.

TEMPLE: It's all right, I'll answer it.

TEMPLE crosses and quietly opens the door.

STEVE: (*Surprised*) Why, Mr Greene!

TEMPLE: Hello, Greene … What is it?

GREENE: I'm awfully sorry to disturb you, Temple – but …

TEMPLE realises GREENE doesn't want to talk on the threshold.

TEMPLE: Come in.

GREENE: Thank you.

GREENE enters. TEMPLE shuts the door.

GREENE: Temple – have you seen my wife?

TEMPLE: (*Apparently astonished*) Your wife?

GREENE: Yes.

TEMPLE: No, I'm afraid we haven't.

STEVE: Isn't she in her room?

GREENE: No. I went along about a quarter of an hour ago: Eileen wasn't there and the bed hadn't been slept in.

STEVE: She's probably in the bathroom.

GREENE: No, I've been to the bathroom.

STEVE: Well, perhaps she's with Mrs Portland or –

GREENE: No, she's not with Mrs Portland or Moira. I've been all over the house and there just isn't a sign of her.

TEMPLE: Have you asked the servants?

GREENE: Yes, I've just come from the servants' quarters.

TEMPLE: Well – what time did she come to bed?

GREENE: She came to bed when I did, just after twelve. You must have heard us, Temple, your light was still on.

TEMPLE: Yes, I did.

GREENE: It's uncanny, I just don't understand it.

STEVE: You say you've been all over the house?

GREENE: Yes. I even woke up Kelly and Chris Boyer in the hope that one of them might have heard –

GREENE is interrupted by a loud thud on the door: it is caused by a knife – or dagger – being driven into the panel of the door.

GREENE: – Good Lord, what's that, Temple?

TEMPLE: Something hit the door …

TEMPLE throws the door open.

STEVE: Paul, what is it?

GREENE: Look!

TEMPLE: It's a knife! Someone must have – thrown it at the door!

GREENE: Do you see anybody?

TEMPLE: No … No, there's no one in the corridor!

STEVE: Paul … Look –

STEVE pulls the knife out of the door: it takes her quite an effort.

STEVE: Stuck – on the – knife – There's a note …

STEVE detaches a small piece of paper.

TEMPLE: So there is …

GREENE: What does it say?

STEVE: It says – "Go to the boathouse".

GREENE: (*Puzzled*) The boathouse?

TEMPLE: Is that all it says?

STEVE: Yes.

TEMPLE: Is there a boathouse near here?

GREENE: Why, yes, of course. Down by the lake.

TEMPLE: How long would it take us to get there?

GREENE:	About ten minutes.
TEMPLE:	Go back to your room and get dressed. I'll meet you downstairs.
GREENE:	Temple, you don't think –
TEMPLE:	Do as I say! I'll meet you downstairs in three minutes! Oh, and Greene!
GREENE:	(*Turning*) Yes?
TEMPLE:	If you've got a torch – bring it!

SCENE 10:   The Lakeside.

A background of night wind and the lapping of water.

TEMPLE:	Where's the boathouse?
GREENE:	It's over there. Look, you can see the outline of it through the bushes.
TEMPLE:	Is it a dilapidated sort of place?
GREENE:	No, it's been pretty well kept. We use it as a storehouse. There should be a boat tied up somewhere along here.

They push through the bushes.

TEMPLE:	Don't flash your torch, Greene.
GREENE:	Why?
TEMPLE:	Because if there's anyone in the boathouse I don't want them to see us.

They arrive at the water's edge.

GREENE:	(*Suddenly*) Here we are! Here's the boat!

GREENE puts his foot on the boat and it bobs up and down in the water.

TEMPLE:	Are there any oars?
GREENE:	Yes, they're both here. Mind your head on that branch, Temple.
TEMPLE:	It's all right, I can manage.
GREENE:	You'll have to bend low or you'll get it in your eyes. I think I'd better get into the boat first otherwise you might – (*He stops dead*)

125

TEMPLE:	What is it? … Greene, what is it?
GREENE:	(*Staring ahead*) I thought I saw something.
TEMPLE:	Where? In the water?
GREENE:	Yes.

A moment.

TEMPLE:	I don't see anything …
GREENE:	No. No, I must be mistaken.
TEMPLE:	(*Watching GREENE*) What was it?
GREENE:	Oh, nothing. I must have been imagining things.
TEMPLE:	No, tell me, what was it?
GREENE:	Well – if you must know …
TEMPLE:	Yes?
GREENE:	I thought I saw – a hand.

END OF EPISODE FOUR

EPISODE FIVE

STEVE TAKES OVER

SCENE 1:	By the Lake, as at the end of Episode 4.

TEMPLE:	Don't flash your torch, Greene.
GREENE:	Why?
TEMPLE:	Because if there's anyone in the boathouse I don't want them to see us.
GREENE:	Mind your head on that branch, Temple.
TEMPLE:	It's all right, I can manage.
GREENE:	You'll have to bend low or you'll get it in your eyes. I think I'd better get into the boat first otherwise you might – (*He stops dead*)
TEMPLE:	What is it? … Greene, what is it?
GREENE:	(*Staring ahead*) I thought I saw something.
TEMPLE:	Where? In the water?
GREENE:	Yes.

A moment.

TEMPLE:	I don't see anything …
GREENE:	No. No, I must be mistaken.
TEMPLE:	(*Watching GREENE*) What was it?
GREENE:	Oh, nothing. I must have been imagining things.
TEMPLE:	No, tell me, what was it?
GREENE:	Well – if you must know …
TEMPLE:	Yes?
GREENE:	I thought I saw – a hand.
TEMPLE:	Where?
GREENE:	I thought I saw it by the boat.
TEMPLE:	Let's move the boat.

With difficulty TEMPLE starts to pull the boat along the bank.

GREENE:	Just over there. Below the bank. Careful, there's a lot of weeds and stuff down there. If you slip off the bank you'll be in a terrible mess.
TEMPLE:	It's all right, I can manage …

GREENE: Temple!

TEMPLE: (*Turning*) What is it?

GREENE: I was right! Look, there's someone in the water!

TEMPLE: Help me get the boat out of the way! Quick!

The boat is dragged to the side.

GREENE: Who is it? Can you see?

TEMPLE: No. Shine your torch on the water over here. That's it! Now give me your hand …

GREENE: I don't think you'll reach.

TEMPLE: Give me your hand! Quickly!

TEMPLE and GREENE link hands. A moment as TEMPLE reaches with difficulty towards the body.

GREENE: Can you reach?

TEMPLE: I think so. No … Leave go! Leave go, Greene, I'm going in!

TEMPLE climbs down the bank and wades into the water.

GREENE: Who is it?

TEMPLE is struggling in the water; trying to lift the body onto the bank.

TEMPLE: It's … a … girl … Give me your hand …

GREENE: Wait a minute, I'll climb down the bank.

GREENE climbs down the bank, partly into the water.

TEMPLE: That's it! Now get hold of my arm.

GREENE: Temple, who is it? Can you see who … It's Eileen! Temple, it's my wife!

TEMPLE: Help me, Greene – I want to get her onto the bank!

GREENE: (*Almost panic stricken*) Temple, it's Eileen! Do you hear what I say, it's Eileen!

TEMPLE: I know. I know. But we've got to get her back on the bank.

GREENE: (*Desperately*) I've got her … I've got her, Temple!

TEMPLE: That's right!

TEMPLE and GREENE lift the inert body of EILEEN out of the water.

GREENE: Quick! Get hold of her arms!

GREENE grabs EILEEN's arms and starts to move them backwards and forwards.

GREENE: Temple, for God's sake help me!

TEMPLE: I'm sorry, Greene, it's no use.

GREENE: What do you mean? (*Desperately*) We've got to do something, we can't just stand here and –

TEMPLE: Look at your hands.

GREENE: (*Bewildered*) What?

TEMPLE: Here's the torch. Look at your hands …

A moment.

GREENE: … They're covered in blood! Temple, they're covered in blood!

TEMPLE: She's been stabbed.

SCENE 2:   A Sitting Room in Brown Acres.

There is gentle conversation which subsides as the door opens and TEMPLE enters.

BOYER: Oh, don't start that again.

STELLA: The whole thing's a nightmare.

TEMPLE: Is Miss Portland here?

STELLA: No, she's in her room. Do you want her?

TEMPLE: Sir Graham would like to have a word with her. He's in the library.

BOYER: I'll tell Moira.

TEMPLE: No, that's all right, Boyer. Would you mind fetching her, Mrs Portland?

STELLA: (*Rising*) No, of course not.

TEMPLE: Thank you.

The door closes behind STELLA.

131

KELLY: Temple, don't think I'm trying to be difficult, but when's the old boy going to break down on this routine stuff? He does nothing but ask us the same questions over and over again.

TEMPLE: You seem to forget, Kelly, a murder has been committed.

KELLY: I know a murder's been committed. We're not likely to forget it, any of us. But the point is this, how long are we going to be under suspicion?

TEMPLE: You're not under suspicion.

KELLY: (*Staggered*) I'm not?

TEMPLE: Why certainly not. Whatever gave you that impression?

KELLY: Say, do you know what's been happening to me since nine o'clock this morning? I've been questioned by two sergeants, an Inspector, a Divisional Superintendent and Sir Graham Forbes himself. And that isn't everything! They took my fingerprints … did you know that?

TEMPLE: Yes, I knew that. They took my fingerprints as well.

KELLY: (*Pleasantly surprised*) They did?

TEMPLE: (*Nodding*) And Mr Boyer's.

KELLY: Oh, well, that's different. I didn't know it was routine stuff. I thought they'd got their knife into me and wanted – (*He realises what he has said*)

TEMPLE: (*Politely*) You thought what?

KELLY: (*A moment, then suddenly, bluntly*) Look, Temple. Let's not play around anymore – let's put our cards on the table. I know why the Yard have got their eye on me. Mrs Greene was stabbed, wasn't she?

TEMPLE: Yes. And so were Inspector James and Archie Brooks.

KELLY: (*Apparently surprised*) Is that so?

TEMPLE: That's so.

KELLY: (*Thoughtfully*) I didn't know that.

BOYER: I may be dense, Temple, but I don't see the significance. Why bring up a thing like that –

KELLY: I used to do a knife throwing act, Mr Boyer – they still think I'm doing it. Catch on?

BOYER: But that's nonsense! Why should you want to murder Eileen?

TEMPLE: Why should anyone want to if it comes to that?

TEMPLE takes a knife from his pocket.

TEMPLE: Kelly, does this knife belong to you?

KELLY: (*Surprised*) Why, yes! Where did you get it?

TEMPLE: What's more to the point – where did you get it?

KELLY: But I've several knives like that. I carry them about with me. I told you, I used to do a circus act.

TEMPLE: Do you still do it?

KELLY: Only as a gag. I take the knives with me when I'm invited anywhere. Well – you know how it is – some people like to do conjuring tricks, others do card tricks.

TEMPLE: And you throw knives?

KELLY: That's right. (*Quickly*) Only in fun!

TEMPLE: Did you throw this last night?

KELLY: (*Resentfully*) What do you mean?

TEMPLE: Did you?

BOYER: Good Lord, you don't mean that the knife – is the knife that killed Mrs Greene?

A moment.

133

TEMPLE: No. This knife was thrown at my bedroom door just after three o'clock this morning. There was a note attached to it: "Go down to the boathouse". Greene and I went down to the boathouse and found Eileen.

KELLY: (*Relieved*) Oh …

TEMPLE: So you see, Kelly, I'm not accusing you of murder. I'm simply asking you whether –

KELLY: Whether I got up at three o'clock in the morning and threw the knife at your bedroom door? The answer's no.

TEMPLE: Then somebody must have stolen the knife from you?

KELLY: That seems to be the obvious explanation.

TEMPLE: How many knives have you?

KELLY: I arrived at Southampton with four.

TEMPLE: That's not what I asked you. How many knives have you?

KELLY: There should be three in my room – the one you've got there makes four.

TEMPLE: Are all the knives the same?

KELLY: They're different weights and sizes but they look more or less the same, I guess.

TEMPLE takes some photographs from a large envelope.

TEMPLE: I want you to take a look at these pictures, Kelly.

BOYER: What are they?

TEMPLE: They're from the police file: close-ups of Archie Brooks and Inspector James. In both instances you can see the knife.

A pause.

KELLY: Well?

TEMPLE: Have you seen those knives before?

KELLY: No.

TEMPLE:	Don't they belong to you?
KELLY:	I've told you, I've never seen them before. In any case, I've only got four. Three of them are upstairs in my room and you've got the fourth.
TEMPLE:	How do you know you've still got three?
KELLY:	(*Rather impatiently*) Because I was looking at them this morning and … (*He stops*)
TEMPLE:	(*Politely*) You were looking at them this morning? Then you must have noticed that this one was missing?
KELLY:	Yes, I – was under the impression I'd left it in town.
TEMPLE:	I see.

The door opens and STELLA enters.

STELLA:	Moira will be down in a few moments.
TEMPLE:	Oh, thank you, Mrs Portland.
STELLA:	Mr Kelly and I would like to catch the 2.45 back to town. Is that possible?
TEMPLE:	I don't see why not. (*Moving to the door*) I'll have a word with Sir Graham.
STELLA:	Thank you. Oh, Mr Temple …
TEMPLE:	(*Turning*) Yes?
STELLA:	Where's Hubert? – we haven't seen him since breakfast.
TEMPLE:	He's in his room.
STELLA:	How's he taking all this?
TEMPLE:	Well, naturally, he's very distressed.
STELLA:	Yes, of course. What a dreadful thing to have happened – really dreadful. Have you any idea who did it?
TEMPLE:	(*Slowly: watching STELLA*) I've got my suspicions, Mrs Portland. (*Closing the subject*) I'll ask Sir Graham about the train.

SCENE 3:   The Library.

SIR GRAHAM and INSPECTOR VOSPER are in the middle of a conversation.

VOSPER: … Of course the whole point is, Sir Graham. If she was murdered in the house and then taken down to the lake, then there's just the possibility that someone –

VOSPER is interrupted by the door opening.

TEMPLE: May I come in?

FORBES: Yes, of course, Temple.

TEMPLE: Moira Portland will be down in a moment.

TEMPLE shuts the door.

FORBES: Oh, good. You know Inspector Vosper, of course?

TEMPLE: Yes, indeed, Inspector. Have you checked the prints?

VOSPER: Yes, we've checked all of them, Mr Temple. No luck, I'm afraid.

TEMPLE: Well, that's unfortunate.

FORBES: Did you show the knife to Kelly?

TEMPLE: Yes.

VOSPER: (*A touch of sarcasm*) Of course he'd never seen it before.

TEMPLE: Oh yes, he'd seen it all right. As a matter of fact it belongs to him.

VOSPER: (*Rather surprised*) Did he say so?

TEMPLE: Yes.

FORBES: What!

TEMPLE: Apparently he's got several like this. He seems to carry them about with him.

VOSPER: What the devil on earth does he do that for?

TEMPLE: When the party gets tame, Kelly livens it up with a demonstration. Our George rather fancies himself as the life and soul of the party.

VOSPER: M'm. What did he say when you produced the knife?

TEMPLE: He seemed surprised. Boyer wanted to know if it was the one that killed Eileen.

VOSPER: I wish we could find that knife, Mr Temple. There was no sign of it I suppose?

TEMPLE: I'm afraid not. I had a pretty good look for it too.

FORBES: Temple, tell me: do you think this is tied up with the murder of Brooks and James, or do you think it's an isolated affair and nothing to do with the Madison case?

TEMPLE: I think it's all part and parcel of the same case, Sir Graham.

FORBES: Then why was she murdered? We know why James was murdered and we've got a pretty good notion why Brooks was taken care of, but this affair isn't quite the same.

TEMPLE: M'm.

VOSPER: If Mr Temple's right, Sir Graham – and I must confess I'm inclined to agree with him – then it seems to me that –

VOSPER is interrupted by a knock at the door.

FORBES: Come in.

The door opens.

MOIRA: I believe that you wanted to see me?

MOIRA sounds tired and rather ill, although her manner is faintly defiant.

FORBES: Oh, yes, come in, Miss Portland.

MOIRA: What is it that you want?

FORBES: Won't you sit down?

MOIRA: I should prefer to stand if you don't mind.

137

FORBES:	Just as you wish. I've been reading through your statement, Miss Portland, and there are one or two points I'm not quite clear about.
MOIRA:	Well?
FORBES:	You say you went to your room last night about quarter past eight, before dinner – you took three aspirins and went to bed.
MOIRA:	Yes.
FORBES:	I understand from Mr Temple that earlier in the evening you caused rather an unpleasant scene.
MOIRA:	Yes, I was tight. I'm afraid I behaved very badly.
FORBES:	Well, you made rather a remarkable statement.
MOIRA:	Did I? I'm afraid I don't remember.
FORBES:	You said that Archie Brooks was a friend of yours, and that he'd been murdered by someone in this room. It was obvious that you were referring to either Mr and Mrs Greene, George Kelly, Mrs Portland or your fiancé Chris Boyer.
MOIRA:	I've told you I don't remember making such a statement.
FORBES:	Nevertheless, you made it.
MOIRA:	I was drunk. I just didn't know what I was saying.
FORBES:	Was Archie Brooks a friend of yours?
MOIRA:	(*Hesitating*) – Yes.
FORBES:	A close friend?
MOIRA:	It depends what you mean by a close friend.
FORBES:	Did you see a great deal of each other?
MOIRA:	No. He came to the Manilla once or twice and … we had … a few drinks together … that's all.
FORBES:	You seem to be fond of having a few drinks.

138

MOIRA:	(*Coldly*) Is there anything else you'd like to know?
FORBES:	Yes, there is.
MOIRA:	Well?
FORBES:	Have you seen this knife before?
MOIRA:	No.
FORBES:	Are you sure?
MOIRA:	Quite sure.
FORBES:	When did you first hear that Mrs Greene had been murdered?
MOIRA:	My fiancé told me. He came to my room.
FORBES:	What time would that be?
MOIRA:	About half past four.
FORBES:	Were you surprised?
MOIRA:	Of course I was surprised! I was stunned. I just didn't believe it.
FORBES:	Is this the first time you've been down here to Brown Acres?
MOIRA:	Good gracious no! I've been down several times.
FORBES:	I understand you work for Mr Greene?
MOIRA:	I'm attached to the London office of the Portland Yeast Company, if that's what you mean.
FORBES:	Mr Greene's office?
MOIRA:	Mr Greene is in charge of the office, yes.
TEMPLE:	Miss Portland, when I met your father on the boat, coming over from America, he told me that Mr Greene had made arrangements for him to meet a man called Madison. Have you heard of Mr Madison by any chance?
MOIRA:	No, I'm afraid I haven't.
TEMPLE:	Mr Greene doesn't seem to have heard of Madison either – it's most odd.

139

MOIRA: You must have misunderstood my father.

TEMPLE: No, I don't think I did.

MOIRA: (*A shrug*) I'm sorry I can't help you. May I go now?

FORBES: Yes, you can go, Miss Portland.

TEMPLE: Oh, just a moment!

MOIRA: (*Turning*) Yes?

TEMPLE: You said last night you'd been down into the village, to the local pub.

MOIRA: Yes.

TEMPLE: (*Quite pleasant*) Which one did you go to?

MOIRA: There is only one. The White Horse.

TEMPLE: (*Still smiling*) The White Swan.

MOIRA: I mean the White Swan.

TEMPLE: If I remember rightly you had three pink gins. Is that right?

MOIRA: (*Hesitating*) Yes.

TEMPLE: (*Laughing*) They must have been under the counter.

MOIRA: What do you mean?

VOSPER: What are you getting at, sir?

TEMPLE: Have you ever tried to order a pink gin at the White Swan, Inspector?

VOSPER: No, sir.

TEMPLE: Well, I have. I tried this morning. By Timothy how I tried.

MOIRA: What are you talking about?

TEMPLE: They only have a beer licence, but apart from that no one seems to remember serving you, Miss Portland. Now I ask you. A very pretty girl in full evening dress strolls into a very quiet bar and orders three pink gins, and yet – no one seems to remember her. It's most odd.

MOIRA: Why?

140

TEMPLE:	Did you really go down to the village last night?
MOIRA:	Of course I did! If I didn't go down into the village how did I manage to get drunk so quickly?
TEMPLE:	(*Slowly; watching MOIRA*) I don't think you were drunk, Miss Portland.

A moment.

MOIRA:	Sir Graham, I'm going back to Town this afternoon – have you any objection?
FORBES:	None whatsoever. We've got your address, I take it?
VOSPER:	Yes, sir, we've got her address.
MOIRA:	(*Leaving*) If you want to get in touch with me during the week you can nearly always find me at the office.
FORBES:	Thank you.

The door shuts.

VOSPER:	What did you mean, Mr Temple, you don't think she was drunk?
TEMPLE:	I went down to the village first thing this morning and called at the White Swan.
FORBES:	Well?
TEMPLE:	She never went near the place.
VOSPER:	I don't get this. When we spoke to Mrs Portland, Hubert Greene, Kelly and her fiancé Boyer they all said she was drunk.
TEMPLE:	She looked drunk and behaved as if she was drunk, but I bet my hat that she wasn't.
VOSPER:	You mean she was putting on an act? But why?
FORBES:	Temple, you don't think she overheard our telephone conversation, became upset and had to pretend she was drunk to conceal her feelings?

TEMPLE: It's a possibility. Sir Graham, I've been meaning to ask you about that phone call. Was that a lot of nonsense about Dr Elzec or did you really come across his photograph?

FORBES: Oh, we came across it all right. It was in the snapshot album you found at Brooks' place. Elzec, or Weiner as he called himself in '37, seems to be quite a character. He'd been mixed up in all sorts of rackets.

TEMPLE: Is he a doctor?

FORBES: Not a medical doctor. He's a doctor of music.

TEMPLE: Why did you tell me about him over the phone – wasn't that risky?

FORBES: I wanted whoever was listening to know that we were on to him. I believe that if Elzec really is mixed up in this business they'll either go for him or drop him like a hot potato. Don't worry, we've got our eye on Dr Elzec – with a bit of luck he might turn out to be a first class decoy.

TEMPLE: I hope you're right, Sir Graham. I sincerely hope you're right.

FADE UP of music.

FADE DOWN of music.

SCENE 4: The Entrance Hall of the Temples' Apartment Block.

The lift arrives and the gates are opened. TEMPLE picks up his and STEVE's luggage.

TEMPLE: It's all right, darling – I can cope.

STEVE: I'll take my hatbox.

TEMPLE: Right, thanks.

TEMPLE enters the lift with the bags. STEVE follows him.

STEVE: I'll close the gates.

142

TEMPLE: Wait a moment, I think there's someone coming …

We hear approaching footsteps. DR ELZEC arrives at the lift.

ELZEC: (*Surprised*) Oh, good evening, Mr Temple …

TEMPLE: Hello, Doctor Elzec! Are you going upstairs?

ELZEC: Yes.

TEMPLE: I don't think you've met my wife.

ELZEC: No, I've not yet had that pleasure. Good evening, Mrs Temple.

STEVE: Good evening, doctor.

TEMPLE: Can you get in all right? It's a bit of a crush with all this luggage.

ELZEC: Yes, I can manage, thank you.

ELZEC gets in the lift and TEMPLE closes the gates.

STEVE: Shall I press the button?

TEMPLE: (*Rather squashed*) Yes, please, darling.

STEVE presses the button and the lift starts.

ELZEC: Have you been away for the weekend?

TEMPLE: Yes, we've only just got back.

ELZEC: I'm glad I bumped into you, Mr Temple, there's something I wanted to speak to you about.

TEMPLE: Oh?

ELZEC: You'll probably think it's a lot of nonsense, but …

TEMPLE: Go on, doctor.

ELZEC: Mr Temple, if I wanted to speak to someone at Scotland Yard, do you think you could arrange it for me?

TEMPLE: Well, it's not really very difficult, you know. All you've got to do is phone Whitehall 1212.

ELZEC: Yes, but – oh, here we are!

The lift stops. STEVE opens the gates.

STEVE: Shall I take the smaller case?

TEMPLE: No, it's all right, darling, I'll see to it. You go ahead.

STEVE: (*Going*) Goodbye, doctor.

ELZEC: Goodbye, Mrs Temple.

TEMPLE: Now, doctor, you were saying – you want me to speak to someone at Scotland Yard.

ELZEC: Well, I was wondering if you could arrange for me to see that man – the man that was in the lift the first time we met?

TEMPLE: Inspector James?

ELZEC: Yes.

TEMPLE: I'm afraid that won't be possible.

ELZEC: (*Disappointed*) No?

TEMPLE: James is dead. He was murdered.

ELZEC: (*Softly*) Oh. Oh, I didn't know that.

TEMPLE: Why did you want to see the Inspector?

ELZEC: Well – (*Suddenly, with a little laugh*) Well, the fact of the matter is, Mr Temple, I think I'm being followed.

TEMPLE: Being followed?

ELZEC: Yes. It really is most odd. The first time I noticed it was yesterday morning. I had an appointment in Regent Street and I picked up a taxi just outside the flat. When I was getting into the taxi I noticed a man standing in one of the doorways.

TEMPLE: Go on.

ELZEC: Later, the same morning, when I was going down Oxford Street, I noticed the same man. He was on the opposite side of the road but I'm quite sure that he was watching me.

TEMPLE: It doesn't mean to say you're being followed just because you see the same man twice in the same day.

144

ELZEC: But I saw him again, this afternoon. I had an appointment in Knightsbridge. I caught the tube from Green Park. When I got into the train he was already there, sitting in the corner, watching me.

TEMPLE: Did you speak to him?

ELZEC: No. No, of course not.

TEMPLE: Have you any idea who he is – or why he's following you?

ELZEC: Not the slightest.

TEMPLE: All right, I'll have a word with the Yard about it. If you see him again or anything else develops give me a ring.

ELZEC: Thank you, Mr Temple. That's very kind of you. Here's your case.

TEMPLE takes the case.

TEMPLE: Oh, thank you.

ELZEC closes the gates and the lift starts to ascend.

SCENE 5:   The TEMPLES' Bedroom.

TEMPLE and STEVE are unpacking.

TEMPLE: Where does this shirt go, darling?

STEVE: To the laundry. Put it over there.

TEMPLE: Golly, I'm tired! If there's anything I hate more than unpacking …

STEVE: (*Laughing*) It's packing! Paul, you really are the limit! Just look what you've done! You've bundled everything onto the bed.

TEMPLE: I'll sort it out later.

The front door buzzer goes.

STEVE: You'll do nothing of the sort. You'll – That's someone at the door, darling.

TEMPLE: Well, isn't Charlie in?

STEVE: No, it's his night out.

TEMPLE: (*Moving out*) By Timothy, how many nights out does that young fellow have!

SCENE 6:   The TEMPLES' Hallway.

TEMPLE opens the door.

FORBES: Good evening, Temple.

TEMPLE: (*Surprised*) Hello, Sir Graham. Come in.

SIR GRAHAM enters.

FORBES: What time did you get back?

TEMPLE: We've only been in about a quarter of an hour. Come along, let me get you a drink.

TEMPLE and SIR GRAHAM move into the drawing room.

FORBES: Is Steve in?

TEMPLE: Yes, she's unpacking, she'll be out in a minute. What would you like, Sir Graham?

FORBES: Nothing, thanks.

TEMPLE: Sure?

FORBES: Yes, quite sure.

TEMPLE: I'm rather glad you called round, Sir Graham. I just bumped into Elzec.

FORBES: Oh? When?

TEMPLE: About twenty minutes ago. (*Faintly amused*) He asked me to have a word with you.

FORBES: What about?

TEMPLE: He's under the impression that he's being followed.

FORBES: Oh, Lord! You mean …

TEMPLE: Yes, he's spotted your man. I'm afraid you'll have to change him.

FORBES: That's annoying. Oh, well, I'll have a word with Vosper in the morning.

STEVE enters.

STEVE: (*Surprised*) Hello, Sir Graham!

FORBES: Oh, hello, Steve.

STEVE: No, don't get up. You look rather pleased with yourself. What's happened?

FORBES takes a telegram from his pocket.

FORBES: When I got back to the Yard, I found this cable waiting for me. Read it, Temple.

SIR GRAHAM hands TEMPLE the cable. A moment as TEMPLE reads it over.

TEMPLE: This doesn't make sense to me. What does it mean?

FORBES: (*Leaning forward: confidentially*) I'll tell you. It means that we really have traced the plane – the one that crashed in Eppingdale. We know where it came from and we know who was flying it.

TEMPLE: That's quick work.

FORBES: Oh, we move quickly sometimes. It was flown by a man called Dordrecht – a Dutchman. I've phoned the authorities in Amsterdam and this time it really looks as if we're onto something.

STEVE: What do you mean?

FORBES: I think it's a pretty safe bet, Steve, that Dordrecht came over here to collect a supply of counterfeit dollars, the head man – call him Madison if you like – got wind of our visit to Eppingdale, and failed to keep his appointment.

TEMPLE: Go on

FORBES: Someone else is going to come over, someone else is going to contact Madison and collect the dollars.

TEMPLE: Is that supposition – or fact?

FORBES: It's a fact – because we know who's coming.

STEVE: What?

TEMPLE: You do?

FORBES:	Yes. Dordrecht worked with a Spaniard, a man called Alfaro.
TEMPLE:	Alfaro?
FORBES:	Yes. He's an export merchant, he lives outside Amsterdam. For weeks now the Dutch police have had their eye on him. They know he's been running a counterfeit racket and they've been waiting for the right moment to drop on him. Two days ago Alfaro booked a reservation. He flies from Amsterdam on Wednesday.
STEVE:	For London?
FORBES:	Yes.
TEMPLE:	What are you going to do – tail him at this end?
FORBES:	Of course. From the moment he steps off the plane we'll watch him like a hawk. In my opinion there's a very good chance, he might lead us straight to Madison.
TEMPLE:	Yes, and there's a very good chance he might vanish into thin air! Someone ought to bump into Alfaro at Schiphol airport, get friendly, and travel over with him on the plane.
FORBES:	Yes, I've thought of that, Temple. That's why I'm here.
TEMPLE:	Oh. You want me to pop over to Amsterdam and –
FORBES:	No. I don't want you to pop anywhere.
TEMPLE:	What do you mean?
FORBES:	I want Steve to go over to Holland. I want her to accidentally bump into Alfaro and –
TEMPLE:	Yes, but just a minute. Why Steve?
FORBES:	Well …
TEMPLE:	Why Steve?

STEVE:	Alfaro's a boy for the ladies. Correct, Sir Graham?
FORBES:	Yes.
TEMPLE:	Yes. Well I don't like it.
STEVE:	You're not supposed to like it, darling. Go on, Sir Graham.
FORBES:	There's absolutely nothing for you to worry about, Temple. You know Steve – when it comes to anything like this she's got her head positively riveted on.
STEVE:	What would you want me to do?
FORBES:	I should want you to play up to him – get to know everything you can. If he falls for you and wants to make a date, then make a date but …
TEMPLE:	What!
FORBES:	Don't worry, I'll have half the Yard tailing her the moment she steps off the plane.
TEMPLE:	Well frankly, I don't like it.
STEVE:	Darling, I could do it standing on my head!
TEMPLE:	What about her passport? If he sees the name Temple …
FORBES:	He won't. I've fixed that with the Foreign Office.
STEVE:	What do you mean?
FORBES:	You'll be travelling under the name of Gloria Wade.
STEVE:	Gloria Wade! What on earth am I supposed to be?
FORBES:	A musical comedy actress – very gay and not exactly out of the top drawer. I'll let you have the passport on Tuesday morning.
TEMPLE:	What time does the plane leave Amsterdam?
FORBES:	Two forty Wednesday afternoon.

TEMPLE: Huh! Gloria Wade.

FADE In of music.

FADE DOWN of music.

SCENE 7:   The Interior of a Large Airliner.

We hear the conversation of passengers as they take their places.

GIRL: Do you mind if I put my coat over here?

MAN 1:   No, not at all.

STEWARDESS: Excuse me, madam – I'll take the coat.

GIRL: Oh, thank you.

MAN 2:   Can we get anything to eat on the plane?

STEWARDESS: Yes, sir. We shall be serving refreshments later.

Suddenly: very full of herself: a musical comedy personality: calling in an affected voice.

STEVE: Stewardess! Stewardess!

STEWARDESS: Yes, madam?

STEVE: I can't sit here! I'm terribly sorry, but I simply can't sit here!

STEWARDESS: Why – what's the matter?

STEVE: I must sit near the front. If I don't I shall be sick – violently sick.

STEWARDESS: I'm afraid all the seats are taken, madam.

STEVE: But I've got to move, I just can't be … Oh, ask that young man over there if he'll change seats. I'm sure he'll be a darling!

The passengers are amused.

YOUNG MAN: (*In very broken English*) You would like to change seats?

STEVE: Would you mind? Would you mind terribly?

YOUNG MAN: No. No, that is quite all right.

STEVE:	Oh, you really are a darling! You're terribly sweet!

STEVE moves into the aisle and drops her bag.

YOUNG MAN:	You've dropped your handbag.
STEVE:	Oh!

The STEWARDESS picks it up.

STEWARDESS:	Here we are.
STEVE:	Oh, thank you.

STEVE crosses to her seat.

ALFARO:	Would you prefer to sit on the inside?
STEVE:	No, I shall be quite all right here.

DON ALFARO is a Spaniard: a man of about forty-five.

ALFARO:	Are you sure?
STEVE:	(*Taking notice of DON ALFARO: a friendly little laugh*) Quite sure. Oh, I hope that young man wasn't a friend of yours?
ALFARO:	No. No, we were not travelling together.
STEVE:	(*Giggling*) I'm terribly nervous.
ALFARO:	There is no need to be nervous. What are you nervous about?
STEVE:	I don't know. Just don't know – haven't a clue.
ALFARO:	English?
STEVE:	(*Faintly aggressive*) What do you mean?
ALFARO:	Are you English?
STEVE:	Of course I'm English! What did you think I was, an Alsatian?
ALFARO:	Haven't I seen you before somewhere?
STEVE:	Now come off it! Come off it!
ALFARO:	No, seriously.
STEVE:	Did you see One of the Girls?
ALFARO:	One of the Girls?
STEVE:	A revue – I did six weeks in Paris.
ALFARO:	Oh! You are on the stage!

STEVE: I say, you are bright, aren't you?

The engines of the plane start up.

ALFARO: What did you do in One of the Girls?

STEVE: What didn't I do? Everything!

ALFARO: I'm sorry I missed it. I should like to have seen you. Don't you think you'd better fasten your belt?

STEVE: My belt? Oh … Oh, my belt … Yes, of course!

A moment.

ALFARO: What have you been doing in Amsterdam?

STEVE: I haven't been doing anything. I'm on my way home from Switzerland. What a country! Have you been there?

ALFARO: But of course!

STEVE: It's heavenly! (*Singing*) Yodelooo!

ALFARO: So, you are a singer?

STEVE: What did you think I was?

ALFARO: (*Laughing*) I did not know. I thought perhaps you were a dancer. You have the – what is the word – the figure of a dancer.

STEVE: (*Flattered*) Oh. Oh, really …

ALFARO: Permit me to introduce myself, senorita. My name is Don Alfaro.

STEVE: I'm Gloria Wade.

ALFARO: I'm pleased to meet you, Miss Wade.

STEVE: I'm pleased to meet you too.

ALFARO: (*Moving closer: significantly*) I'm so glad you changed your seat.

The engine starts to roar.

SCENE 8:   The Same, later.

The plane is now cruising at altitude.

STEVE: Well, so far so good! Thank goodness it's not a bumpy flight.

152

ALFARO:	You'll be all right now. The worst is over.
STEVE:	Famous last words!
ALFARO:	Pardon?
STEVE:	I said famous … Stop it! You're not Dutch, are you?
ALFARO:	(*Amused*) I am a Spaniard.
STEVE:	A Spaniard! Really? I don't think I've ever met a real Spaniard before!
ALFARO:	Well, you've met one now.
STEVE:	Do you live in Spain?
ALFARO:	No, I live just outside Amsterdam. I'm in the export business, that's why I'm coming to England.
STEVE:	Oh, just fancy! How nice. It's all export now, isn't it?
ALFARO:	(*Amused by STEVE*) Yes.
STEVE:	What do you export?
ALFARO:	Oh, all sorts of things. What are you going to do when you get back to England?
STEVE:	Oh, I don't know. Probably go into a show.
ALFARO:	I know one or two theatre people – they may be able to help you.
STEVE:	Oh, really? That is nice of you.
ALFARO:	Do you live in London?
STEVE:	Yes. I live with a girl friend in St John's Wood.
ALFARO:	St John's Wood? Is that nice?
STEVE:	Oh, ever so nice. Very select, of course. How long are you staying in England?
ALFARO:	Two or three days.
STEVE:	With friends?
ALFARO:	Yes, with friends.
STEVE:	Where?
ALFARO:	In the country. Look, why don't we have dinner together one evening?

STEVE:	Oh, I couldn't do that!
ALFARO:	Why not?
STEVE:	Oh, really I couldn't.
ALFARO:	Wouldn't you like to have dinner with me?
STEVE:	Yes, of course, but –
ALFARO:	Well?
STEVE:	Really, I don't know what to say!
ALFARO:	Why don't you say yes?
STEVE:	All right! All right! I'll try anything once!
ALFARO:	Where shall we meet? Do you know the Plaza Hotel?
STEVE:	Yes.
ALFARO:	I'll meet you in the lounge tonight, at eight o'clock.
STEVE:	I say, you are a quick worker, aren't you?
ALFARO:	(*Moving closer to STEVE*) Why not tonight?
STEVE:	(*Giggling*) Oh Mr Alfaro!

FADE UP of music.

FADE DOWN of music.

SCENE 9:   The Plaza Hotel Lounge.

There is background conversation.

ALFARO:	Hello, senorita! I'm so sorry I'm late!
STEVE:	Late! Do you know what time it is? It's nearly a quarter to nine.
ALFARO:	I know, but – well – after all, business is business.
STEVE:	What have you been up to? You've been up to something, I'll bet. You're as cute as a box of monkeys.
ALFARO:	No. No, I've just been getting things organised.
STEVE:	What things?

A dance orchestra starts to play.

ALFARO: Oh, just little things. Don't you trouble your pretty little head about business. Now what would you like to do?

STEVE: What would you like to do?

ALFARO: I've ordered a table at the Ritz. As a matter of fact I promised to see someone there at ten o'clock.

STEVE: A girl?

ALFARO: No. No, no, of course not! A business associate – it won't take me more than ten or fifteen minutes. I promise you, Gloria, I'll be finished in a quarter of an hour.

STEVE: (*Pouting*) All right – then we'd better go to the Ritz.

ALFARO: You don't have to come if you don't want to. But I've kept the taxi waiting.

STEVE: I said all right, didn't I?

ALFARO: Now don't be tiresome about this, my dear. I've got to see this man. When I've seen him we'll have plenty of fun.

STEVE: You men, you're all the same – work, work, work! Who is this man anyway?

ALFARO: (*Laughing: yet irritated*) I've told you, he's just a business associate – it's not important. It doesn't matter. Come along, Gloria, don't act like a little baby. Would you like a drink before we leave?

STEVE: Well, all right!

ALFARO: Waiter?

WAITER: Monsieur?

ALFARO: Two champagne cocktails.

WAITER: Two champagne cocktails, monsieur.

SCENE 10:   A Taxi.

En route to The Ritz.

ALFARO: I'll tell you what we'll do, Gloria. When we've had dinner together, we'll –

STEVE: (*Interrupting ALFARO: chatty*) What do they call this man?

ALFARO: Which man?

STEVE: The man you're meeting.

ALFARO: I've told you, it's not important.

STEVE: Well, if it's not important why are you meeting him?

ALFARO: (*Controlling himself*) Sweetheart, I want to speak to him for five or ten minutes. It won't take more than five or ten minutes.

STEVE: Five or ten minutes? You said a quarter of an hour.

ALFARO: All right a quarter of an hour! What does it matter?

STEVE: I know you foreigners, you're all the same!

ALFARO: (*Moving closer to STEVE*) Gloria, don't be cross with me.

STEVE: I am cross with you. We make a date for eight o'clock, you turn up at a quarter to nine, and now – (*Hurt*) – you're going to leave me for another woman.

ALFARO: (*Exasperated*) I am not going to leave you for another woman! I've told you, I'm meeting a man …

STEVE: What man?

ALFARO: Does it matter what man? If I told you his name you wouldn't be any the wiser!

STEVE: No, I'll bet I wouldn't!

ALFARO: Don't you believe me?

STEVE: Well – I don't know. Phew! Isn't it hot in here?

156

ALFARO:	Are you warm?
STEVE:	Yes, I am! Can't we have a window down?
ALFARO:	(*Watching STEVE*) It will be very cold with the window open.
STEVE:	Well then let's have it open! Phew! It's like an oven ...
ALFARO:	I don't think it's warm.
STEVE:	You don't?
ALFARO:	No. No, I think it is just nice ...
STEVE:	You're hot blooded that's why you don't ... don't ... (*She is beginning to feel faint*) ... notice it ...
ALFARO:	What's the matter?
STEVE:	I don't know, I ... (*A little gasp*) Put the window down.
ALFARO:	(*Slowly*) You look very pale.
STEVE:	Yes, I ... I feel dizzy ... I can't ... see ... properly ... I ... What's the matter with me? What is it? What's happening?
ALFARO:	Is there anything you would like me to do?
STEVE:	Yes ... Yes, I'd like ... like ... you ... to ... put ... the window ... down.
ALFARO:	It will be very cold with the window down, senorita.
STEVE:	Please ... do ... as ... I ...

STEVE gives a quick little gasp and faints.
ALFARO slides back the glass and speaks to HARRY the driver. ALFARO's manner is quiet and very business-like. He is no longer the Don Juan.

ALFARO:	Harry!
HARRY:	(*Turning*) Yes?
ALFARO:	She's asleep.
HARRY:	Oh. It worked all right?
ALFARO:	Yes. You know where to go?

HARRY:	Sure. I know where to go. How long will she be out?
ALFARO:	About an hour.
HARRY:	She's a good looker.
ALFARO:	Yes.
HARRY:	Who is she?
ALFARO:	(*Completely matter of fact*) Her name's Temple. She picked me up on the plane coming over from Amsterdam.

END OF EPISODE FIVE

EPISODE SIX

JUST A RED HERRING

SCENE 1:   In the Taxi, as at the end of Episode 5.

ALFARO: I don't think it's warm.
STEVE: You don't?
ALFARO: No. No, I think it is just nice …
STEVE: You're hot blooded that's why you don't … don't … (*She is beginning to feel faint*) … notice it …
ALFARO: What's the matter?
STEVE: I don't know, I … (*A little gasp*) Put the window down.
ALFARO: (*Slowly*) You look very pale.
STEVE: Yes, I … I feel dizzy … I can't … see … properly … I … What's the matter with me? What is it? What's happening?
ALFARO: Is there anything you would like me to do?
STEVE: Yes … Yes, I'd like … like … you … to … put … the window … down.
ALFARO: It will be very cold with the window down, senorita.
STEVE: Please … do … as … I …

STEVE gives a quick little gasp and faints.

ALFARO slides back the glass and speaks to HARRY the driver. ALFARO's manner is quiet and very business-like. He is no longer the Don Juan.

ALFARO: Harry!
HARRY: (*Turning*) Yes?
ALFARO: She's asleep.
HARRY: Oh. It worked all right?
ALFARO: Yes. You know where to go?
HARRY: Sure. I know where to go. How long will she be out?
ALFARO: About an hour.
HARRY: She's a good looker.

ALFARO:	Yes.
HARRY:	Who is she?
ALFARO:	(*Completely matter of fact*) Her name's Temple. She picked me up on the plane coming over from Amsterdam.
HARRY:	Is she with the Yard?
ALFARO:	(*Puzzled*) I don't know. Frankly, I can't make it out.
HARRY:	What are you going to do with her?
ALFARO:	I'll decide when we get down to the cottage. (*Quietly*) Harry …
HARRY:	Yes?
ALFARO:	Are we being followed?

A pause.

HARRY:	No, I don't think so.
ALFARO:	You'd better make certain.
HARRY:	(*A moment*) I can't see anybody.
ALFARO:	Have you arranged for the launch?
HARRY:	Yes, I phoned Elzec.
ALFARO:	What did you say?
HARRY:	I said we'd be there by nine.
ALFARO:	Did you tell him about our little friend here?
HARRY:	No.
ALFARO:	Good. I'm afraid we're going to be late.
HARRY:	We shall be in a 'ell of a mess if he doesn't wait for us.
ALFARO:	You'd better step on it.
HARRY:	O.K.

HARRY accelerates.

FADE UP music.

FADE DOWN music.

SCENE 2: The Deck of a Cabin Cruiser moored to a river jetty.

There is a slight background of river noises. The engine of the cruiser is ticking over. ELZEC and BENNETT – a middle-aged, timid little man – are waiting on the jetty.

During the following dialogue, the taxi approaches, comes to a standstill, and the engine is switched off.

ELZEC: They're late. I'm giving them another five minutes.

BENNETT: It's not like Alfaro to be late.

ELZEC: Well, he's late tonight.

BENNETT: I don't like it. I've got a feeling that …

ELZEC: I'm not interested in your feelings, Bennett. Keep them to yourself.

BENNETT: I shouldn't be doing this. This isn't my job. (*Petulantly*) I wish I was back on the newspaper!

ELZEC: There's nothing to stop you going back.

BENNETT: (*Dejected: a little laugh*) Oh! And what happens when I mention it? You know what he threatens to do. You know what happened to Kendell.

ELZEC: Kendell had an accident. He was knocked down by a car.

BENNETT: An accident? Do you believe it was an accident?

ELZEC: Yes, I do. I know it was an accident because –

ELZEC stops, having heard the taxi.

BENNETT: (*Nervously*) What is it?

ELZEC: Here they are …

BENNETT: Are you sure it's Harry?

ELZEC: (*Going*) Yes, I know the taxi. You stay here.

BENNETT: (*Relieved*) O.K. (*Suddenly*) Elzec …

ELZEC: What is it?

BENNETT: There's someone watching us. Look!

ELZEC: It's only a little girl. Take no notice of her.

The noise of the cruiser recedes as ELZEC leaves the jetty and crosses to the taxi.

The taxi door opens and HARRY gets out.

ELZEC: You're late!

HARRY: Yes, I know.

HARRY shuts his door.

ELZEC: Is Alfaro with you?

Another door opens as ALFARO climbs out.

ALFARO: I'm here. Good evening, Mr Weiner – or should I say Dr Elzec?

ELZEC: It doesn't matter what you say. I'm tired of hanging about – come on, let's get to the cottage.

ALFARO: One moment!

ELZEC: What is it?

ALFARO: I've brought someone with me.

ELZEC: What do you mean? (*Tensely*) Who is it?

ALFARO: You'd better take a look.

ELZEC moves to the taxi and looks in.

ELZEC: Good Heavens! Do you know who this is?

ALFARO: Yes, her name's Temple. She picked me up on the plane coming over from Amsterdam. I don't know what the idea is, I'm sure.

ELZEC: Why did you bring her here?

ALFARO: Because I intend to ask Mrs Temple one or two questions. I couldn't very well do that in the lounge of the Plaza Hotel.

ELZEC: I don't think Madison would like that.

ALFARO: I'm not interested in what Madison likes or dislikes. Which boat have you brought – the one with the cabin?

164

ELZEC:	Yes.
ALFARO:	Good. Have you got anyone with you?
ELZEC:	Bennett.
ALFARO:	All right, tell him to give Harry a hand and put the girl in the cabin.
ELZEC:	I don't want her to see me.
ALFARO:	That won't be necessary. Don't worry! Come along, let's go down to the launch.

FADE UP music.

FADE DOWN music.

SCENE 3: The Deck of the Cruiser.

The cruiser is now on the river, travelling very fast.

ALFARO:	Is everything ready for me?
ELZEC:	Yes.
ALFARO:	What is it this time – tens or twenties?
ELZEC:	They're mostly ten dollar bills.
ALFARO:	Good. (*Curious*) What's in this case?
ELZEC:	I understand it's new radio equipment. Madison told me to take it down to the cottage.
ALFARO:	Did he bring it on board?
ELZEC:	Yes.
ALFARO:	When?
ELZEC:	About an hour ago. (*Pause*) I was sorry to hear about Dordrecht.
ALFARO:	Yes.
ELZEC:	How are you going to get the stuff back? It won't be easy without him.
ALFARO:	I'm seeing Madison tomorrow – we're discussing the whole proposition. (*Turning*) Hello, here's Bennett.
ELZEC:	What is it, Bennett?
BENNETT:	(*Approaching*) That woman …
ALFARO:	Yes?

165

BENNETT: She's coming round.

ALFARO: Oh. I'll go and talk to her.

ALFARO starts moving to the cabin.

BENNETT: Whatever happens don't let her scream. You can hear everything at this time of night.

ALFARO: (*Smiling*) Don't worry …

SCENE 4:   The Cruiser Cabin.

ALFARO enters the cabin: as he closes the door behind him the noise of the engine fades down slightly.

STEVE: Where am I? Where are you taking me?

ALFARO: There's no need for alarm. Please sit down.

STEVE: If you don't tell me where you're taking me I'll –

ALFARO: (*With authority*) Now sit down, Mrs Temple, and listen to what I'm saying.

STEVE: So – you know who I am then?

ALFARO: Didn't I tell you on the plane that I thought I'd recognised you? If you don't wish to be recognised you know you shouldn't have your photograph in the glossy magazines.

STEVE: What is it you want?

ALFARO: What's more to the point, Mrs Temple, what do you want?

STEVE: I … I demand that you turn the boat round and take me back!

ALFARO: You have a sense of humour. Oh, forgive me! Can I offer you a drink? (*Significantly*) A champagne cocktail, perhaps? (*He laughs*)

STEVE: Where are you taking me?

ALFARO: You'll find out all in good time. But first of all I want to have a little chat. Why did you catch that particular plane from Amsterdam? Because you wanted to get friendly with me?

166

STEVE: Yes.

ALFARO: Why?

STEVE: My husband's investigating the Madison mystery and there are certain things which we should like to know, Mr Alfaro.

ALFARO: What, for instance?

STEVE: Well, for instance – who is Mr Madison?

ALFARO: (*Smiling*) Go on – what else would you like to know?

STEVE: Why did your colleague Mijnheer Dordrecht carry an English penny on a keychain – a penny with the date 1919 on it?

ALFARO: (*Still smiling*) Go on …

STEVE: Who murdered Eileen Greene?

ALFARO: Eileen Greene? I've never heard of anyone called Eileen Greene.

STEVE: And there's another interesting point. Why did you arrange for your –

This sentence is a bluff, and STEVE suddenly makes a wild dash for the door of the cabin. ALFARO throws himself at her.

ALFARO: Why, you little devil!

STEVE: (*Struggling with the door*) Open this door! Do you hear what I say? Open this door!

ALFARO grabs STEVE by the arm and swings her round.

ALFARO: If you raise your voice again I'll –

STEVE: Leave go of my arm!

STEVE suddenly smacks him across the face: a loud, resounding smack.

ALFARO: Oh! Why, you …

ALFARO is stunned.

STEVE: Now please let go of my arm. (*After a moment*) Thank you.

167

ALFARO: You'll regret that, Mrs Temple. Now sit down
             and listen to what I'm saying. How did you
             know that I should be travelling on that
             particular plane? (*No reply*) All right. I'll ask
             you another question. How did you know that I
             was mixed up in this business?

STEVE: (*Bluffing*) Someone told my husband.

ALFARO: Who?

STEVE: Don't you know?

ALFARO: (*Moving closer to STEVE, threateningly*) Who
             told your husband that I was mixed up in this
             business? Answer me! Who told him?

STEVE: Do you want the truth?

ALFARO: Yes. Yes, I want the truth. If you don't tell me
             the truth I'll take you by the neck and I'll –

STEVE: (*With contempt in her voice*) All right! All
             right, you can have it! For weeks now the
             Dutch police have had their eye on you, they
             know you're mixed up in the counterfeit racket,
             they knew that Dordrecht was mixed up in it …

ALFARO: You're lying!

STEVE: I'm not lying. I'm telling you the truth.

ALFARO: If you're telling me the truth why haven't they
             arrested me – why didn't they arrest Dordrecht?

STEVE: Because the Dutch, like Scotland Yard, are not
             interested in small fry, Mr Alfaro.

ALFARO: (*Tensely: rising anger: almost to himself*) I'm
             beginning to understand. I've been used as a
             bait, a decoy! They thought I would lead you to
             Madison, they thought I would deliberately
             lead you …

*ALFARO is interrupted by the sound of excited voices on deck
and a sudden banging on the door.*

ALFARO: What is it? What's the matter?

STEVE: What's happened?

HARRY: (*From outside the door*) It's the police! They're on board!

ALFARO: What!

HARRY: It's the police, Alfaro! You'd better –

HARRY gives a sudden groan as something hits him on the back of the head.

ALFARO: Harry, what's happened? Harry!?

STEVE: (*Springing to life*) Help! Paul! Help!

ALFARO grabs STEVE and tries to put his hand over her mouth.

ALFARO: Shut up! Shut up!

STEVE: Paul! Help! Help!

There is a sudden bang on the door, a splintering of wood as the lock gives way, and the door bursts open. TEMPLE and VOSPER rush into the cabin.

STEVE: Paul, look out!

TEMPLE: Drop that gun!

STEVE: Darling, look out!

VOSPER: Oh no you don't, my friend!

VOSPER hits ALFARO with a tremendous punch. ALFARO gives a groan and collapses.

TEMPLE: Oh, good man, Vosper!

VOSPER: Good Lord, I've knocked him cold!

STEVE: Oh, Paul!

TEMPLE: Darling, are you all right?

STEVE: Yes … yes, I'm all right.

TEMPLE: Are you sure?

STEVE: Yes, darling, honestly!

SIR GRAHAM arrives, a little out of breath.

FORBES: Oh, here you are, Steve! Is she all right, Temple?

STEVE: Hello, Sir Graham!

TEMPLE: Yes, she's all right.

169

FORBES: Thank heavens we've found you!

TEMPLE: Have you rounded them all up?

FORBES: Yes, but there's no sign of ... (*He stops: surprised*) Is this Alfaro?

TEMPLE: Yes.

ALFARO is groaning: slowly coming round.

FORBES: What happened to him?

VOSPER: He bumped against my fist, sir.

FORBES: (*Smiling*) Oh, I see.

TEMPLE: How many of them are there?

FORBES: Four – with Alfaro. That includes our friend Dr Elzec.

VOSPER: Elzec? Was he one of them?

FORBES: Yes.

TEMPLE: That's interesting.

VOSPER: What shall we do, Sir Graham?

FORBES: I want you to stay on board and take over, Vosper. I'm leaving you Taylor and Smith.

VOSPER: Very good, sir.

FORBES: Keep on our tail. Don't get too far away in case there's any trouble.

VOSPER: There'll be no trouble, sir – don't you worry.

FORBES: Nevertheless, keep pretty close to us. Come along, Temple, let's get back to the police launch. Let me give you a hand, Steve.

FADE UP music.

FADE DOWN music.

SCENE 5:   The Deck of the Police Launch.

The launch is travelling at an average speed. In the near background can be heard the noise of the cabin cruiser. There are distant background river noises.

SERGEANT FINLEY is a Scot: about thirty-seven or eight.

FINLEY: He's keeping pretty close, sir.

FORBES:	Yes, I told him to.

A pause.

TEMPLE:	Where are we aiming for, Sergeant?
FINLEY:	I'm making for Millgate Steps. Is that all right, Sir Graham?
FORBES:	Yes, that's all right.
FINLEY:	I've contacted Superintendent Bradley. He's meeting us here.
FORBES:	Good. Are you feeling cold, Steve?
STEVE:	Just a little bit.
FORBES:	There's an overcoat over there, Temple.
TEMPLE:	(*Moving off*) I'll get it.
FORBES:	I'm sorry things turned out like this.
STEVE:	They might have turned out much worse. How on earth did you manage to find me?
FORBES:	Well, we followed the taxi from the Plaza and then suddenly lost sight of it. Fortunately when we got down to the river a little girl told Vosper about the launch. She apparently saw you being carried out of the taxi.

TEMPLE returns with the coat and puts it round STEVE's shoulders.

TEMPLE:	Here we are, Steve.
STEVE:	Oh, thanks.
TEMPLE:	Have you any idea where they were taking you to?
STEVE:	I heard one of the men mention a cottage.
FORBES:	You've no idea where it is, I suppose?
STEVE:	Not the slightest.
FORBES:	Did you know Elzec was on board?
STEVE:	No, but funny enough I thought I recognised his voice.
TEMPLE:	When did Alfaro spot you, darling?

STEVE: On the plane. Apparently he'd seen a photograph of me in a glossy magazine.

TEMPLE: That was bad luck.

STEVE: Well, I've discovered one thing, Paul.

TEMPLE: What's that?

STEVE: Both Alfaro and Elzec know the identity of Madison. They're not working in the dark.

FORBES: I sincerely hope you're right, Steve.

STEVE: Why do you say that?

FORBES: (*A little laugh*) Well, we've got Elzec and we've got Alfaro. All we've got to do now is make them talk.

STEVE: (*Shaking her head*) They won't talk, Sir Graham.

TEMPLE: (*Quietly*) I wouldn't be too sure about that, darling. (*Suddenly*) Steve, I'm rather curious about one point. Why did Alfaro …

As TEMPLE speaks there is a tremendous explosion followed by a gigantic upheaval of water. The explosion has taken place on board the cabin cruiser: a time-bomb has exploded and the boat has practically disintegrated. The swirling river causes the police launch to rock and sway.

The following four speeches are spoken almost simultaneously.

TEMPLE: Good Lord, what's happened?!

FINLEY: What the devil …

FORBES: Temple, what is it?

STEVE: Paul, what's happened?

TEMPLE: Be careful, Steve – hold on!

The launch steadies itself.

FINLEY: There must have been a time bomb on the other boat, Sir Graham.

TEMPLE: Look there's Vosper!

FORBES: I don't see him.

172

FINLEY: There he is, sir!
FORBES: Oh, yes, I see him! Swing her round, Sergeant!

The engine roars and FINLEY turns the launch.

TEMPLE: I don't see any of the others.
FORBES: It'll be a miracle if any of them survive.
TEMPLE: I wonder what the devil happened?
FORBES: I'm damned if I understand it.
STEVE: There's someone else in the water! Look! Over there! He's clinging to part of the wreckage.
FORBES: She's right!
TEMPLE: It's Smith.
FINLEY: (*Calling*) Are you all right, Smith?
FORBES: He can't hear you.
FINLEY: I think he can, sir! (*Calling*) Can you hold on?
TEMPLE: He's waving!
STEVE: I think he's all right, Paul.
FINLEY: Fred'll be all right – he's a first class swimmer.
FORBES: (*Grimly*) It doesn't look like Vosper is.
FINLEY: I don't see any sign of Taylor.
FORBES: No.
TEMPLE: Here's Vosper! He's over on the stern – give me your hand, Sir Graham! Quickly!
FORBES: Slacken speed, Sergeant!

The engine slows, and TEMPLE and FORBES lean over the side to haul VOSPER aboard.

STEVE: Be careful, Paul!
TEMPLE: It's – all right …
FORBES: Steady!
TEMPLE: I've got him! Hold on! Hold on, Sir Graham!
FORBES: That's it!
VOSPER: (*Struggling to get out of the water*) I can manage – if you can just –
TEMPLE: Get hold of his arm, Sir Graham … That's it!
VOSPER: (*Collapsing onto the deck*) I'm all right now …

TEMPLE: What happened, Vosper?

VOSPER: (*Breathless: exhausted*) There must have been
            a time-bomb in the suitcase. Lucky for me I
            was over on the other side of the launch when it
            went off. I – I don't know what happened to the
            others …

FORBES: Turn the launch, Sergeant, we've got to pick up
            Smith.

FADE UP music.

FADE DOWN music.

SCENE 6:   The TEMPLES' Dining Room

*TEMPLE and STEVE are having breakfast. TEMPLE is
reading the paper.*

STEVE: Would you like some more coffee, Paul?

TEMPLE: Oh, yes, yes please darling.

STEVE: (*Pouring coffee*) Is there anything in the paper
            about last night?

TEMPLE: They refer to a mysterious explosion in which
            five people lost their lives. There aren't any
            details.

STEVE: (*Handing TEMPLE his cup*) My word, I was
            lucky!

TEMPLE: You certainly were. Just how lucky I don't
            suppose you'll ever know.

STEVE: I can guess.

TEMPLE: (*Looking up: quietly*) What do you mean?

STEVE: I know what a temptation it must have been for
            you.

TEMPLE: What are you talking about?

STEVE: If you'd left me on the launch and simply
            followed us there's a sporting chance we
            should have taken you straight to their
            headquarters.

174

TEMPLE: A sporting chance my foot! You don't think I'd take a chance like that, do you? Why good heavens, even if the explosion hadn't have happened it's more than likely we should have lost you on the river.

STEVE: Do you think Vosper was right? Do you think it was a time-bomb in the suitcase?

TEMPLE: Yes, I do.

TEMPLE drinks his coffee.

STEVE: What are you going to do this morning, Paul?

TEMPLE: Well, I've got an appointment with Sir Graham at ten. It's rather a pity. I was hoping to start my new novel this morning.

STEVE: What's it all about?

TEMPLE: The novel?

STEVE: Yes.

TEMPLE: It's all about a man who murders his wife because she always forgets to put sugar in his coffee.

STEVE: (*Laughing*) Oh, darling, I'm sorry!

The telephone rings.

TEMPLE: It's all right. I'll take it.

TEMPLE crosses to the phone and lifts the receiver.

TEMPLE: Hello?

We hear the sound of someone pressing button 'A' and the pennies dropping.

MOIRA: (*Nervous: over-wrought*) Is that Mr Temple?

TEMPLE: Yes, who is that?

MOIRA: This is Moira Portland.

TEMPLE: (*Pleasantly*) Oh, good morning, Miss Portland. I'm sorry, I didn't recognise your voice.

MOIRA: Mr Temple, I don't want to make a nuisance of myself, but – do you think I could see you sometime? I'd – rather like to talk to you.

175

TEMPLE:	Yes, of course, Miss Portland. As a matter of fact, I'd rather like to talk to you.
MOIRA:	Could you – meet me tonight?
TEMPLE:	Yes, certainly. Would you like to come to my flat?
MOIRA:	No, I should prefer to meet you at the Manilla.
TEMPLE:	Well, why not come to the flat? We can talk much better here than at the Manilla.
MOIRA:	(*Hesitating*) No. If I come to the flat I might be noticed.
TEMPLE:	What do you want me to do – bump into you 'accidentally'?
MOIRA:	Yes. I shall be there from nine o'clock onwards.
TEMPLE:	All right – I'll be there about ten.
MOIRA:	Thank you. Oh, Mr Temple?
TEMPLE:	Yes?
MOIRA:	(*Haltingly: still over-wrought*) I'm awfully sorry I was rude to you at the weekend but you see I haven't been feeling very well recently and I'm afraid I've been rather overdoing things.
TEMPLE:	Yes, I think you have, Miss Portland. If I were you, I should take it easy. (*A moment*) You know what I mean, don't you?
MOIRA:	(*Softly*) Yes.
TEMPLE:	I'll see you tonight.
MOIRA:	No, wait a minute! Don't ring off, please! There's – something else I wanted to tell you.
TEMPLE:	What?
MOIRA:	I – didn't murder Eileen …
TEMPLE:	I never thought you did, Miss Portland.
MOIRA:	No, but the police think so, at least they will think so when they find …

TEMPLE:	When they find what?
MOIRA:	… Nothing. I'll tell you tonight.
TEMPLE:	All right.
MOIRA:	(*Rather sadly*) Oh, and Mr Temple, whatever happens please don't change your mind about me.
TEMPLE:	What do you mean?
MOIRA:	I – didn't murder Eileen, honestly I didn't. I'm … just a red herring.

MOIRA rings off. TEMPLE replaces the receiver.

TEMPLE:	(*To himself*) Well, what an extraordinary thing to say.
STEVE:	Was that Moira Portland?
TEMPLE:	Yes.
STEVE:	What did she say?
TEMPLE:	(*Thoughtfully*) She wants me to meet her tonight at the Manilla.
STEVE:	Yes, but what else did she say? You seemed so surprised.

The door opens and CHARLIE enters.

TEMPLE:	(*Still deep in thought*) She said, I didn't murder Eileen I'm … (*Looking up*) What is it, Charlie?
CHARLIE:	There's a Mr Kelly would like to see you, sir.
STEVE:	(*Faintly surprised*) Mr Kelly?
TEMPLE:	Yes, all right, Charlie – ask him in.
CHARLIE:	(*Going*) O.K.
STEVE:	What does Kelly want, I wonder?
TEMPLE:	I don't know.
STEVE:	Did you expect him?
TEMPLE:	No.

KELLY is in the doorway.

TEMPLE:	(*Pleasantly*) Ah, hello, Kelly! Come on in!
KELLY:	Am I interrupting your breakfast?
TEMPLE:	No, we've just finished.

STEVE: You can take the tray, Charlie.

CHARLIE: Yes, ma'am.

STEVE: (*Rising*) Will you excuse me, Mr Kelly, I'm –

KELLY: Oh, don't go away, Mrs Temple, please! I wanted to have a word with you.

STEVE: With me?

KELLY: Yes.

STEVE: What about?

KELLY: (*Smiling*) You said I telephoned you one night at the Manilla.

STEVE: (*Facing KELLY*) That's right. You did.

KELLY: (*Emphatic, yet laughing*) But I didn't, Mrs Temple.

STEVE: Well, if you didn't, who did? It sounded remarkably like you, Mr Kelly.

KELLY: That's just the point. Who did? Temple, I've been doing quite a lot of thinking during the past few days and I've kind of reached a decision. Do you know what I think? I think somebody's trying to make a monkey out of me!

STEVE: (*Politely*) A monkey out of you, Kelly?

KELLY: Yes. Somebody impersonated me that night, somebody tried to give you the impression that I was mixed up in this – what do you call it? – Madison affair.

TEMPLE: (*Watching KELLY*) Aren't you mixed up in the Madison affair?

KELLY: (*Faintly aggressive*) Most certainly not! And I'll tell you another thing I'm not mixed up in either.

TEMPLE: What's that?

KELLY: This Greene murder. Now, I don't know what your opinion is, Temple, but I've a hunch the police are trying to pin that rap on me.

STEVE: What do you mean, Mr Kelly?

TEMPLE: The police aren't trying to pin a rap on anybody, as you so elegantly put it.

KELLY: (*Faintly aggressive*) Well, they've asked me an awful lot of questions – they keep on asking me an awful lot of questions.

TEMPLE: Does that surprise you?

KELLY: Certainly it surprises me. Why pick on me of all people? Why not pick on Hubert Greene, or Stella or Moira Portland for that matter?

TEMPLE: (*Quietly*) You know how Eileen was murdered – she was stabbed.

KELLY: All right, she was stabbed! But does that mean that I stabbed her? Listen, Temple, if I wanted to commit a murder would I use a knife? No sir, you bet your bottom dollar I wouldn't!

STEVE: What would you do, Mr Kelly?

KELLY: Why, I'd shoot the guy or strangle him or something. I certainly wouldn't throw suspicion on to myself by using a dagger.

STEVE: Are you suggesting then that someone is deliberately trying to throw suspicion on to you?

KELLY: That's exactly what I am suggesting, Mrs Temple! And what gets me – what really get me – is the fact that Scotland Yard can't see through it. I'm not mixed up in this Madison mystery, not really mixed up in it, I'm just … well, I'm just a red herring.

TEMPLE: Is that why you came here this morning, Kelly, to tell us that you were just a red herring?

KELLY: No. No, of course it isn't. I came here because I
            wanted you to have a look at this brooch.

A pause.

TEMPLE: Where did you find this?

KELLY: I came across it in the bushes, down by the
            lake, not so far from where you found Mrs
            Greene.

TEMPLE: Were you looking for it?

KELLY: No! I went down to the lake because – well – I
            wanted to see the scene of the crime. I guess
            you can put it down to morbid curiosity. I was
            probing among the bushes when I suddenly
            found the clip. (*Significantly*) It's been rather
            badly knocked about, Temple.

TEMPLE: Yes, I can see that.

STEVE: Have you any idea who it belongs to?

KELLY: Yes, as a matter of fact I have.

TEMPLE: Well?

KELLY: It belongs to Moira Portland.

FADE UP music.

FADE DOWN music.

SCENE 7:   An Office in Scotland Yard.

*A knock at the door. It opens and the SERGEANT shows
TEMPLE in.*

SERGEANT: Mr Temple, sir.

FORBES: Ah, come in, Temple. Thank you, Sergeant.

The door closes.

TEMPLE: I'm afraid I'm a little late, Sir Graham.

FORBES: That's all right. Greene hasn't arrived yet.

TEMPLE: Is that why you wanted me here, because
            you're going to question Greene?

FORBES: Not exactly. As a matter of fact, Greene made
             the appointment himself. I want to have a chat.
             Sit down.

TEMPLE: Thank you.

FORBES: (*Worried, yet with a note of authority in his
             voice*) Temple, we don't seem to be getting
             anywhere with this Greene murder. I had
             another talk with Kelly yesterday and he still
             sticks to his original story.

TEMPLE: Well, you've succeeded in 'rattling' Mr Kelly,
             if nothing else.

FORBES: Have you seen him?

TEMPLE: Yes, I saw him this morning. He produced this
             rather interesting trinket.

TEMPLE shows the brooch to FORBES.

FORBES: What is it – a clip?

TEMPLE: Yes, apparently he found it by the lake, near
             where Mrs Greene was found.

FORBES: It looks to me as if it's been trodden on.

TEMPLE: Yes.

FORBES: Who does it belong to?

TEMPLE: Well, according to Kelly it belongs to Moira
             Portland, but personally I rather doubt it.
             Anyway, I'm seeing her tonight, I'll mention it.
             She asked me to meet her at the Manilla.

FORBES: The Manilla? Why?

TEMPLE: I don't know why – but I've got my suspicions.
             (*Changing the subject*) Any news of Elzec or
             the other man – Alfaro?

FORBES: We picked up Alfaro shortly after you left us.
             There was no sign of Elzec.

TEMPLE: Was Alfaro dead?

FORBES: Yes. So is Sergeant Taylor – his body was
             picked up this morning.

181

TEMPLE: Oh, I'm sorry about that. He seemed a nice young fellow.

FORBES: Yes. He was indeed.

TEMPLE: Do you think Elzec was lucky and escaped or do you think it's just the fact that you haven't found him yet?

FORBES: I don't know. According to Vosper, he was standing about two or three yards from him when the thing exploded. I'm inclined to think Elzec was thrown clear of the actual explosion.

TEMPLE: In which case it's just a question of whether he was drowned or not.

FORBES: Yes.

TEMPLE: You heard what Steve said about the cottage?

FORBES: Yes, and I'm determined to find that place if it's the last thing I do.

TEMPLE: If you do find it you'll probably discover the whole set-up – the printing press and everything.

There is a knock and the door opens.

FORBES: Yes, I agree. Well, we're combing every inch of the river, Temple – we can't do more. Yes, Sergeant?

SERGEANT: Mr Greene has arrived, sir.

FORBES: Ask him in.

SERGEANT: Yes, sir. (*Showing GREENE in*) This way, please.

FORBES: (*Pleasantly*) Ah, come in, Greene.

GREENE: Good morning, Sir Graham (*Faintly surprised*) Hello, Temple! I didn't expect to find you here.

TEMPLE: I didn't expect to find you here either. Would you like to see Sir Graham alone?

GREENE: No. Actually, I'm rather glad to see you, Temple.

FORBES: Won't you sit down, Greene?

GREENE: Oh, thank you. (*Nervously*) Do you mind if I smoke?

FORBES: No, of course not.

GREENE: (*Offering cigarette*) Sir Graham?

FORBES: No, thank you.

GREENE: Temple?

TEMPLE: Er – thank you. (*He takes a cigarette*)

GREENE: I'll tell you why I wanted to see you, Sir Graham … (*He strikes his lighter*) Light?

TEMPLE: Oh, thanks. (*He lights his cigarette*)

GREENE: (*Lighting his cigarette*) I've been thinking about last weekend – in fact I can't stop thinking about it. Sometimes, you know, it's difficult for me to realise that Eileen isn't … (*He stops himself*) I'm staying in Town as much as possible. I just can't bear the thought of going back to the house.

TEMPLE: I can understand that.

FORBES: (*To the point but quite gently*) What did you want to see me about?

GREENE: I wanted to tell you about something that happened, or rather something that was said, the night before my wife was – murdered.

FORBES: Go on.

GREENE: We were in the library: Stella, Eileen, Chris Boyer and myself. It was before Moira Portland and Mr and Mrs Temple joined us. I overheard a remark which Chris Boyer made to my wife. I didn't think anything of it at the time but in the light of what's happened I …

FORBES: What did Boyer say to your wife?

183

GREENE: He said: "We'll have to talk about this, Eileen. We'll try and get together ... I'll meet you later tonight."

A moment.

FORBES: Is that all he said?

GREENE: Yes.

FORBES: Have you any idea what he was referring to?

GREENE: Not the slightest.

TEMPLE: Was Boyer a friend of your wife's – a personal friend?

GREENE: Good heavens, no! They hardly knew one another.

FORBES: (*Slowly*) You're quite sure that was what you overheard?

GREENE: Quite sure.

TEMPLE: Did you speak to your wife about it?

GREENE: No, I didn't think it was important. I thought the whole thing was unimportant. In any case, it went completely out of my mind. You remember what happened, Temple, Moira came down and we had that awful scene in the library.

TEMPLE: Yes. (*Thoughtfully*) Boyer said "We'll have to talk about this, Eileen. We'll try and get together."

GREENE: That's right.

FORBES: And you haven't the slightest idea to what he was referring?

GREENE: Not the slightest.

TEMPLE: Have you spoken to Boyer about it? Have you asked him what he meant?

GREENE: No, I haven't seen Boyer since the weekend.

TEMPLE: Well, next time you see him I should ask him, if I were you.

GREENE: Yes, all right I'll do that. (*Rising*) I'm sorry to have bothered you, Sir Graham, I thought perhaps it might be important.

FORBES: It still might be important.

TEMPLE: Greene, tell me. Have you seen this clip before?

TEMPLE passes GREENE the clip.

A moment.

GREENE: No.

TEMPLE: You're sure?

GREENE: Yes.

TEMPLE: It didn't belong to your wife by any chance?

GREENE: No, I'm sure it didn't. (*He is studying the brooch: quietly*) I'm quite sure.

FADE UP music.

FADE DOWN music.

SCENE 8:   The Hall of the Manilla Club.

In the background we hear lively conversation and a dance orchestra from the restaurant.

STEVE: I don't see any sign of Moira Portland.

TEMPLE: No, I don't either.

STEVE: Do you think she's in the cocktail bar?

TEMPLE: Possibly. Let's go and have a look.

STEVE: (*Suddenly*) Wait a minute, Paul!

TEMPLE: What is it?

STEVE: Isn't that Mrs Portland over there?

TEMPLE: Yes, so it is. She's spotted us!

STELLA approaches.

STELLA: Hello, Mr Temple! (*To STEVE*) Good evening!

STEVE: Good evening, Mrs Portland.

STELLA: (*Pleasantly*) I didn't know you were a member here?

185

TEMPLE: I'm a very new member. I only joined a couple of days ago. Would you care to have a drink with us?

STELLA: Well, that's very sweet of you but I'm in a party and I hardly feel I can break away quite so early in the evening.

TEMPLE: Well, later on perhaps.

STELLA: Yes, I'd love to.

TEMPLE: Is Moira in your party?

STELLA: Moira? (*With a laugh*) Good gracious, no! I haven't seen Moira since – (*She stops speaking, realising that STEVE is staring at her dress*) Is anything the matter with my dress, Mrs Temple?

STEVE: I wasn't looking at your dress, Mrs Portland. I was looking at your clip.

STELLA: Oh?

STEVE: It's awfully nice, isn't it?

STELLA: Sam bought it for me in New York. Well, actually, he bought me a pair, but unfortunately I …

TEMPLE: … Lost the other one.

STELLA: (*Surprised*) Yes. How did you know?

A pause.

TEMPLE: Is this it?

STELLA: (*Taken aback*) Why, yes! Wherever did you find it?

TEMPLE: I didn't find it. Mr Kelly did.

STELLA: Where?

TEMPLE: He found it by the lake not very far from where Mrs Greene was murdered.

STELLA: (*After a moment: quite simply*) How very odd.

TEMPLE: (*Watching her*) Have you any idea where you lost it?

186

STELLA:	(*Hesitatingly*) No, I'm afraid I haven't.
TEMPLE:	Mr Kelly was under the impression it belonged to Moira.
STELLA:	(*With a little laugh*) Oh, yes, I can understand that. I lent the clips to Moira and George must have seen her wearing them.
TEMPLE:	When did you lend the clips to Miss Portland?
STELLA:	That night – the night before the murder. Don't you remember seeing them?
TEMPLE:	(*Thoughtfully*) No, I can't say I do.
STEVE:	(*Suddenly*) Yes, I do! She wore a black dress with a sort of ruffle across the top and a clip on each shoulder.
STELLA:	That's right, Mrs Temple.
TEMPLE:	Mrs Portland, let's get this straight. Did you lose the clip or did Moira lose it?
STELLA:	(*Rather vaguely*) Well I don't really know how it happened. You see, I lent her the clips and then she returned them to me. Actually, she put them on my dressing table when she went to bed. You remember, she went up rather early that night because …
TEMPLE:	Yes, I remember.
STELLA:	The next morning I packed the clips – at least I think I packed them – (*Rather lamely*) and when I got back to Town I found there was one missing. (*With charm*) Sorry to be rather hazy about it, but I'm afraid that's what happened.
TEMPLE:	I see.
STELLA:	(*With just a faint suggestion of embarrassment*) Now, if you'll excuse me, I think perhaps I'd better join my friends. Goodbye, Mrs Temple.
STEVE:	Goodbye.
TEMPLE:	We shall probably see you later.

187

STELLA: Yes, I hope so.

A pause.

STEVE: Paul …

TEMPLE: Yes, darling?

STEVE: Do you believe her story?

TEMPLE: Well, she seemed rather vague about it, didn't she? Come along, let's go into the cocktail bar.

CHRIS BOYER calls to them from the background. He stops them from entering the cocktail bar.

BOYER: Hello, there!

TEMPLE: (*Turning*) Oh, hello, Boyer!

BOYER: (*Laughing*) I thought it was you! I've been expecting to see you, Temple. I hear you're a member now.

TEMPLE: Yes.

BOYER: That's fine – I'm glad to hear it. How are you, Mrs Temple?

STEVE: I'm very well thank you.

TEMPLE: Is Moira with you?

BOYER: No, she's not here tonight.

TEMPLE: She'll probably be along later.

BOYER: I doubt it. She's usually here by this time if she's coming. (*Seriously*) Temple, I'm glad I bumped into you. There's something I wanted to ask you.

TEMPLE: Yes?

BOYER: I saw Inspector Vosper this afternoon – he came to my flat.

TEMPLE: Oh?

BOYER: (*Curious*) You know, Temple, I've got a hunch that the police think I'm mixed up in this business.

TEMPLE: Which business?

BOYER: Why – this – murder.

188

TEMPLE:	The Greene murder?
BOYER:	Yes. Of course.
TEMPLE:	Whatever gave you that idea?
BOYER:	Well, Vosper was very curious. He asked me a great many questions – some very embarrassing ones, I'm afraid.
TEMPLE:	That isn't entirely unusual when a murder's being investigated.
BOYER:	Temple, I'd like to be frank with you about this business.
TEMPLE:	By all means.
BOYER:	I know that this Greene case, the murder of Chunky Brooks, the death of Mark Kendell are all part and parcel of the same thing – the Madison mystery.
TEMPLE:	Well?
BOYER:	Well, I want you to know that I'm not mixed up in the Madison mystery, Temple.
TEMPLE:	No?
BOYER:	No!
TEMPLE:	Tell me, why did you say to Mrs Greene, the night before she was murdered: "We'll have to talk about this, Eileen. We'll try and get together … I'll meet you later tonight."
BOYER:	(*Tensely*) How do you know I said that?
TEMPLE:	You were overheard.
BOYER:	Well, whoever overheard me must have deliberately … Look here, Temple, if you think I'm behind all this – if you think I'm the mysterious Mr Madison – then you've got another think coming! (*Shrewdly*) It's perfectly obvious that somebody's trying to throw suspicion onto me. You know what I am, don't you?

TEMPLE: No. What are you, Mr Boyer?
BOYER: I'm just a red herring!

END OF EPISODE SIX

EPISODE SEVEN

THE FOUR SUSPECTS

SCENE 1:   A Telephone Box in the hall of the Manilla Club.
There is distant sound of conversation and the dance orchestra from the restaurant.

VOSPER: (*Distort*) This is Inspector Vosper speaking. Mr Temple, listen … don't leave the Manilla Club. Sir Graham's on his way over. He wants to see you.

TEMPLE: What is it, Vosper? Is anything wrong?

VOSPER: It's Moira Portland – she's dead.

TEMPLE: Dead.

VOSPER: Yes. We found the body about twenty minutes ago.

TEMPLE: Where did you find her?

VOSPER: In a flat just off the Charing Cross Road.

TEMPLE: What flat?

VOSPER: Chris Boyer's.

TEMPLE: I see – well thanks for letting me know, Vosper. I'll talk to Sir Graham when he arrives.

TEMPLE replaces the receiver and opens the door of the telephone box. He returns to STEVE and CHRIS BOYER.
FADE UP music.

FADE DOWN music.

SCENE 2:   The Manilla Club.

STEVE: Who was it on the phone, darling?

TEMPLE: (*Quietly*) It was a message from Sir Graham. He wants to see me.

STEVE: (*Rather surprised*) Tonight?

TEMPLE: (*Not wishing to pursue the subject*) Yes, he's calling in here … Boyer, when did you last see Moira Portland?

BOYER: This afternoon. Why do you ask?

TEMPLE: I wondered, that's all …

BOYER:	Look here, Temple, I think it's about time I took you into my confidence. (*Facing TEMPLE: bluntly*) What's your honest opinion of me?
TEMPLE:	(*Rather taken aback*) Well …
BOYER:	Come along, let's be frank about it. You've met me several times, we spent the weekend together down at Hubert Greene's place.
TEMPLE:	The first time I met you, I thought you were a nit-witted young man who danced divinely. Now, I'm not so sure.
BOYER:	What are you not so sure about – my dancing?
TEMPLE:	No – that you are nit-witted, Mr Boyer. I've an idea that you're playing a part – and playing it very well, if I may say so.
BOYER:	(*Laughing*) You may say so, Mr Temple, and how right you are! And if it affords you any personal satisfaction you're the first person that's spotted it. Now let me tell you a little about myself. Before the war I was an actor. I did four years with a weekly Rep. Company and two years in the West End. When the war broke out I went into the Fleet Air Arm. I was demobbed in 1945.
TEMPLE:	Go on.
BOYER:	I came back to the theatre brimming with enthusiasm. After eighteen months I was eventually offered the part of a butler in a French farce. I had two lines. I stuck it for the best part of twelve months and then one night I decided to change my tactics. I'd always been a good dancer and, to be frank, women were never exactly allergic to me. The rest you can guess.

194

TEMPLE:	Yes.
STEVE:	And how does Moira Portland fit into the picture?
BOYER:	She doesn't.
STEVE:	What do you mean?
BOYER:	I broke off our engagement this afternoon. You see, Temple, I quite enjoy playing the part of a gigolo, but –
TEMPLE:	But you don't like to be called one – at least not to your face?
BOYER:	Exactly.
TEMPLE:	Is that the real reason why you broke off your engagement with Miss Portland?
BOYER:	What other reason could I have?
TEMPLE:	The fact that she takes drugs.

A moment.

BOYER:	When did you discover that?
TEMPLE:	I guessed it – the night she pretended to be drunk.
BOYER:	I don't know why but Moira's changed a great deal during the past few months. She seems worried and almost – almost frightened at times.
TEMPLE:	Have you any idea what she's frightened about?
BOYER:	No, I haven't, but curiously enough Chunky Brooks must have noticed something. He asked me a great many questions about Moira and he spoke to Eileen Greene about her as well. That was the significance of the remark – the one that Greene overheard. I wanted to have a word with Eileen about it and simply said – "We'll have to talk about this, Eileen. I'll meet you later tonight."

TEMPLE: And did you meet her?

BOYER: Of course not – she was murdered, you know that.

TEMPLE: You said just now that Hubert Greene overheard that remark – how do you know it was Greene?

BOYER: You said so.

TEMPLE: No, I didn't. I simply said your remark was overheard.

BOYER: (*With a nervous little laugh*) Well, I took it for granted it was Greene.

SIR GRAHAM is approaching.

STEVE: Oh. Here's Sir Graham.

TEMPLE: Hello, Sir Graham.

FORBES: Did you get my message, Temple?

TEMPLE: Yes, I've just been speaking to Vosper.

STEVE: Has anything happened, Sir Graham?

FORBES: Yes, there's been a new development. Boyer, I'm afraid I've got some very bad news for you.

BOYER: What is it? Is it Moira?

A moment.

FORBES: Yes – she's committed suicide.

A moment.

STEVE: Oh, how horrible.

BOYER: (*Quietly*) I was afraid of that …

TEMPLE: There's no doubt that it <u>was</u> suicide?

FORBES: No doubt, several people saw it happen.

BOYER: (*Softly*) What time did she do it?

FORBES: About eight o'clock this evening. What did you mean just now when you said – I was afraid of that?

BOYER: Moira's been acting very strange lately. She's been terribly over-wrought and at times quite

	impossible to talk to. I was talking to Temple about it only a few moments ago.
STEVE:	Mr Boyer was saying that he'd just broken off his engagement.
FORBES:	Oh? When did that happen?
BOYER:	This afternoon.
FORBES:	Was Miss Portland upset?
BOYER:	We were both upset. It wasn't exactly a pleasant afternoon.
FORBES:	Where did you see Miss Portland?
BOYER:	At her flat. I arrived about a quarter to three and left just after four.
FORBES:	Did anyone else call on her while you were there?
BOYER:	No, but there was a telephone call.
FORBES:	Who was it, do you know?
BOYER:	Yes, it was Mrs Portland.
FORBES:	Did you hear the conversation?
BOYER:	Part of it. They seemed to be making an appointment to see each other.
FORBES:	M'm – I'd like to see Mrs Portland.
STEVE:	She's here, Sir Graham.
FORBES:	What – here at the Manilla?
TEMPLE:	Yes, we were talking to her only a few minutes ago. She's in the cocktail bar.
FORBES:	Good. Boyer, would you mind asking Mrs Portland if she can spare me a moment?

BOYER hesitates momentarily.

| BOYER: | Very well. |

BOYER leaves.

| STEVE: | Oh dear, that poor girl. Why do you think she did it, Sir Graham? Because Boyer broke off the engagement? |

197

FORBES:	I don't think the engagement had anything to do with it. I may be wrong of course.
TEMPLE:	I agree with you, Sir Graham, I don't think it had either. According to Boyer she's been desperately worried for some little time now.
FORBES:	Did he tell you why she was worried?
TEMPLE:	No.
FORBES:	She'd been taking drugs – did you know that?
TEMPLE:	Yes.
STEVE:	Why did you want to talk to Mrs Portland, Sir Graham?
FORBES:	A woman visited Moira this afternoon just after Boyer left her. From the description we've received it sounds remarkably like Mrs Portland.
STEVE:	Well, that rather ties up with the phone call, doesn't it?
FORBES:	Yes. You know, Temple, I've been doing quite a lot of thinking about the Madison mystery, and it seems to me that we've got four class suspects.
TEMPLE:	We may have four suspects, Sir Graham, but there's only one Mr Madison!
STEVE:	Who are the four – Stella Portland, Hubert Greene, George Kelly …?
TEMPLE:	And Chris Boyer.
STEVE:	But you both said that you didn't think he had anything to do with Moira committing suicide.
TEMPLE:	We don't think the broken engagement had anything to do with it.
FORBES:	Exactly.
STEVE:	Yes, but if he deliberately did that this afternoon –
TEMPLE:	(*Stopping STEVE*) Here's Mrs Portland …

STELLA PORTLAND approaches.

FORBES: She looks upset.

STEVE: Boyer must have told her.

STELLA: (*Obviously distressed*) Sir Graham, is this true what Chris just told me about Moira?

FORBES: Yes, I'm afraid it is, Mrs Portland.

STELLA: Oh, the stupid silly girl! Whatever made her do it, I told her that – (*She suddenly stops*)

A moment.

FORBES: (*Quietly*) Mrs Portland, when did you last see your step-daughter?

STELLA: I – I beg your pardon?

FORBES: When did you last see your step-daughter?

STELLA: Oh, er – several days ago. As a matter of fact I haven't seen her since the weekend.

FORBES: Are you sure?

STELLA: (*Indignantly, but not too sure of herself*) Whatever do you mean? Of course I'm sure!

FORBES: You haven't seen Miss Portland since the weekend?

STELLA: No.

FORBES: You didn't visit her this afternoon?

STELLA: (*Almost a little frightened*) No – I didn't. I've told you, I haven't seen her for several days.

FORBES: Have you spoken to her on the telephone?

STELLA: No, I – (*Suddenly, changing her mind*) – Yes. Yes, I have. I spoke to her this afternoon.

FORBES: Did she ring you or …?

STELLA: No, I rang her. I wanted to arrange a luncheon date.

FORBES: Did you arrange it?

STELLA: Yes, for next Friday.

FORBES: Mrs Portland, you must forgive me if I ask you a rather personal question.

STELLA: I'm getting quite used to personal questions, Sir Graham.

FORBES: How did you get on with your step-daughter?

STELLA: (*Almost a note of defiance in her voice*) I got on quite well with her. I don't expect you to believe that, I don't expect anyone to believe it, but the fact remains that I did.

FORBES: I see.

STELLA: When we first met we took an instant dislike to one another and then gradually things began to change. (*Thoughtfully*) I think she realised …

STELLA hesitates.

STEVE: Realised what, Mrs Portland?

STELLA: … That I was a friend and not an enemy.

FORBES: Had she many enemies?

STELLA: I should ask Mr Boyer that question. After all, he was her fiancé.

TEMPLE: Boyer broke off the engagement this afternoon.

STELLA: Oh!

TEMPLE: Didn't you know that?

STELLA: No, I didn't.

TEMPLE: What was Moira like on the phone – did she sound worried or depressed at all?

STELLA: No more than usual. Frankly, she hadn't a lot to say. I had the impression that there was someone with her.

STEVE: Boyer said he was with her, Mrs Portland.

STELLA: Oh. Oh, I see.

FORBES: Have you any idea why she committed suicide?

STELLA: No, I haven't unless – she was terribly upset about what happened this afternoon.

FORBES: You mean it was the breaking of her engagement.

STELLA: Yes.

FORBES:	You can't think of any other reason why she should have taken her life?
STELLA:	(*Hesitantly*) No. No, I can't.
FORBES:	(*Watching STELLA*) You don't sound very convincing, Mrs Portland.

FADE IN music.

FADE DOWN music.

SCENE 3: The Corridor outside the TEMPLES' Flat.

TEMPLE and STEVE are standing outside their front door: TEMPLE is pressing the buzzer impatiently.

TEMPLE:	Come on, Charlie!
STEVE:	Haven't you got your key?
TEMPLE:	(*Feeling in his pocket*) I've got it somewhere, but – where on earth did I put it?

STEVE presses the buzzer.

STEVE:	I can't understand why Charlie doesn't come.
TEMPLE:	He's probably in bed.
STEVE:	Come on!
TEMPLE:	I don't know what on earth's the matter with Charlie these days, he seems to deliberately go out of his way to …
STEVE:	Here he is!

The door opens.

STEVE:	We thought you'd gone on your holidays, Charlie.
CHARLIE:	(*Taking STEVE literally*) What – me? I 'ad my holidays in August.
STEVE:	You were such a long time answering the door!
CHARLIE:	Oh. (*Smiling*) That was on account of Mr Kelly.
TEMPLE:	Mr Kelly?
CHARLIE:	Yes, I was in the bathroom, sir, 'elping him to tidy up.

TEMPLE: (*Still puzzled*) Mr Kelly?

STEVE: Don't keep on saying 'Mr Kelly', darling. What's happened, Charlie?

CHARLIE: Mr Kelly's 'ad a bit of a rough house. He's been tidying up in the bathroom.

TEMPLE: Come on, Steve, let's see what it's all about.

SCENE 4:   The TEMPLES' Bathroom.

GEORGE KELLY is at the wash-hand-basin, running his hands under the tap. The door opens and TEMPLE and STEVE enter.

KELLY: (*Pleasantly*) Oh, hello, there! Say, I'm glad you're back.

KELLY turns off the tap.

TEMPLE: What on earth have you been up to?

KELLY: You might well ask!

STEVE: You've torn your shirt.

KELLY: I've torn darn nearly everything.

TEMPLE: You look as if you've been in a fight.

KELLY: I have – and I got the worst of it.

STEVE: But what happened?

KELLY: I don't know what happened! It seemed to me I was hit by a hurricane. One minute I was standing on my feet – the next I was fighting for dear life. (*Looking in the mirror*) Just look at my face! Uncle Sam certainly took an awful beating.

TEMPLE: Kelly, I'm not very bright this evening. Supposing you start at the beginning. What are you doing here, anyway?

KELLY: I wanted to have a talk. I was passing your apartment so I thought I'd drop in for a few minutes. The elevator was on the top floor and I rang for it.

202

TEMPLE: Go on.

KELLY: It came down: the light wasn't on, so I took it for granted it was empty.

STEVE: Well, wasn't it empty?

KELLY: It certainly was not! Just as I put my hand on the gate it was thrown open and – wham! For a moment I just didn't know what had hit me.

STEVE: You mean to say someone stepped out of the lift and hit you?

KELLY: He certainly did.

STEVE: But why?

KELLY: You're asking me! Either the guy was nuts or he just didn't want me to see him. Anyway, we went at it hell for leather; suddenly he landed me a real Joe Louis – Oh, what a humdinger! – did I hear music! When I recovered, the guy had disappeared.

TEMPLE: Would you recognise him again?

KELLY: No, I don't think I would. You see, we were more or less in the dark and the whole thing happened so quickly.

STEVE: I bet you'd like to get your hands on him.

KELLY: Get my hands on him? I don't want to go near the guy – look what he's done to me!

TEMPLE: (*Smiling*) All right, Kelly, join us when you're ready. I daresay you can do with a Scotch and soda.

KELLY: And how!

SCENE 5:   The TEMPLES' Drawing Room
TEMPLE siphons some soda into a glass.
TEMPLE: How's that?

KELLY: That's dandy. (*Taking the glass*) Thanks. That certainly looks good. (*He drinks*) My, tastes good, too!

TEMPLE: You know, Kelly, that's rather a remarkable story of yours.

KELLY: Remarkable? It's fantastic! If I was in your shoes I just wouldn't believe a word of it.

TEMPLE: When did it happen, exactly?

KELLY: The fight?

TEMPLE: Yes.

KELLY: About ten minutes ago. Gee, I wish you and Mrs Temple had turned up ten minutes earlier.

TEMPLE: Yes, I wish we had. You're quite sure you wouldn't recognise the man again?

KELLY: I'm sure. (*Suddenly*) Say, I wonder if it's any use asking the people up above if they knew him?

TEMPLE: There isn't anybody above.

KELLY: No? (*Puzzled*) What do you mean?

TEMPLE: The flat immediately above this belongs to a Major Hartley – he's in Washington. He sublet it to a man called Elzec.

KELLY: Well, maybe this guy was a friend of this Elzec's.

TEMPLE: Elzec disappeared several days ago. We have reason to believe he was drowned.

KELLY: Oh. (*Politely*) Was he a friend of yours?

TEMPLE: (*Watching KELLY*) Not exactly. (*Changing the subject*) Anyway, what was it you wanted to see me about?

KELLY: Well – you know that brooch, or rather clip, I found – the one I handed over to you this morning?

TEMPLE: Yes?

KELLY: I told you it belonged to Moira Portland.

TEMPLE: That's right.

KELLY: Well, I've been thinking about that. Maybe that was a tactless thing for me to say in view of the fact that I found the brooch very near the spot where Mrs Greene was murdered.

TEMPLE: Why tactless?

KELLY: Well, I don't want to throw suspicion onto Moira Portland – I don't want to throw suspicion on to anybody.

TEMPLE: Don't worry, Mr Kelly, you won't throw suspicion onto Miss Portland … She's dead.

KELLY: (*Staggered*) Who are you kidding?

TEMPLE: (*Almost matter of fact*) I'm not kidding. I'm telling you the truth. Miss Portland committed suicide.

KELLY: When?

TEMPLE: Tonight.

KELLY: (*Stunned*) A young kid like that, why … Whatever made her do such a stupid thing? For God's sake, what made her do it?

TEMPLE: Your guess is as good as mine, Kelly … It might even be better.

A moment and then the telephone starts to ring.

TEMPLE: Excuse me.

TEMPLE lifts the receiver.

TEMPLE: Hello?

There is no reply from the other end of the line.

TEMPLE: Hello?

Suddenly, from the other end, we hear a low moan – someone is in pain and endeavouring to speak.

TEMPLE: Who is that? Who's there?

ELZEC: Is … that … you, Temple?

TEMPLE: Yes, who is that?

ELZEC:	This is … Elzec.
TEMPLE:	Dr Elzec …?
ELZEC:	Temple, listen … I've got to see you … There's something I – must – tell – you …
TEMPLE:	What's the matter? What's the matter with you?
ELZEC:	I've been … beaten up … I … I …

Silence.

TEMPLE:	Elzec! Elzec, where are you?!
KELLY:	(*Bewildered*) Temple, what is it?
TEMPLE:	Sh! Be quiet! (*On the phone*) Elzec, can you hear me?
ELZEC:	Yes – yes, I – can – hear – Temple. I want to tell you about Madison, I want to tell you about the cottage at Lockdale and …
TEMPLE:	At Lockdale?
ELZEC:	Yes, that's … where … we were going the night Madison … double-crossed us …
TEMPLE:	Elzec, listen! Where are you? Where are you speaking from?
ELZEC:	I'm … in … the flat …

ELZEC gives a gasp and the telephone receiver can be heard falling from his hand.

TEMPLE:	By Timothy!

TEMPLE hurriedly puts down the phone.

KELLY:	What is it? What's happened?
TEMPLE:	Elzec's been beaten up! He's in the flat above! Come on, Kelly – follow me!

SCENE 6: Outside ELZEC's Flat.

TEMPLE is shaking the handle of the door.

KELLY:	Is this the flat?
TEMPLE:	Yes.
KELLY:	Is the door locked?

TEMPLE: Yes! We've got to break it down. Come on, Kelly!

TEMPLE and GEORGE KELLY start throwing their weight against the door.

KELLY: Boy, this is some door!

TEMPLE: Come on! … That's it!

The door collapses and both TEMPLE and KELLY rush into the flat.

KELLY: Gee, what's hit this place? There's been a whale of a fight by the looks of things!

TEMPLE: Yes.

A moment.

KELLY: I don't see any sign of your friend Elzec.

TEMPLE: (*Off*) He's over here in the bedroom.

KELLY: Oh, Let's have a look.

KELLY joins TEMPLE and gives a low whistle of surprise.

KELLY: He's certainly been beaten up … Is he …?

TEMPLE: Yes. (*Rising from the floor*) We're too late, Kelly.

KELLY: That's terrible! (*Suddenly*) Temple, you know that character I bumped into? The fellow I told you about – the one that went for me in the elevator?

TEMPLE: Yes?

KELLY: (*Keyed up: tense*) Do you think he's responsible for this? Do you think he murdered Elzec?

TEMPLE: It's possible. (*Watching KELLY*) Quite possible …

FADE UP music.

FADE DOWN music.

SCENE 7: The TEMPLES' Drawing Room.

207

The door opens and TEMPLE enters. He is in a bright mood:
he sounds very pleased with himself.

TEMPLE: Are you ready?

STEVE: Yes.

TEMPLE: You look – very glamorous this morning!

STEVE: Well, I don't feel very glamorous. Look, have I
            <u>got</u> to go out this morning?

TEMPLE: Yes, Steve, you have. And don't forget what I
            told you.

STEVE: Do you really want me to do that?

TEMPLE: Yes, I do, Steve.

STEVE: But it doesn't make sense.

TEMPLE: Doesn't it, darling? Well, don't let it worry
            you.

The door opens.

TEMPLE: What is it, Charlie?

CHARLIE: (*Brightly*) I'm off now, Mr Temple!

TEMPLE: All right, Charlie. Have a good time.

CHARLIE: Ta. You bet I will, Mr T.

STEVE: (*Amazed*) And where do you think you are
            going?

CHARLIE: I'm having the day off.

STEVE: Oh, you are, are you?

CHARLIE: S'right. Mr Temple said it'll be o.k.

STEVE: Oh, he did.

CHARLIE: S'right.

TEMPLE: That's all right, Charlie. Run along!

CHARLIE: (*Giving TEMPLE the wink as he goes*) Okey-
            doke, Mr T.

The flat buzzer sounds.

TEMPLE: (*Calling to CHARLIE*) Just see who that is,
            would you?

CHARLIE: (*Calling back from the hall*) Will do, sir.

CHARLIE opens the front door.

STEVE:	Now look here, Paul, I don't know what's going on here this morning, but I intend to know –
CHARLIE:	(*Back in*) There's Inspector Vosper to see you, Mr T.
TEMPLE:	Why, hello, Inspector! Come in.
VOSPER:	(*Entering*) Good morning, sir. Good morning, Mrs Temple.
STEVE:	Good morning, Inspector. (*Leaving*) I'm going now then, Paul.
TEMPLE:	Yes, all right, darling. Don't forget what I told you.
STEVE:	I won't.

A pause as STEVE leaves.

TEMPLE:	Well, how did you get on upstairs?
VOSPER:	We've turned the place upside down.
TEMPLE:	Have you found anything?
VOSPER:	Frankly, very little of the stuff seems to belong to Elzec – it's mostly Major Hartley's.
TEMPLE:	Any fingerprints?
VOSPER:	Nothing worth worrying about. But that's not why I wanted to see you, Mr Temple.
TEMPLE:	Why did you want to see me?
VOSPER:	(*Perturbed*) Are you sure – quite sure – that Elzec said: "the cottage at Lockdale"?
TEMPLE:	Yes.
VOSPER:	It was Lockdale?
TEMPLE:	Yes, I'm quite sure it was Lockdale. Why?
VOSPER:	Well, we've been turning the village upside down, sir. If there's a cottage down there being used for this counterfeit racket then by George we've yet to find it.
TEMPLE:	Are there many cottages down there?
VOSPER:	Only about half-a-dozen.

TEMPLE:	(*Puzzled*) Only half-a-dozen. You must have checked them by now.
VOSPER:	Yes, we have, sir. I just don't understand it.
TEMPLE:	Well, I'm sure Elzec said Lockdale.
VOSPER:	He didn't say Laleham by any chance, sir?
TEMPLE:	Laleham? Where's Laleham? Is that on the river?
VOSPER:	It's about three quarters of a mile from Chertsey.
TEMPLE:	No, I'm pretty sure he said Lockdale, Inspector.
VOSPER:	All right, we'll go on checking. We'll move the whole of Scotland Yard down there if necessary. (*Changing the subject*) Mr Temple, you remember that fellow Mark Kendell – the chap that broke into your flat?
TEMPLE:	Yes?
VOSPER:	I've got a theory about him.
TEMPLE:	What's that?
VOSPER:	Well, I think that Kendell was under the impression that Elzec was doing a double-cross. It's my opinion that he didn't intend to break into your flat that night but into Elzec's.
TEMPLE:	You mean in other words, he picked the wrong flat?
VOSPER:	Exactly. Don't forget Elzec had only moved in the day before.
TEMPLE:	Yes, I agree with you, Inspector.
VOSPER:	And there's another point, Mr Temple. You remember that explosion on the river?
TEMPLE:	I shan't easily forget it, Inspector.
VOSPER:	Well, I think I know what happened that night. Madison took a suitcase down to the launch, he told Elzec it was something for the cottage. In actual fact it was a time bomb. Madison wanted

	to get rid of Elzec, Alfaro and the rest of the gang.
TEMPLE:	In other words he's going into liquidation?
VOSPER:	Exactly.
TEMPLE:	You may be right, Inspector. If you are …
VOSPER:	We've got to move fast.
TEMPLE:	Fast is hardly the word. We've got to move like greased lightning.
VOSPER:	Yes. Mr Temple, what do you think happened last night?
TEMPLE:	With Elzec?
VOSPER:	Yes.
TEMPLE:	I think when Elzec realised that Madison was trying to double-cross him he decided to get his own back. He sent for Madison – with the intention of letting him have it. Unfortunately for Elzec, and for us too, Madison turned the tables on him.
VOSPER:	In other words Kelly was beaten up by Madison who was making a getaway after the attack on Elzec?

The flat buzzer sounds.

TEMPLE:	Er – yes.
VOSPER:	That's one theory of course. There is another.
TEMPLE:	Yes, there is another, Inspector. (*Suddenly*) What time is it?
VOSPER:	I make it just gone twelve.
TEMPLE:	I think that's George Kelly at the door. Will you excuse me, Inspector?
VOSPER:	Oh, I'd like a word with Kelly.
TEMPLE:	Well, I rather wanted to see him alone.
VOSPER:	I can wait.
TEMPLE:	No, I'd – (*With a little laugh*) – er – prefer you to see him some other time. If you don't mind?

211

VOSPER: (*Puzzled*) No, of course not. (*Watching TEMPLE*) Are you up to something, Mr Temple?

The flat buzzer sounds again.

TEMPLE: What me? Good gracious, no. Look here, Inspector, I'll take him into my study and you can slip out of the front door. You can let yourself out all right, can't you?

VOSPER: Yes, of course I can. I say, what's going on here? Why the devil shouldn't I see Kelly?

TEMPLE: (*Disarmingly pleasant*) No reason at all if you'd really like to see him.

A moment.

VOSPER: All right, Mr Temple. You play it your own way.

TEMPLE: (*Laughing*) Thanks, Inspector.

SCENE 8: The Hallway.

TEMPLE opens the front door.

TEMPLE: Ah, come in, Kelly!

KELLY: Am I late?

TEMPLE: No, no, you're in nice time.

KELLY: Sorry I was out when you phoned. I only got your message about an hour ago.

TEMPLE: That's all right. I'm glad you could make it., Let's go into my study.

TEMPLE and KELLY move into the study.

KELLY: Say, this is some den!

TEMPLE: Do you like it?

KELLY: Yes, sir! Is this where you write all those thrillers?

TEMPLE: Well, some of them. Would you like a glass of sherry?

KELLY: Yeah – I think maybe I would.

TEMPLE pours the drinks.

TEMPLE: This is a very dry sherry, I hope you like it.

KELLY: Can't be too dry for me. (*Impressed: looking about him*) Say, you've written some books, Temple.

TEMPLE: One or two.

KELLY: Do you know, funny enough I've never read one of yours.

TEMPLE: There's nothing funny about it, Mr Kelly – quite a lot of people haven't read any of my books. (*Offering KELLY his drink*) Here you are.

KELLY: Thank you. I go in for Westerns. You know the sort of thing. Riders Over Arizona, The Sheriff of Melton Creek.

TEMPLE: Shades of Zane Grey.

KELLY: Sure!

TEMPLE: (*Raising his glass*) Well, your very good health!

KELLY: (*A little taken aback by Temple's exuberance*) Yours too.

TEMPLE and KELLY drink.

TEMPLE: Sit down, Kelly. (*A moment*) I'll tell you what I wanted to see you about. I've been having a talk to Inspector Vosper. He's got a theory about last night. He thinks that Elzec was murdered by a man called Madison and that it was Madison that bumped into you coming out of the lift.

KELLY: Well, that's exactly what I said! I told you – in my opinion the guy who murdered Elzec was the bird who knocked the stuffing out of me.

TEMPLE: Yes, well I'd like you to go down to the Yard, Kelly, and look at some photographs.

KELLY: What sort of photographs?

TEMPLE: Oh, just pictures of one or two people. I've got a hunch you might be able to pick him out.

KELLY: What – the man who attacked me?

TEMPLE: Yes.

KELLY: There's not a hope! I wouldn't recognise him if he walked into this room. I told you, it was dark. I hardly saw the guy.

TEMPLE: Nevertheless, I'd like you to have a look at the photographs.

The telephone starts to ring.

TEMPLE: Oh, excuse me.

TEMPLE picks up the receiver.

TEMPLE: Hello?

STEVE: (*Distort*) Well, here I am, darling. You told me to ring up.

TEMPLE: (*Very surprised tone of voice*) Oh, hello, Steve!

STEVE: (*Amused*) Well, don't sound so surprised!

TEMPLE: Is anything the matter, darling?

STEVE: No, of course there isn't anything the matter. Remember you told me to –

TEMPLE: (*Cutting in on STEVE*) I say, that is too bad! Where did it happen?

STEVE: Where did what happen?

TEMPLE: Have you tried the starting handle?

STEVE: Paul, what is this? What are you talking about?

TEMPLE: (*Taking absolutely no notice of STEVE*) Oh, Steve, you should have tried the starting handle, that's the first thing you should have done! Where are you, darling? Where are you speaking from?

STEVE: Where do you think I'm speaking from? I'm in the call box at the end of the road!

TEMPLE: Good Lord, what an extraordinary place to pick!

STEVE: What do you mean, what an extraordinary place to pick? You told me to ring you up from …

TEMPLE: Look here, Steve, I'd better come down and have a look at you! Go back and sit in the car, darling!

STEVE: What do you mean, go back and sit in the car? I haven't got the car, I walked down to the box!

TEMPLE: Yes, all right you can try that, but I shouldn't get your hands dirty.

STEVE: I haven't the slightest intention of … Try what? What are you talking about?

TEMPLE: (*Pleasantly*) All right, Steve. I'll do that. Shan't be long, darling.

TEMPLE rings off.

KELLY: Is anything the matter?

TEMPLE: Yes, my wife's having a spot of trouble with the car. Not exactly an unusual occurrence, Mr Kelly. Look here, would you excuse me if I popped out for five or ten minutes? I'd better give her a hand.

KELLY: Sure! I'll come with you.

TEMPLE: No, I'd rather you didn't. The flat's empty and I'm expecting a call from Scotland Yard.

KELLY: Do you want me to take it?

TEMPLE: I should be very grateful if you would. It'll be Sir Graham Forbes. Tell him I'll see him as arranged – nine o'clock tonight.

KELLY: O.K. I'll do that.

TEMPLE: I shan't be long.

KELLY: If you need any help with the car, give me a ring.

215

TEMPLE: I think I know what's wrong with it. The trouble with my wife is she never uses any imagination! (*Suddenly laughing at himself*) I shan't be long, Kelly.

KELLY: (*Laughing*) O.K.

TEMPLE: If you feel like another glass of sherry just help yourself.

KELLY: I might do that. It's <u>very</u> nice.

They laugh.

FADE UP music.

FADE DOWN music.

SCENE 9:   TEMPLE's Study. Later.

The door opens and TEMPLE enters.

TEMPLE: Kelly, I'm sorry we've been such a long time!

KELLY: It's o.k.

TEMPLE: I hope you helped yourself to the sherry!

KELLY: I nearly started on the whisky.

STEVE: You should have done, Mr Kelly – it would have taught my husband a lesson! Leaving you alone in the flat like that!

TEMPLE: Did anyone call?

KELLY: No, and there wasn't a phone call either.

TEMPLE: Oh – didn't Sir Graham ring?

KELLY: No. What was the matter with the car, Mrs Temple?

TEMPLE: (*Amused*) Tell him, darling!

STEVE: You beast! No you tell him – you'll enjoy it more.

TEMPLE: She ran out of petrol!

KELLY: Oh that's just too bad!

TEMPLE: Come on. Kelly – let's go into the drawing room.

KELLY: No, Temple, I'm afraid I've got to be making a move. I've got a luncheon date.

TEMPLE: Oh, what a pity! Well, look here, Kelly, will you drop in the Yard and have a word with Vosper? I'd like you to check on those photographs.

KELLY: O.K., but I've told you it's no use. I'm sure I shouldn't recognise the guy again.

TEMPLE: Well – you never know.

KELLY: Goodbye, Mrs Temple.

STEVE: Goodbye, Mr Kelly.

TEMPLE: I'll see you to the lift. When you see Vosper, tell him that you've had a chat to me and that I suggested he showed you a series of photographs. If you can give him some idea of the height of the man who attacked you …

FADE UP music.

FADE DOWN music.

SCENE 10:   The TEMPLES' Drawing Room.

TEMPLE is whistling softly to himself. STEVE enters.

TEMPLE: (*Looking up*) Is lunch ready, darling?

STEVE: It will be in a few minutes.

TEMPLE: (*Pleasantly*) Oh, you've changed your dress!

STEVE: Now look here, Paul – don't you start giving me the run around!

TEMPLE: (*Innocently*) The run around?

STEVE: Yes, the run around! Now what's this all about? First of all you give Charlie the day off, then you make me go down to the call box and put through a phoney phone call, then you invite Mr Kelly to the flat and leave him high and dry …

217

TEMPLE: Hardly dry, darling! (*Laughing at STEVE*)
             Don't you know what it's all about?

STEVE: Of course I don't know what it's all about!

TEMPLE: Well, where's that intuition of yours?

STEVE: You keep my intuition out of this!

The telephone starts to ring.

TEMPLE: You keep it out, darling – you're the one who
             always boasts about it.

TEMPLE lifts the receiver.

TEMPLE: Hello?

GREENE: (*Distort*) Is that you, Temple?

TEMPLE: Who is that?

GREENE: This is Hubert Greene.

TEMPLE: Oh, hello, Greene!

GREENE: Temple, I'm awfully sorry I couldn't make it
             this morning.

TEMPLE: Make it? Make what?

GREENE: Our appointment.

TEMPLE: Appointment? Had we an appointment this
             morning?

GREENE: (*With a little laugh*) Yes. I got your note last
             night. You said would I call round and see you
             at twelve o'clock this morning.

TEMPLE: (*Surprised*) I did?

GREENE: (*Laughing*) Yes.

TEMPLE: My dear fellow, I never sent you a note.

GREENE: But I've got it here – now – in front of me.

TEMPLE: I sent you a note asking you –

GREENE: Asking me to call round at twelve o'clock this
             morning – yes! Unfortunately, I was kept at the
             office and couldn't make it.

TEMPLE: But, Greene, I never sent you a note. I didn't
             want you to call round this morning!

218

GREENE: But I tell you – I've got the note here in front of me!

TEMPLE: You may have this note in front of you, Greene – I'm quite prepared to believe that you have – but the fact remains that I didn't send it.

GREENE: (*Angry*) Then who did?

TEMPLE: Was it posted?

GREENE: No, it was delivered by hand.

TEMPLE: Who delivered it?

GREENE: I don't know. I found it in the letter box.

TEMPLE: Is it typewritten?

GREENE: No, it's handwritten.

TEMPLE: Bring it round to the flat this evening. You know my address?

GREENE: Yes, of course. (*Almost perturbed*) I say, this is very odd, isn't it, Temple? Why should anyone send me a note like this?

TEMPLE: (*With quiet authority*) Do as I say, Greene – bring the note round this evening.

GREENE: Yes, all right, I will. Goodbye, Temple.

TEMPLE: Goodbye.

TEMPLE replaces the receiver.

STEVE: What is it, Paul? What's happened?

TEMPLE: Greene received a note asking him to call here this morning. He apparently couldn't keep the appointment because he was detained at the office.

STEVE: Did you send him a note?

TEMPLE: No, I didn't.

STEVE: Then who did? Do you know?

The flat buzzer goes.

TEMPLE: (*Faintly amused*) Yes, I've got a very good idea … It's alright, darling, I'll see who that is.

TEMPLE goes into the hall and opens the front door.

STELLA:	Good morning, Mr Temple.
TEMPLE:	Mrs Portland ... is anything the matter?
STELLA:	Yes, I've got to see you. I've got to see you now, this minute, before – it's too late.
TEMPLE:	What's happened?
STELLA:	I want to tell you why Moira committed suicide, I want you to know what she told me yesterday afternoon. (*Tensely*) I want to tell you ... about Madison.

END OF EPISODE SEVEN

EPISODE EIGHT

INTRODUCING
MADISON

SCENE 1:	The TEMPLES' Hallway, as at the end of Episode 7.
TEMPLE:	Why, hello, Mrs Portland … is anything the matter?
STELLA:	Yes, I've got to see you. I've got to see you now, this minute, before – it's too late.
TEMPLE:	What's happened?
STELLA:	I want to tell you why Moira committed suicide, I want you to know what she told me yesterday afternoon. (*Tensely*) I want to tell you … about Madison.
A moment.	
TEMPLE:	Please, do come in.
STEVE:	(*Coming into the hall*) Darling, who is it?
TEMPLE:	It's Mrs Portland.
STEVE:	(*Surprised by STELLA's appearance*) Is anything the matter?
STELLA:	Yes, I – I – (*Faintly*) May I sit down for a few moments?
TEMPLE:	Yes, of course. Come along.
STEVE:	Give me your arm.
SCENE 2:	The TEMPLES' Drawing Room, a short while later.
STEVE:	… Do you feel better now?
STELLA:	Yes, I'm all right now. I was so upset about Moira. It came as a great shock to me – you see I was only talking to her just before she committed suicide.
TEMPLE:	(*Quietly*) What did Moira tell you, Mrs Portland?
STELLA:	Well, yesterday afternoon: the poor girl was obviously on the verge of a nervous breakdown. She told me the whole story – the

story about herself and my husband Sam and Chris Boyer …

TEMPLE: Go on.

STELLA: Well, you know the story about Sam, about his loss of memory and how he was discovered wandering down Portland Avenue in Chicago.

TEMPLE: Yes.

STELLA: Well, for many years Sam tried to discover his true identity. It was almost an obsession with him. He told you the story of the penny. He told nearly everyone he met. He attached great importance to that penny. One morning, some months ago, Chris Boyer told Moira that he'd discovered Sam's identity. He told Moira that Sam was the son of a man called Clint. Dawson

TEMPLE: Clint Dawson?

STELLA: Yes. Dawson was a swindler – he was a notorious sharepusher and company promoter. He was sent to prison in 1914. Mrs Dawson, together with Sam, left England, shortly after her husband was sentenced. At the time, no one knew where she went or what happened to her. It's pretty obvious now, of course, that she went to the States.

TEMPLE: Yes. Go on.

STELLA: When Boyer told Moira this story she asked me not to tell anyone about it, her common sense told her that such a story would not only distress Sam, but probably have drastic repercussions on the Portland Yeast Company.

STEVE: But why should it do that?

STELLA: Well – if it became known that the head of the company was the son of a swindler, then …

TEMPLE: Like father like son?

224

STELLA: Exactly.

TEMPLE: Go on, Mrs Portland.

STELLA: To Moira's astonishment, Boyer started to blackmail her. He must have had literally thousands of pounds out of the poor girl. Suddenly Moira could stand it no longer and she told Boyer to send for her father and tell him the whole story. You know what happened …

TEMPLE: Boyer pretended that a private investigator called Madison had discovered Sam's identity and he wired for your husband to come over here.

STELLA: Yes – he put Hubert Greene's name to the cable because he realised that Sam would take more notice of it. What would have happened if Sam hadn't died, it's difficult to say. I believe that Boyer would have told him the whole story and then blackmailed him.

STEVE: Do you think Boyer really <u>did</u> discover the identity of your husband or was he just bluffing?

STELLA: (*Thoughtfully*) From what Moira told me, I'm pretty sure he was on to something. You see, Sam was right, that particular penny was an important link. If Boyer could have got hold of that penny he could have proved without any shadow of doubt that Sam was the son of the notorious Dawson.

STEVE: Is that why the penny was changed?

STELLA: Yes.

STEVE: Who changed it?

STELLA: Moira did. As soon as we arrived in London she came straight to the hotel. She asked to see

Sam's watchchain. I thought at the time, it was just for sentimental reasons. I realise now, of course, that she changed the penny.

TEMPLE: Where is the penny, Mrs Portland – the actual penny that Sam carried about with him?

STELLA: (*Hesitating*) It's here – I got it from Moira yesterday afternoon.

STELLA passes the coin to TEMPLE who studies it.

TEMPLE: … 1885 … Well, the date's all right anyway, Portland could certainly have had this penny in his pocket in 1914 – but that doesn't prove that this is the penny.

STELLA: There's an inscription on the bottom. It's very, very faint, but if you look closely you can just see it.

TEMPLE: (*Reading*) "To my …" My word, it certainly is faint … (*Peering*) "To my son – Good Luck – C …" Is it a B or a D?

STELLA: Well, I always thought it was a B and so did Sam, but if Boyer's story is true, then …

STEVE: C.D.! Clint Dawson! Paul, the coin must have been given to Portland by his father!

STELLA: 1885 – that's probably the year that Sam was born – he always reckoned he was about sixty-four or five.

TEMPLE: (*Thoughtfully*) Yes.

STEVE: You know, it seems to me, you know everything there is to know about Boyer without having so much as a shred of evidence.

STELLA: I agree, Mrs Temple! And that's the most dreadful part of the whole business! (*Suddenly, looking up*) Unless, of course, your husband …

TEMPLE: Unless what, Mrs Portland?

STELLA: Unless you've got the evidence, Mr Temple?

TEMPLE: (*Quietly: watching STELLA*) I know the
            identity of Madison, Mrs Portland, and I've got
            quite enough evidence to arrest the gentleman –
            when the time comes.

SCENE 3:   The Deck of a Motor Launch.
The launch is moored to a river jetty, its engine ticking over.
VOSPER and SIR GRAHAM are on deck, watching
TEMPLE's car arrive.

VOSPER: This looks like Mr Temple, Sir Graham.
FORBES: Yes, I think it is. What time do you make it,
            Vosper?
VOSPER: It's just gone four.
FORBES: He certainly hasn't wasted any time.
The engine is switched off and TEMPLE opens the car door.
VOSPER: (*Laughing*) It's only an hour since I phoned
            him.
The car door is shut.
TEMPLE: (*Approaching*) Sorry to have kept you waiting
            …
FORBES: We were just saying how quick you've been!
TEMPLE: So you finally found the place, Inspector!
VOSPER: One of my men found it – there was a message
            for me when I got back to the Yard.
TEMPLE: Was it at Lockdale?
VOSPER: Yes, but no wonder we couldn't spot it. The
            cottage was built on the site of what must have
            been a country mansion. The Madison outfit
            have been using the cellar.
TEMPLE: Is the cottage deserted?
VOSPER: It's derelict – you wouldn't look twice at the
            place.
TEMPLE: What's the cellar like?

FORBES:	You've never seen anything like it, Temple! And talk about equipment!
VOSPER:	It's an eye-opener. No wonder they've been able to flood the continent with counterfeit dollars.
TEMPLE:	How long will it take us to get there?
VOSPER:	Are you in a hurry?
TEMPLE:	I want to be back by seven at the latest.
VOSPER:	Oh, that's easy.
FORBES:	Jump aboard, Temple!

TEMPLE climbs onto the launch.

VOSPER:	We're ready, constable! Cast off!
CONSTABLE:	(*Off*) Very good, sir!

The engine revs and the launch leaves the jetty.

FORBES:	(*Confidentially*) How did you get on in town?
TEMPLE:	(*Same tone*) Oh, very well.
FORBES:	Did Kelly turn up?
TEMPLE:	Yes. (*With a laugh*) As a matter of fact he turned up while I was talking to Vosper.
FORBES:	Oh!
TEMPLE:	I think Vosper wondered what on earth was going on.
FORBES:	I can imagine that! Did you tell him?
TEMPLE:	No, I didn't want to take any chances. I haven't even told Steve about it.
FORBES:	Perhaps you're right. Madison's a clever devil – at least you'll certainly think so when you've seen this place at Lockdale.
TEMPLE:	If he'd stuck to his counterfeit racket I doubt very much whether we would have caught him.
FORBES:	I doubt it, too. (*As an afterthought*) But we haven't caught him yet, Temple.
TEMPLE:	No, Sir Graham. But we shall.

SCENE 4:   Another Jetty.

The launch arrives and comes to a standstill. The engine is switched off. As they greet the waiting SERGEANT, TEMPLE, SIR GRAHAM and VOSPER climb onto the jetty.

VOSPER: Good afternoon, Sergeant!

BAKER: Good afternoon, sir! (*Noticing FORBES*) Oh, good afternoon, Sir Graham!

FORBES: Good afternoon, Sergeant.

VOSPER: Anything to report?

BAKER: (*Faintly puzzled*) Yes, sir. There's someone in the cottage, sir.

VOSPER: In the cottage?

BAKER: Yes, sir. A young fellow came down the towpath about five minutes ago and went up to the cottage. We let him carry on because we didn't want to arouse his suspicions.

TEMPLE: What was he like, this young fellow?

BAKER: Oh, rather a good-looking chap. We thought he was selling something, he carried a small case.

VOSPER: Is he in the cottage now?

BAKER: He's either in the cottage or in the cellar.

FORBES: All right, Sergeant. Come along, Temple.

SCENE 5:   Outside The Cottage.

VOSPER is quietly trying the handle of the front door.

VOSPER: The door's latched.

TEMPLE: Wait a minute …

TEMPLE presses against the door.

VOSPER: Can you open it?

TEMPLE: I think so …

The latch is released.

FORBES: You've done it!

TEMPLE: Sh!

TEMPLE slowly opens the door.

229

A moment.

TEMPLE: (*Pleasantly: normal voice*) Good afternoon, Mr Boyer!

BOYER: (*Startled*) Why, Temple! Sir Graham! What is this? What are you doing here?

FORBES: May I ask what you are doing here?

BOYER: I have an appointment. At least – I think – I have.

FORBES: You don't seem very sure.

BOYER: Well, I don't know, you see … This place isn't at all what I expected. Why, it's almost derelict!

TEMPLE: (*Quietly*) What did you expect?

BOYER: Well, I expected a cottage by the river, a sort of weekend place. When Kelly spoke to me on the phone he said that …

TEMPLE: What did Mr Kelly say?

BOYER: (*Hesitatingly*) He said that he'd taken the cottage for weekends. He asked me to meet him here. He also asked me to bring this case along. Apparently he left it at the Manilla two or three nights ago.

TEMPLE: Have you any idea why Kelly wanted to see you?

BOYER: Yes, of course – I wouldn't have come otherwise. He said that he had a message for me from Moira – a note which she was supposed to have written shortly before she committed suicide.

TEMPLE: Did you say this case belongs to Kelly?

BOYER: Yes.

FORBES: What's in it, do you know?

BOYER: I believe it's just books and things.

TEMPLE: Let me have a look at it.

TEMPLE picks up and examines the case.

VOSPER: Is it locked?

TEMPLE: Yes. By Timothy …

FORBES: Temple, what is it?

TEMPLE: Listen! Listen to this!

We can hear a faint ticking noise from inside the case.

TEMPLE: Do you hear it?

FORBES: Yes!

VOSPER: Good Lord, is that from the case?

TEMPLE: Yes!

FORBES: You mean –

TEMPLE: Look out! Stand clear! Get away from the window, Boyer! Quick!

TEMPLE hurls the case through the window: there is the sudden smashing of glass followed by an explosion.

BOYER: Good Lord. Temple! What was in it?

TEMPLE: Well – it wasn't books.

FADE UP music.

FADE DOWN music.

SCENE 6:   TEMPLE's Study.

TEMPLE is at his desk typing. The door opens and Steve enters.

STEVE: What time is it, Paul?

TEMPLE stops typing and looks at his watch.

TEMPLE: It's just gone half-past eight.

STEVE: (*Puzzled*) I feel awfully tired.

TEMPLE: Well, if you feel tired I should go to bed.

STEVE: I've a jolly good mind to.

TEMPLE: Did you finish the drink I mixed you?

STEVE: Yes.

TEMPLE: Would you like another?

STEVE: No. (*Yawning*) No, I don't think so. Paul, I feel peculiar …

231

TEMPLE: What do you mean – peculiar?

STEVE: Unsteady.

TEMPLE: I expect you've been over-doing things. I should go and lie down, Steve.

STEVE: Yes. I'm afraid if you want anything you'll have to get it yourself. Charlie hasn't come in yet.

TEMPLE: All right, darling.

STEVE: (*Stopping: puzzled*) Paul …

TEMPLE: Yes?

STEVE: What happened this morning when Mr Kelly –

TEMPLE: (*Laughing at STEVE*) I thought you said you were feeling off colour. Go and lie down, Steve!

STEVE: Yes, all right … Gosh, I'm sleepy! It's funny I should feel like this! Goodnight, Paul.

TEMPLE: Goodnight, darling.

STEVE leaves and TEMPLE starts typing again.

After a short while the flat door buzzer sounds.

TEMPLE stops typing, goes through to the hall and opens the front door.

TEMPLE: Ah, hello, Greene! I've been expecting you. Come in!

GREENE enters.

GREENE: I hope I'm not too early.

TEMPLE shuts the door.

TEMPLE: No, you're in nice time. Shall I take your coat?

GREENE: Thanks.

TEMPLE takes the coat and hangs it up.

TEMPLE: Let's go into the study.

They move into the study.

GREENE: This is a very pleasant room.

TEMPLE: Yes, it is, isn't it?

TEMPLE shuts the door.

TEMPLE: Would you like a drink?

GREENE: Well – er …

TEMPLE: I'm having a whisky and soda.

GREENE: I don't think I will, thank you. I say, it was very odd about that note, wasn't it? I can't imagine why anyone else should send it.

TEMPLE: May I see it?

GREENE: Yes, of course, I've brought it for you.

GREENE hands over the note.

TEMPLE: (*Reading*) "Dear Mr Greene, I should be grateful if you would call round and see me this morning at twelve o'clock. Yours sincerely, Paul Temple." … Did you call round this morning?

GREENE: No, I told you over the telephone I was detained at the office, I couldn't make it.

TEMPLE: Yes, of course.

GREENE: Temple, who did send this note?

TEMPLE: Don't you know who sent it?

GREENE: No.

TEMPLE: Sir Graham Forbes.

GREENE: Sir Graham?

TEMPLE: Yes.

GREENE: Are you joking?

TEMPLE: No.

GREENE: (*Bewildered*) But why should Sir Graham send it?

TEMPLE: Because I asked him to.

GREENE: Because you … Look here, Temple, what is this?

TEMPLE: (*Simply*) I asked Sir Graham to send you a note because I wanted you to call round at twelve o'clock this morning.

GREENE: But why didn't you write the note yourself?

TEMPLE: Ah, yes! Why didn't I? That's quite a point.

GREENE: What do you mean?

TEMPLE: (*Smiling*) Well, if I'd written the note myself I couldn't truthfully have said that I hadn't written it, could I? And if I couldn't have said that I hadn't written it, you wouldn't be here.

GREENE: I'm afraid I don't follow you.

TEMPLE: (*Pleasantly*) Don't you? It's really quite simple. You came here this evening because you were quite genuinely puzzled about the note. If you hadn't been puzzled you wouldn't have come. That's true, isn't it?

GREENE: Yes, but – do you mean to say that the note was a – well – a hoax to get me here this evening?

TEMPLE: No, to get you here this morning – at twelve o'clock.

GREENE: But I didn't come here this morning!

TEMPLE: I'm sorry to contradict you, but I feel quite sure that you did.

GREENE: What do you mean? If I say I didn't come then I didn't come!

TEMPLE: Greene, I think it's about time you realised that the game is up.

A tense pause.

GREENE: What?

TEMPLE: For quite a while now, I've suspected that you were Madison, that you were head of the counterfeit racket and that you were responsible for the deaths of Chunky Brooks, Inspector James, <u>and</u> – Eileen.

GREENE: Good lord, man, are you crazy?

TEMPLE: (*Slowly, seriously, watching GREENE*) Let me tell you something, Greene. I've met a great many people in my time – a great many

234

criminals – but I don't think I've ever met one quite like you before. I believe if only you'd stuck to the counterfeit racket you'd have got away with it. Unfortunately you went in for blackmail.

GREENE: (*Lightly, in control of himself*) I'm supposed to be a blackmailer as well, am I? My word, I do sound an unpleasant customer. Just as a matter of interest – who am I supposed to have blackmailed?

TEMPLE: You blackmailed Mrs Portland into telling me a very interesting story – a perfectly true story too except for one interesting detail.

GREENE: What do you mean?

TEMPLE: It was you and not Chris Boyer who discovered that Sam Portland was the son of a notorious swindler! It was you and not Mr Boyer who blackmailed Moira! When Moira refused to be blackmailed any longer you sent for Sam. When Sam died you tried to get hold of the penny to substantiate your story: you knew that if you had possession of the penny you could go on blackmailing Mrs Portland and eventually gain control of the Portland Yeast Company.

GREENE: (*With sarcasm*) This is a most interesting story. Tell me, it's a small point, but why am I supposed to have murdered Eileen?

TEMPLE: Eileen found out that you were mixed up in the counterfeit racket and she told a friend of hers – a C.I.D. man, Archie Brooks. Brooks asked your wife to keep an eye on you. Eileen did, and she found out about Eppingdale.

235

	Unfortunately in the course of finding out she gave herself away.
GREENE:	So I – er – just eliminated her?
TEMPLE:	So you just eliminated her, making certain of course, in the process of doing so, to throw suspicion on to Mr Kelly.
GREENE:	(*Apparently very intrigued*) Oh, so Mr Kelly comes into the picture?
TEMPLE:	Very much so. Mr Kelly, I regret to say, fell for your little story.
GREENE:	Which story?
TEMPLE:	(*Watching GREENE*) The story you told him the day after he arrived.
GREENE:	(*No longer amused*) I repeat: which story?
TEMPLE:	You told Kelly that you had the upper hand so far as Moira and Mrs Portland were concerned. You promised Kelly that if he threw in his lot with you and got on the right side of Mrs Portland he'd be well taken care of.
GREENE:	Did Kelly tell you that?
TEMPLE:	No – not exactly.
GREENE:	If I were you, Temple, I should stop writing thrillers and concentrate on –
TEMPLE:	(*Interrupting GREENE*) Don't you think this is rather an attractive vase?
GREENE:	What are you talking about?
TEMPLE:	About this vase – don't you think it's attractive?
GREENE:	Temple, have you taken complete leave of your … Why, you swine!
TEMPLE:	You see the point?
GREENE:	You cunning devil!
TEMPLE:	Out of the mouth of babes …
GREENE:	Stand away from that phone.

TEMPLE: I have no intention of touching it. Greene, I think perhaps you ought to know that there are three men watching the block and a fourth man in the lift, so if you have any melodramatic ideas in your head I should –

GREENE has produced a revolver.

GREENE: I should – what, Temple?

TEMPLE: I should get rid of them. I should also get rid of that revolver too.

GREENE: (*Calmly*) Temple, there's a rather important point, which you appear to have overlooked.

TEMPLE: Yes?

GREENE: If I'm caught – and incidentally I haven't the slightest intention of being caught – I shall pay the maximum penalty so I might just as well – (*Smiling*) dispose of you. Give me that key.

TEMPLE: Which key?

GREENE: The key in the door.

TEMPLE: What do you want it for?

GREENE: Give it to me!

A pause.

TEMPLE: All right.

TEMPLE goes to the door, removes the key from the lock and throws it on the desk. GREENE picks it up.

GREENE: Thanks. Now turn round so that you're standing with your back to the desk …

The door is thrown open.

TEMPLE: Steve! Why I thought I'd put you to sleep!

STEVE: Yes, I know you did, darling. Good evening, Mr Greene. Drop that revolver or I shall fire. (*A moment*) You heard what I said – drop it!

GREENE: You wouldn't have the nerve.

STEVE: Wouldn't I? I'll give you five seconds – drop it.

A pause.

GREENE drops the revolver.

GREENE: Now, would you mind turning that revolver just a little to the right. I'm not exactly a nervous person but somehow –

GREENE makes a run for the door.

TEMPLE: Steve, look out!

GREENE knocks over a chair. STEVE fires her gun.

STEVE: (*Hurt*) Oh … Paul! Oh, my leg!

TEMPLE: Steve, what is it?!

While TEMPLE rushes to STEVE, GREENE escapes, locking the study door behind him.

TEMPLE: Are you alright?

STEVE: (*Rubbing her leg*) The chair – hit my leg and – I couldn't – get a proper aim …

TEMPLE moves to the door and tries to open it.

TEMPLE: Confound it! He's locked the door!

TEMPLE starts to throw his weight against the door.

STEVE: What are you doing?

TEMPLE: We've got to get out of here, Steve!

TEMPLE continues to try and force the lock.

STEVE: There's someone coming!

CHARLIE: (*From outside the door*) Is that you, Mr Temple?

STEVE: It's Charlie!

TEMPLE: Yes, get the door open, Charlie! Quick.

There is a concerted attack on the door by TEMPLE and CHARLIE and the lock gives way.

CHARLIE: (*Breathlessly*) Blimey, what's going on 'ere?

TEMPLE: (*Urgently*) Did you see Mr Greene?

CHARLIE: Greene? Was that the bloke in the grey suit and –

TEMPLE: Yes! Did you see him?

CHARLIE: Course I saw him! Blimey, he wasn't 'alf in a hurry! He ran upstairs like a scalded cat!

TEMPLE: Upstairs?

CHARLIE: S'right.

TEMPLE: Are you sure?

CHARLIE: Course I'm sure.

VOSPER arrives: he is out of breath.

VOSPER: What's happened, Mr Temple?

TEMPLE: He's made a dash for it, Vosper – he's gone
            upstairs!

VOSPER: Is there an exit up there?

TEMPLE: There's a fire-escape from the roof that goes
            down into a cul-de-sac.

VOSPER: Where's the cul-de-sac – at the back of the
            building?

TEMPLE: Yes! Let's get down there, Vosper.

SCENE 7:   The Cul-De-Sac.

*TEMPLE, STEVE, SIR GRAHAM and VOSPER are in the
cul-de-sac staring up at the roof.*

VOSPER: There's no sign of him.

FORBES: No. Are you sure there isn't another fire
            escape?

TEMPLE: That's the only one, Sir Graham.

VOSPER: Of course he might still be on the roof.

FORBES: Yes. We'll give him another three minutes and
            then we'll send Evans and Tyler up there.

TEMPLE: You've got the front entrance covered?

FORBES: Yes, don't worry about that.

STEVE hands TEMPLE the gun.

STEVE: (*Quietly*) You'd better take this, Paul.

TEMPLE: What is it? Oh, the revolver. Thanks.
            (*Suddenly*) By the way, Steve, I thought you'd
            gone to sleep?

STEVE: You mean you thought you'd put me to sleep!
            You don't think I fell for that corny old gag. I

239

knew you were up to something so I poured the drink away … (*She stops*) What is it, Inspector?

VOSPER: (*Peering down the mews*) I was just looking down the mews. There's someone in a car …

TEMPLE: There are quite a lot of cars down there.

VOSPER: Yes, but it looked to me as if he was watching us …

In the background the car starts up and starts to move towards TEMPLE and party: it gathers speed very quickly.

FORBES: Look out. He's coming down … Stand on one side, Steve!

The car draws nearer: gathering speed all the time.

TEMPLE: By Jove, he's letting it rip!

The car roars past them.

VOSPER: Sir Graham, look!

FORBES: It's Greene!

STEVE: Paul, it's Hubert Greene!

FORBES: He's beaten us, Temple!

TEMPLE: Oh, no he hasn't. (*He takes aim*) Watch that back tyre!

TEMPLE fires twice: the revolver shots are followed by the loud report of a bursting tyre.

There is a screeching of brakes.

VOSPER: You've done it!

STEVE: You've hit it, darling!

The car crashes to a halt.

FORBES: Now, we've got him.

SCENE 8: The TEMPLES' Drawing Room.

STEVE, TEMPLE and SIR GRAHAM FORBES are sitting in front of the fire: they are having tea.

TEMPLE: Give Sir Graham another cup of tea, darling.

FORBES: Thank you.

STEVE: (*Pouring the tea*) Paul, I've been thinking …

240

TEMPLE:	Now don't start talking about the Madison mystery!
STEVE:	There's an awful lot you haven't explained.
TEMPLE:	What is it you want to know?
STEVE:	Well, in the first place, what made you suspect Greene?
TEMPLE:	Didn't you suspect him? Hubert Greene was an extraordinary individual. The first time I met him, down at Southampton, I was impressed by his personality. I remember thinking that he was the sort of man that might exercise a strong influence over certain people.
STEVE:	He certainly exercised it over Moira Portland.
FORBES:	Yes, I agree. Moira wasn't only blackmailed by Greene, she was definitely under his influence.
TEMPLE:	Do you remember the night we met Greene at the Manilla – when he persuaded Moira to go down to his place for the weekend?
STEVE:	Yes. I've often wondered about that night. Why did Greene go to the Manilla – to see Moira?
TEMPLE:	Yes, but that wasn't his only reason. Greene had been told by Elzec, who was a member of his gang, that another member – a man called Mark Kendell – was double-crossing them and had an appointment at the Manilla with Archie Brooks. Greene wanted to take a look at Brooks, he'd already heard quite a bit about him and he knew that his wife, Eileen, was a very old friend of Chunky's. Well – I don't have to tell you what happened to poor old Chunky.
STEVE:	Well, why did Greene invite us down to his place for the weekend?

TEMPLE: He wanted us at Brown Acres because he'd already made up his mind to murder Eileen and he'd every intention of throwing suspicion on to Kelly. He wanted us as witnesses – that he had nothing whatever to do with the murder. Don't forget, Steve, it was our room he came to immediately after the murder.

STEVE: Well, if Greene murdered Eileen and threw suspicion on to Kelly – who threw the knife at our bedroom door?

TEMPLE: Kelly did.

STEVE: (*Surprised*) Kelly!

TEMPLE: Yes.

STEVE: But how do you know it was Kelly?

TEMPLE: When Sam Portland died of a heart attack George Kelly was, to all intents and purposes, out of a job.

FORBES: And a very soft job too.

TEMPLE: Greene very quickly weighed up the situation and made Kelly a proposition. He told Kelly that if he played in with him, he had simply nothing to worry about. Kelly was obviously flattered by this and for a time at any rate did precisely what Greene wanted him to do.

FORBES: Even to the extent of ringing you up at the Manilla and telling you to keep out of the Madison case.

TEMPLE: Yes. Then Kelly began to get ambitious – for one thing he'd discovered that Greene was not only a blackmailer but the head of an international counterfeit racket. He told Greene that he wanted to be in on this; Greene immediately realised that Kelly was getting out of hand and decided to double-cross him. He

242

told Kelly to go down to Eppingdale and meet a man called Dordrecht – Greene gave Kelly a 1919 penny and told him to show this to Dordrecht as a means of identification. You know what happened at Eppingdale: the plane crashed and Dordrecht was killed. Kelly saw the crash and panicked – as he was running away he dropped the penny.

STEVE: Yes, but I still don't see why Kelly had to take a 1919 penny down to Eppingdale.

FORBES: Greene knew perfectly well that if we picked up George Kelly at Eppingdale and discovered that he carried a 1919 penny attached to a key ring or a watch chain then we'd assume that Kelly was down at Eppingdale because of something to do with the Madison mystery: we'd assume that the penny was a symbol and that more than likely both George Kelly and Sam Portland were members of the same organisation.

TEMPLE: In other words, Greene wanted us to take our eyes off the counterfeit racket and concentrate on the so-called Madison mystery.

STEVE: I see. Tell me: did Chunky Brooks know that Greene was Madison?

FORBES: No, I don't think so, but he was getting pretty warm. Brooks mixed with quite a lot of people and made contacts which the ordinary C.I.D. man would never dream of making. For instance, he was quite friendly with Moira Portland – that's why she was so upset when she discovered he'd been murdered.

STEVE: You mean the night she made the scene in the library – the night she was drunk?

FORBES:	Yes, except that she wasn't drunk, Steve – she'd taken an overdose of benzedrine.
STEVE:	How did Moira discover about Chunky?
TEMPLE:	I don't think there's any doubt that she must have overheard our conversation with Eileen.
FORBES:	Yes, that's the only possible explanation.
STEVE:	(*Thoughtfully*) Paul …
TEMPLE:	(*Laughing*) Yes, I know, darling. This morning!
STEVE:	What happened this morning? First of all you gave Charlie the day off, then George Kelly arrived, then you made me ring you up from a call box and pretend –
TEMPLE:	Let me explain, Steve. I invited Kelly to the flat and I also told Sir Graham to send Greene a note asking him to call here at about twelve o'clock. As soon as Kelly arrived I received your telephone call – which was exactly what I wanted – and I left the flat.
STEVE:	In other words you left Kelly alone in the flat?
TEMPLE:	Exactly!
STEVE:	But why?

TEMPLE moves to a nearby table.

TEMPLE:	Do you know what this is, darling?
STEVE:	Of course I do. It's the thing you use for dictation – the magnetic recorder.
TEMPLE:	That's right – it records your voice, quite noiselessly, on a plastic record. The record plays for a quarter of an hour. All you do is switch it on.
STEVE:	(*Puzzled*) That's right.
TEMPLE:	Well, I put it under the desk, placed the microphone on top of the vase and switched it on.

STEVE: You put it under your desk? ... Oh! You mean while Kelly was here?

TEMPLE: Yes. At twelve o'clock precisely, Hubert Greene turned up. Kelly took him into my study. Listen to this – it's just part of the recording.

TEMPLE switches on the voice recorder. We hear the recorded voices of GEORGE KELLY and HUBERT GREENE. KELLY and GREENE are tense and at times aggressive.

GREENE: I can't understand why Temple isn't here.

KELLY: I told you – his wife had an accident with the car.

GREENE: Is that servant fellow in the flat?

KELLY: No, the flat's empty. (*Aggresively*) Greene, there's something I want to ask you. I've been wanting to speak to you about it for some time. When you murdered Eileen – why did you try to throw suspicion on to me?

GREENE: What are you talking about?

KELLY: You know what I'm talking about! I saw you stab Eileen – I saw you carry her down to the lake.

GREENE: Oh?

KELLY: Yes, I did!

GREENE: Is that why you threw the knife at the door – the one with the note?

KELLY: Yes, I thought if Temple got down to the lake in time there was just a chance that he might save her.

Suddenly there is a note of desperation in GREENE's voice: taking KELLY into his confidence.

GREENE: Kelly, listen! I had to get rid of Eileen! Don't you understand, things were getting desperate!

245

	She'd been talking to Chunky Brooks – Brooks knew about Elzec and Mark Kendell.
STEVE:	Why, that's a confession, darling! You could …
TEMPLE:	Sh!
KELLY:	It was you that murdered Elzec – wasn't it?
GREENE:	Yes, and I had a very narrow squeak. I bumped into Temple getting out of the lift.
KELLY:	It wasn't Temple you bumped into, you fool! It was me!
GREENE:	You!
KELLY:	Yes! Now listen, Greene, you've played me for a sucker long enough. Now it's my turn!
GREENE:	What do you mean?
TEMPLE:	Listen to this, Steve!
KELLY:	I'm going to make you a proposition. I'm broke – dead broke. I want five hundred pounds and an air passage back to the States.
GREENE:	In return for what, exactly?
KELLY:	In return for keeping my mouth shut! If you don't come over with the five hundred I shall go straight to the Yard and tell them about Eileen.
GREENE:	(*Smiling*) But the Yard think that you murdered Eileen …
KELLY:	Well, I'll soon disillusion them! In any case, for your information, they think that Moira Portland did it.
GREENE:	Moira!
KELLY:	Yes. As soon as I knew you were throwing suspicion on to me, I got busy and, with the help of a diamond brooch, I transferred the suspicion on to Moira.

GREENE:	Kelly, listen! I'll give you the five hundred and I'll buy you an air passage – on one condition.
KELLY:	What's the condition?
GREENE:	I want you to ring up Chris Boyer and arrange to meet him at a certain address. You can tell him that shortly before she committed suicide Moira left him a note –
STEVE:	(*Cutting in on the word "address"*) So that's why Kelly telephoned Boyer ...

TEMPLE stops the recording.

TEMPLE:	Yes. Greene wanted to dispose of the counterfeit printing plant and at the same time continue to throw suspicion on to Boyer.
STEVE:	Well, Greene certainly seems to have been quite a character!
TEMPLE:	Quite a character. That's putting it mildly!
STEVE:	What happened to Kelly?
FORBES:	We picked him up at the airport just over an hour ago.
STEVE:	Oh! I don't know why, but I feel rather sorry about that. I was quite fond of Kelly.
FORBES:	Yes – Kelly had quite a way with him.
TEMPLE:	Well – that's the end of the Madison mystery, Steve. (*Yawns*) And by golly, I'm tired!
FORBES:	What are you going to do now, Temple?
TEMPLE:	Oh, I expect I shall write another book, Sir Graham, or, as Sam Dodsworth would say, sit back with my feet on the mantelpiece and think of nothing more important than ... (*Yawns*) By Timothy, I'm tired!
FORBES:	Temple ... I suppose you wouldn't be interested in ... taking on another case?
TEMPLE:	(*Sleepily*) Straight away?
FORBES:	Yes.

TEMPLE:	(*Trying to arouse interest*) That depends. (*Yawns*) What's it all about?
FORBES:	Well; I'll tell you. Two days ago, Inspector Vosper received a telephone call from a girl who called herself Mademoiselle Didre. She told Vosper that she had vital information concerning the identity of a man reputed to be the leader of the largest White Slave organisation in … (*He stops: a moment*) I say, Temple? Temple? Why, he's asleep!
STEVE:	Of course he's asleep.
FORBES:	What do you mean?
STEVE:	(*Laughing*) Didn't you see me drop the tablet into his cup of tea?
FORBES:	You mean – you've put him to sleep?
STEVE:	That's right. It makes a nice change, doesn't it, Sir Graham?
FORBES:	But, Steve, why on earth …
STEVE:	I'll tell you why! Because I want to have a nice heart to heart talk with you, Sir Graham.
FORBES:	With me, Steve?
STEVE:	Yes, with you! From now on we're not going to get mixed up in any more of your mysterious cases, so you and the rest of the bright little boys at Scotland Yard can just go and –
FORBES:	All right! All right, Steve! I just thought this particular case might interest your husband, that's all. It doesn't matter. If you feel like that about it.
STEVE:	I do feel like that about it!
FORBES:	All right, Steve. That's perfectly all right. There's nothing to worry about. Just forget it.
STEVE:	(*Apparently disinterested*) What happened to this Mademoiselle Didre anyway?

248

FORBES: (*Casually*) This what?
STEVE: Mademoiselle Didre.
FORBES: Oh, she was murdered.
STEVE: How original. Where?
FORBES: In Soho.
STEVE: It gets worse and worse.
FORBES: Yes, but the extraordinary part about it, Steve, is that she was strangled with a silk scarf, one of those coloured scarves with pictures on it – you know the kind of thing.
STEVE: (*Vaguely interested now*) Yes.
FORBES: We found the scarf in the basement of the house where she was murdered. It was an English scarf but oddly enough it has pictures of Paris on it.
STEVE: Pictures of Paris?
FORBES: Yes. The Arc de Triumph – the Madeleine – the Eiffel Tower …
STEVE: (*More interested*) Go on …
FORBES: Wrapped in the scarf was a small white carnation.
STEVE: A small white … (*Suddenly, galvanised into action, shaking TEMPLE*) I say, darling, wake up! Paul, this is the most extraordinary business! Apparently a young girl called … Paul, wake up! Don't be stupid – wake up! (*Shaking TEMPLE wildly*) Oh, isn't he infuriating! (*Livid*) Just look at him – his feet on the mantelpiece! Paul, wake up! Wake up, darling! Wake up!

THE END

Press Pack

Press cuttings about Paul Temple and the Madison Mystery

Paul Temple Returns by Francis Durbridge

With the production of *Paul Temple and The Madison Mystery* Paul Temple celebrates his eleventh birthday. It was in the spring of 1938 that I created the character of Paul Temple and Martyn C. Webster produced the first serial *Send For Paul Temple*.

The idea for the present serial occurred to me in March of this year while I was on a trip to the United States. Immediately on my return I discussed the idea with Martyn C. Webster and after making one or two alterations to my original draft started work on the story. In the light of recent events the story is highly topical. It deals with the dollar situation – the counterfeit dollar situation.

Please note, however, that Paul Temple and Steve are not in any way Americanised. Almost the entire action of the story takes place in London and the Home Counties and apart from such well-known radio favourites as Marjorie Westbury, Ivan Samson, Kim Peacock, Olaf Olsen and Lester Mudditt, the cast includes Wendy Gibb, a young Australian actor who is making her first radio appearance in this country. Lester Mudditt, who has appeared in all the Temple serials, will once again be playing his original role of Sir Graham Forbes.

The story of *The Madison Mystery* starts on board a large Atlantic liner. Paul Temple and Steve are returning to England after a visit to the United States and they make the acquaintance of a certain Mr Sam Portland. Portland appears to be just a typical self-made American businessman but one morning he bumps into Temple on the promenade deck and proceeds to tell him a very curious story. If you listen to Episode 1 you will hear Sam Portland's story and you will realise why I have called the first episode of the mystery *A Penny For Your Thoughts*.

Paul Temple's Casebook by Maurice Wiltshire

Puzzled by the complexities of *The Madison Mystery*, Scotland Yard's most special branch has again called on the services of Paul Temple, the 42-year-old novelist-detective, who has helped them so effectively in the past.

Though his exploits are the property of everyone with the strength to turn a radio dial, little is generally known about the man who is about to make his 11th descent into the twilight of the underworld in as many years.

The son of the late Lieut-General Ian Temple, he was born in Ontario and at the age of ten came to England, where he was later educated at Rugby and Magdalen College, Oxford.

Since the age of 22 he has earned his living as a writer of good-class detective fiction and, because of his insistence on studying the criminal mind at dangerously close quarters, has built up a reputation as one of the most brilliant criminologists in the world.

For obvious reasons all his books are published under a pen-name, though strangely enough, *There Is No Mystery*, his only signed novel, has turned out to be his most successful to date. Paul Temple has made only one attempt at the theatre. His play, *Over My Dead Body*, ran for only seven performances in London in 1936.

The most important phases in Temple's life read like one of his own books. The first time he was asked to help the Yard on a slight but infinitely baffling case of murder he was helped by a well-known Fleet Street journalist of the time who wrote under the name of Steve Trent.

Her real name was Louise Harvey, and she and Temple were married at St Mary Abbot's Church, Kensington, S.W., in 1938. Since that date they have lived at Temple's country home, Bramley Lodge, near Evesham, but they are now looking for a house nearer London, preferably in the Godalming or Guildford district.

Six-feet-one-inch of brawn, and weighing 14st, Temple looks, with his hair still unflicked with grey, five years younger than his age. He is still a scratch golfer and has carried off the most coveted prizes at his local club.

But in recent months fishing has claimed more of his free time. He says that of all the sports he knows this permits the highest degree of contemplative relaxation.

At work in his London flat, or in his study at Bramley Lodge, he sometimes dictates his stories, but he is happiest when pounding the beloved portable typewriter on which he has turned out most of his novels. His main ambition at the moment is to wipe out his 1936 failure with a hit play.

In his career as a criminal investigator he has developed a close friendship with Sir Graham Forbes, of Scotland Yard, but one of Temple's most intimate companions in all his adventures is 36-year-old Francis Durbridge, another writer of thrillers. It is to him that Paul Temple owes his life.

Francis Durbridge, a Birmingham writer of BBC programmes, was on the lookout twelve years ago for a detective character who would move in eccentric circumstances without any eccentricities of his own. He had to be an intellectual man of action, tough but not brutal. With a snap of his fingers Paul Temple was born.

Since then this highly adult child of Durbridge's fertile mind has thrilled radio listeners and thriller readers not only in Britain, but in Canada, Australia, South Africa, and nine European countries.

He is granted a peak listening hour in Holland where he meets with phenomenal success under the name of Paul Vlaanderen.

Now Durbridge has sent for him to solve his latest case – a strange affair of counterfeit dollars entered in the files of Scotland Yard as *The Madison Mystery*. The first episode will be heard in the Light Programme tomorrow.

Hats Off To Paul Temple by **Our Radio Correspondent** (contains spoilers)

The man at the bus stop yesterday morning seemed rather pleased with himself. It would not, indeed, be an exaggeration to say that the fellow was actually smirking.

"Well," he began, "were you right about Greene, too?"

Just in time I recalled his enthusiasm for Mr Paul Temple and those endless mysteries in which he has succeeded in getting himself wrapped ever since 1938, when his creator, Francis Durbridge, first put his inventive pen to paper to write the Paul Temple No. 1.

Meekly I had to confess that the identity of the strange Mr Madison had eluded me right up to the triumphant denouement by radio's ace sleuth round about 9.15 on Wednesday evening.

That was enough to set the Temple fan off on a lengthy explanation on how he had successfully anticipated the solution to the eight-weeks' mystery, an experience that the arrival of our transport happily cut short.

Seriously, there can be no two opinions as to the ability of Durbridge to turn out, apparently almost effortlessly, a succession of taut, suspenseful thrillers for radio.

To Martyn C. Webster must, of course, go considerable credit for the success of the series since he has handled every one of them so far.

His secret, or at least part of it, must be in his insistence that his cast, no less than the listeners, are kept in the dark as to the identity of the villain right up to the end.

This keeping-them-guessing policy led to John McLaren, Canadian actor who has had film experience too, confessing to *Astra* on a recent visit to Northampton, that he must be the murderer for, as George Kelly, he seemed in the earlier episodes, to possess all the attributes of the bad man.

Well, it wasn't him. Ivan Samson, alias Hubert Greene, stood revealed on Wednesday as the man who did it.